D1459809

TROUBLE

Also by Kate Christensen

In the Drink
Jeremy Thrane
The Epicure's Lament
The Great Man

doubleday

new york
london
toronto
sydney
auckland

TROUBLE

a novel

Kate Christensen

ᑕᗪ
DOUBLEDAY

Published in the United States by Doubleday, an imprint of
The Doubleday Publishing Group, a division of Random House, Inc.,
New York.
www.doubleday.com

DOUBLEDAY and the DD colophon are registered trademarks
of Random House, Inc.

Book design by Gabe Levine

Library of Congress Cataloging-in-Publication Data
Christensen, Kate, 1962–
Trouble : a novel / By Kate Christensen. — 1st ed.
p.   cm.
1. Middle-aged women—Fiction. 2. Female friendship—Fiction.
3. Mexico City (Mexico)—Fiction. I. Title.
PS3553.H716T76 2009
813'.54—dc22
2008031416

ISBN 978-0-385-52730-9

PRINTED IN THE UNITED STATES OF AMERICA

1   3   5   7   9   10   8   6   4   2

First Edition

For Cathi Hanauer

PART ONE

*O*n a Thursday night in late December, I stood in my friend Indrani Dressler's living room, flirting with a man I had just met.

"Oh, come on," Mick, the Englishman I was talking to, was saying, "business acumen and a finger on the zeitgeist are not the same as innovation or originality. She's a clever parasite."

"I heard one of her songs the other day in a deli," I said. "It brought back that feeling of being young and wild and idiotic. You just can't take her too seriously."

"She's got a fake accent," Mick said, his mouth gleaming with mirth and wine, firm and half-sneering. His breath smelled like corn. "She irons her hair and she's had too much plastic surgery and she's pasty. She looks like an emaciated Wife of Bath."

"She's got the body of a thirteen-year-old gymnast and she's almost fifty," I said.

"She's a maggot," he said. He was not much taller than I, but broad in the shoulders and solid. His head was large, his face half ugly, half handsome, more French-looking than English, nose too big, eyes narrow, chin jutting forward. We were talking as if the words themselves didn't matter. I had forgotten this feeling.

"A maggot," I repeated, laughing, egging him on.

"Tunneling her way through personas till they're totally rotten and riddled with holes, then moving on to the next one. She went from soft white larva to shriveled maggot in twenty-odd years."

"Obviously," I said with mild triumph, "you're obsessed with her."

"I'm writing an opera about her," he told me in a way that made it impossible to tell whether he was kidding or serious. "Back before she made it. Back when she was young and soft and nasty. I'm calling it *Madonna of Loisaida*. Madonna when she was a newborn vampire, a baby whore."

I realized with a shock of surprise who he was. About a year ago, one of my clients, a pale, severely chic young concert violinist named Alison Fisher, had precipitously quit therapy after five years and moved to Canada to take care of her dying aunt. She had spent many sessions complaining eloquently and, I'd thought, with very good reason, about her boyfriend, Mick Logan; he was British, he wrote avant-garde operas that told melodramatic fictional stories about famous people, and he made Alison feel clumsy and plain and dull with his devastatingly sharp but subtle put-downs. With much guidance and feedback on my part, she had finally managed to get rid of him. According to what Alison had told me, he was in his mid-thirties, about ten years younger than I was; he was very bad news. She'd said once that breaking up with Mick felt like being let out of jail. And now, here he was at a Christmas party, bantering with me, leading me into a sexually charged, ultimately nonsensical argument that seemed to be rapidly leading somewhere I knew I couldn't go, somewhere I hadn't even thought of going in a very, very long time.

Just then, I caught sight of a reflection of a woman in the tilted gilt-edged mirror across the room. She was dressed similarly to me, so I tilted my head to get a better look at her. As I did so, the woman tilted her head to match the movement of mine. I raised my wineglass; she raised hers along with me.

It was then, in that instant, that I knew that my marriage was over.

My heart stopped beating. I almost heard it squeak as it constricted with fear, and then it resumed its steady rhythm and life went on, as it usually does.

"She's not a villainess, though; she's not interesting enough," Mick was saying. "That's the challenge of this opera. She's all too human, just quite vile really."

"*Vile*," I repeated, laughing, mouth open, neck bared, my rib cage pulsing with my hard-beating heart. My laughter had a freaky sound in it, like the yelp of a wild dog. I had to move out, I thought with horror. Or Anthony did. No, I did. Our apartment was his when I married him. And I had to take Wendy with me. Where, though? Where would we go? She'd hate me even more than she did already. Of course, she'd blame me, because it was all going to be my fault. "Then why would you write an opera about her?"

"Because," he said, "like a maggot, she's got under my skin and it's the only way to get her out. That revoltingly nasal little voice. Those dead-fish eyes. Those ropy muscles . . ."

I felt the vastly gigantic, frightening wheels that drive the world begin to turn. Lawyers, custody, settlement, alimony. I'd always been someone who made decisions with agonizing thoroughness and caution; to have such a momentous realization thrust upon me with no control whatsoever felt the way being in an earthquake or avalanche might have felt.

Anthony had stayed home that night, ostensibly because he had a lot of research to do for his new book, but in truth, he was relieved not to have to go out. He hated parties in general and didn't much like Indrani; he thought she was boring, which she wasn't, but you couldn't argue with him when he got an idea about someone. Right then, he was probably sitting in his armchair, happily engrossed in some book about post-Communist Eastern Europe, his current preoccupation, sipping at a water glass filled with neat whiskey, reading glasses on the end of his nose, frowning, gently scratching and rubbing his sternum under his shirt in that abstracted way he had. Anthony was a political scientist and New School professor. When I first met him, he had been a dynamic, passionate man, but over the past years, as he got closer to death and the world continued to go down the tubes, his old fired-up passion had been gradually replaced by bitterness, fatalism, and weariness. I had watched it happen, powerless to stop it.

This attitude of defeated resignation now extended from his work to everything in his life, including our marriage. He was becoming, somehow, an old man. I was apparently still a youngish woman; I looked at my reflection again to make sure I hadn't been mistaken about this, and there I still was, radiant, my hair upswept, my eyes wide and sparkling. If that reflection had belonged to a stranger, I would have been intimidated by her. I had had no idea.

"You wrote an opera about Nico," I said giddily to Mick, just to say something; I had just realized that he seemed to be awaiting a reply from me.

He looked surprised. "How did you know that?"

"Oh," I said, realizing what I'd just revealed. "God. Well."

He looked at me, waiting.

"I just realized who you are," I said. I had never before made a slip like this in eighteen years of being a therapist. "I know a friend of yours."

"Which friend?"

"Alison."

"Alison," he said, as if he were hoping it weren't *that* Alison.

"Alison Fisher."

He shook his head. "How the hell do you know *her*?"

"Oh," I said, waving a casual hand sideways. "You know, New York."

"Right," he said.

"I haven't seen her in ages," I added by way of reassurance.

"She dumped me cold. Never happened to me before or since. Little witch." He looked briefly into his empty glass, then took my half-full glass from me, grazing his knuckles against mine so all the little hairs on his crackled electrically against all the little hairs on mine. He drank from my glass, his eyes audaciously on mine over the rim. "Enough about Alison. What do you do,

Josephine? Doesn't everyone here ask that question before the topic turns to real estate?"

"Oh, I'm a painter," I lied. I had always wanted to be a painter, and I couldn't tell the truth after that slip about Alison; he might have put together that I was the very therapist involved in that little witch's cold dumping of him and surmised that I therefore knew certain things about him, certain highly unflattering things. And that would have been awkward, and the last thing I wanted in this conversation was awkwardness. What I did want, I wasn't yet sure.

Mick handed my glass back to me. My body curved to match the curve of his, as if we were two commas separated by nothing but air. "What sort of painting?"

"Abstract," I said.

"Abstract," he said.

"Abstract," I replied. Repeating each other's words was like sex, I was remembering. My reflection, I noticed, was leaning alluringly into him. I hadn't realized how willowy I was, how darkly elegant. I had to leave Anthony: I owed it to this woman in the mirror.

"Painting is sexy," said Mick. "Writing operas, on the other hand, is lonely and pointless. Who gives a fuck? Aria, schmaria."

"Painting *is* sexy," I repeated. "You stand in your studio half-naked, smearing paint all over the canvas until you explode from the sheer pleasure of it."

He laughed; there was a glint, a predatory edge, in his laughter, and I noticed that he was standing a little closer to me now. "Alison Fisher," he said malevolently, looking at me as if I were now inextricably associated with her, but he was willing to overlook it. I had a sudden urge to suck his cock.

"I need some more wine," I said. "You rudely guzzled my last glass."

"Wait here," he said, and plucked the glass from my hand. I watched him walk over to the dining room table, where all the bottles were. He was wearing a black turtleneck sweater and well-fitting brown jeans and black Doc Martens. He had a good ass. I glanced over at the mirror and again beheld my reflection. My new best friend, I thought with tipsy seasonal sentimentality.

"Josie," said Indrani, standing at my elbow. Her cheeks were flushed. Her blond hair shone. She wore red velvet. I had known her since college, and to me, she still looked exactly the same as the day I'd met her. She smelled of expensive, slightly astringent perfume. "Hi! Where's Anthony?"

"Hi," I said, kissing her. "He's swamped with work. He's so sorry to miss it. You look so beautiful!"

She looked at me. "You do, too," she said. "I mean it."

"Thanks," I said. "I've been talking to your friend Mick. He's a big flirt, isn't he?"

"Is he? I hardly know him; he's a friend of Ravi's." This was her much younger brother. Her parents had had a penchant for exotic names; the two older brothers were Giacomo and Federico. Ravi was a handsome, cheeky, disreputable Lothario type who was at that moment getting sloshed on vodka in the kitchen with Indrani's teaching assistant. "Seriously, you look really good, not that you don't always look good," said Indrani. "What's going on?"

"I'm flirting," I said recklessly. "I haven't flirted in about ten years."

"Are you going to fuck him?" she whispered. She was tipsy, obviously, and kidding; Indrani tended to be idealistic and even moralistic about marriage, probably because she was single.

"No." I laughed, but I did not say it emphatically.

Mick handed me a full glass of wine, which I took without looking at him.

"Hello, Indrani," he said. "Your apartment is lovely."

"Well, thanks. I was lucky; I bought at the right time." Indrani had a soft, round, open face and doelike brown eyes. Her shoulder-length hair was golden and shiny and straight, like a little kid's; her tall body was charmingly ungainly, slightly plump, and breasty. Although she was now a middle-aged professor at an Ivy League school, she had never lost the disarmingly naïve ingenue quality that had instantly endeared her to me and won my trust when I was a shy eighteen-year-old in a strange new place.

She was not Indian; she was English and Danish. She had been born in Costa Rica to hippie parents who had later moved to the Bay Area, where she had grown up. Unfortunately for Indrani, given this upbringing, she was by nature deeply reserved and emotionally conservative. As a kid, she had chafed with embarrassment and discomfort at all the naked tripping adults at happenings, the peach-and-lentil burger suppers, the patchouli-scented, jerry-rigged VW vans, the peace marches, having to wear used clothes from the People's Park free box. Her mother was the only daughter of a very rich man, but Indrani hadn't fully realized this until she was given access to her trust fund at the age of twenty-one.

"Hey, Josie," she said, turning her lambent gaze on me, "I've been meaning to ask, have you heard anything from Raquel lately? What's going on with her new boyfriend? She wouldn't even tell me his name, but she said he's exactly half her age."

"So it's Josie, then, not Josephine," said Mick. "Suits you, actually."

I was so turned on by the sound of his voice in my ear, I could have raped him right there. I was feeling loose and wild and punchy. I had spent the past ten years, it seemed to me now, with my muscles clenched, eyes narrowed, shut up in a dark, too-small, sterile room, trying desperately but vainly to make it feel homey and capacious. The door out of my cage, my cell, had been right there all along and I had just flung it open; now that I could see outside to light, color, life, freedom, I felt that there was no closing it, ever again.

"Yeah," I said, almost giggling like a kid. "I haven't talked to her for a couple of weeks, but she said the thing with the new boyfriend is very hush-hush for some reason, and she wouldn't tell me who he was, either. And she's got a new album in the works. It's her big comeback. Apparently, she's put together an amazing band, and they've been in the studio all fall." Raquel had also told me that she was getting a little sick of Indrani's earnest, self-involved E-mails, but I didn't mention that bit of news.

"Raquel Dominguez?" Mick asked.

"The very same," I said.

He looked impressed, the starfucker. "How do you know her?" he asked.

"College," I said.

"We were all three best friends," Indrani added warmly.

I thought of what Raquel had just said to me about her and felt guilty and complicit, even though I was innocent.

In the fall of 1980, more than a quarter of a century ago, Indrani and Raquel and I had been newly arrived freshmen with consecutive alphabetical last names at a small liberal-arts school tucked away in a leafy suburban corner of a small northwestern city. Sensing a shared ironic yet romantic outlook, we had immediately formed a solid, seemingly permanent triumvirate. The three of us had rented a ramshackle old house together off campus. We majored unanimously in English, wore one another's thrift-store clothes, cooked big meaty dinners, and threw parties at which we all took mushrooms or MDA and played the Talking Heads, the Specials, Elvis Costello, Al Green. We passed boyfriends around amicably and casually—at least two and sometimes all three of us had slept (but never at the same time) with Joe the chem major, Stavros the history major, Dave the anthro major, Jonathan the anthro major, and Jason the anthro major (we'd had a thing for anthropologists, for reasons we could never quite fathom). We never slept with one another. Straight girls sleeping together just for youthful sport was, we all tacitly agreed, a cliché, and of course we called ourselves girls, not women—feminist didacticism, along with earnest vegetarianism, was emphatically not our aesthetic, which set us somewhat apart from the majority of the student body, which suited us fine.

We'd known, with the absolute certainty of undergraduates everywhere, that we were all going to be famous. I studied painting as a sort of unofficial minor, avidly but with only the most obligatory encouragement from my teachers. Indrani ran the school newspaper, the *Quest*; and Raquel, who even then was a compelling, original singer and songwriter, fronted her own band, the Shitheads. Back then, she had been exactly the same singer she was now, as if she had been born singing that way. Her voice was at once raucously passionate and tenderly thoughtful, like an improbable, best-of-both-worlds cross between Janis Joplin and Keely Smith, both of whom had, not coincidentally, been her greatest formative influences. The Shitheads had started performing her sultry, inventive jazz/rock songs at coffeehouses and at the student union; then they'd played at a couple of Friday-night socials, then started getting gigs downtown at a club called Satyricon. In our senior year, they were signed to a recording contract with a local label; the summer after graduation, they went on tour with a few other bands on their label and became college-radio favorites. After graduation, Indrani and I moved to New York, Raquel to Los Angeles with her band.

Of the three of us, only Raquel, not surprisingly, had made it as any sort of artist. I, with typical pragmatic efficiency, instead of getting a shitty day job and using every spare moment to paint, which I wanted to do but knew I had no real talent for or future in, got my Ph.D. in psychology and became a shrink. Indrani, who knew she was too reserved and thin-skinned to be a journalist, had likewise gone for a Ph.D. and now taught English at Columbia.

Meanwhile, Raquel lived in Silver Lake in an airy bungalow with a view. Her name was as familiar as Bonnie Raitt's or PJ Harvey's. Every time we saw her photo or name in an online review or article, Indrani and I sent it to each other by E-mail, our messages often crossing in midair in cyberspace. Even though she had never won a Grammy, her first solo album, *Big Bad*, had gone platinum in 1992; two more albums had quickly followed, and, although she'd been lying low, to put it politely, for the past decade or so, she was still a rich and famous rock star who looked a lot younger than forty-five. Not that Indrani and I looked like cows, ourselves, and not that we did nothing whatsoever to maintain our own looks as far as possible past their natural expiration dates, but Raquel was expertly professional about it in a way Indrani and I didn't have to be. She'd had Botox and Restylane injections and got regular facial peels and dermabrasion treatments; she ate a stringently ascetic diet and followed disciplined regimes of Pilates and yoga and strength training. She both needed and deserved to look as good as she did.

"Is she as crazy as they say?" Mick asked.

"Every bit," I said. "She's cuckoo."

"Josie!" said Indrani, laughing.

"Well, isn't she?" I said, laughing, too. "Not that we don't love her. Not that she's not smart as hell. But she's a whack job!"

"You should know," said Indrani merrily. "You're the shrink."

There was a very brief silence.

"Shrink," said Mick. "I thought you were a painter."

"She's just kidding," I said without looking at Indrani. If I had said that to Raquel, she would have picked up on it right away.

But Indrani said, true to form, "Are you really still painting, Josie? That's great! I thought you'd quit all that a long time ago."

I looked directly at Mick. "I'm a painter manqué," I said with rueful, flirtatious bluntness. "The closest I get to actually being one is telling fibs to handsome men at parties."

"I accept the compliment," said Mick, "but the necessity of fibbing puzzles me. A shrink, is it." I could see by the glint in his eye that he was not puzzled at all.

"It's a living," I replied.

"Yes, I'm sure it pays far better than painting. It was a pleasure to meet you, Doctor." And then he slipped off into the kitchen.

"What was that all about?" Indrani asked. "Is he afraid of therapists or something?"

"I think I'd better go," I told her. "I've had too much wine."

"Poor Josie," she said anxiously, "but please don't go. Do you want some seltzer or coffee?"

"I don't think they'll help," I said. "I have a wicked headache. I'm sorry, Indrani, I just need to lie down."

"Go lie down on my bed," she said. "You can close the door. There's Advil on the nightstand."

"Indrani!" I said, laughing.

"All right," she said. "I'm just disappointed that you're going. I was looking forward to hanging out with you after everyone left."

"I'm so sorry," I said. "Things are just a little tense at home lately."

"All the more reason to stay here," she replied, but she said it with a laugh, offering it as a joke about her own pushy neediness. "You can tell me all about it."

"I will," I said. It wasn't her fault that I'd been caught in a stupid fib and just realized I had to leave my husband. "I'll come and help you clean up tomorrow. My last client leaves at two, and then I'm free till the second week of January."

She looked overjoyed at the thought of having company amid the dregs of her party. "That's all right," she said. "I know you're busy. What about Wendy?"

"I'll bring her along if she wants to come, but she'll probably be glad to get rid of me. I'll get here around three at the latest."

"You think people had fun?"

"They're still having fun," I said. "It's early." I gave her a hug and a kiss on the cheek, then went to find my coat and bag. I did not see Mick on my way out the door. Five minutes later, I was out in the icy air of Riverside Drive, heading down toward the subway stop at 103rd Street and Broadway. I inhaled the bracingly fresh air through my nose and hunkered down into my warm, sensible knee-length down coat, glad I'd worn it over my rather tight bottle green dress and thin tights. I tripped along the sidewalk, unaccustomed to heels. On Broadway, I considered hailing a cab, then thought about walking as far as I could until my feet gave out. Instead of either option, I suddenly swerved and ducked into a bar, pulled in by the inviting yellow-and-blue neon I'd glimpsed out of the corner of my eye.

Inside, it was festive, warm, and loud, a crowd of people drinking together. Whether or not they had arrived together or had known one another before, alcohol and holiday cheer had caused them to form a cohesive-feeling group. I took off my coat and slung it over my arm, then squirmed my way up to the bar and waited for the bartender to notice me. I could use another glass of wine before I head home, I thought. I almost never got to misbehave; I hadn't had a night out by myself in who knew how long. Tomorrow was my last day of work before vacation. Who cared if I was hungover? I'd go to Indrani's after my last client and have a hair of the dog. Then I'd go home and face Anthony, who'd be asleep when I got home and probably gone by the time I woke up. He often did radio talk shows in the early morning or went down to his office at the New School, where he taught political science.

I sensed, rather than saw, the man sitting to my left at the bar notice me and keep his eyes on my face. Hoping to discourage him from talking to me, I gazed fixedly at the bartender, a busty but skinny girl in a low-cut minidress.

"What are you drinking?" the guy next to me asked, shouting a little over the din.

I ignored him, for lack of any better option. The bartender, in turn, ignored me, but she had plenty to occupy her attention.

"Hey," he shouted into my ear. "Lemme buy you a drink."

I shook my head without making eye contact.

He slapped a ten-dollar bill down on the bar and hailed the bartender. She came right over and shot him an inquiring look. He jerked his thumb in my direction.

I leaned over the bar and yelled, "A glass of red wine, please, but I'll pay for it."

She raised her eyebrow at my new pal with a disbelieving smile and took his ten. I still did not look at him. When the bartender returned with my glass of red wine and three ones, he waved away the change. She flashed him a smile. No wonder she was on his side here; she knew I wouldn't have tipped so well. I decided not to thank him; he had forced this on me. I took a sip of wine and tried, unsuccessfully, to forget about him.

"Merry Christmas," he shouted, leaning in toward me. His rocks glass appeared in my peripheral vision; it held something amber, probably whiskey. The ice was crisp and fresh; the drink was almost gone. He was downing them fast.

With a sigh, I knocked my glass with desultory dismissal against his, then took another gulp of wine and fished my cell phone out of my bag, ostensibly to see whether I had any messages, but really, of course, to shake him off.

"Hello, darling, it's your mother," he shouted. "You never call! You never write!"

I kept a straight face, but inside I couldn't help laughing; he was so unrelentingly obnoxious. I put my cell phone back into my bag and gave him my most professional stare. My brief impression of him was that he was a lot younger than I'd suspected. Why was he hassling me? There were plenty of girls there who looked like Columbia students. I picked up my glass and my bag and struck off through the crowd to find another spot farther down the bar. I stood near the pool table, watching two boys take turns shooting balls into pockets. I felt myself melt with the almost-forgotten pleasure of solitary anonymity in a close, noisy crowd. I had been tense and brittle for so long, I almost collapsed with this release, this softening. I finished my wine and turned around to catch the bartender's eye. It took a while to get her to acknowledge me, but I managed to procure another full glass of red wine. I tipped her two bucks, then turned back toward the room and breathed the sharp, yeasty smell of my glass of wine and took a sip. It tasted harsher and not as good as the first one, the one my unwanted pursuer had bought me.

One of the boys playing pool noticed me and looked at me for a beat or two longer than necessary. The most flattering interpretation of this was that he was stunned by my foxiness, but he was probably wondering why someone old enough to be his mother was infiltrating his hangout. I looked back at him, and he dropped his eyes. It was just past midnight. Wendy was, no doubt, still awake, texting her friends on her cell phone under the covers, pretending to be asleep if Anthony checked on her, which he wouldn't. This was because he was, no doubt, dozing in his chair, book fallen open facedown on his chest, whiskey dregs warming in his forgotten glass. The thought of our quiet apartment, the two of them isolated in their separate worlds, made the wine in my mouth taste bitter. If I were home now, I thought, I would be in my own hermetic cave, in bed with a novel and a cup of mint tea; I would get up and open Wendy's door every now and then and listen to her faking being asleep, phone glowing under her comforter.

Throughout her childhood, I had done my best to love and be loved by Wendy. Anthony and I had brought her home from a Chinese orphanage when she was not quite a year old. As a baby, she was very bright, verbal, and curious. As a toddler, she developed strong opinions about what she did and did not want to do, eat, and wear, but she could be reasoned with and convinced to do my bidding with some effort. About the time she started school and realized there were other people in the world, teachers, friends, she began looking quizzically at me, evidently wondering why I was bossing her around like that. It was around this time that she seemed to become aware of me as someone she disdained and preferred not to be around. When she was six, I administered her first IQ test and learned that her IQ was 177. In first grade, she quietly, subversively began to challenge and resist my authority as her mother, but she had continued to tolerate me with a stoic reserve. The instant she'd turned eleven, it seemed, her ability to bide her time with me as her mother had dissolved and given way to a frank yearning to be away from me, out of my clutches, free at last. "I'm counting the seconds till I can leave," she had told me flatly more than once. She was closer to Anthony, but only marginally, if only because he wasn't me.

It was the oddest relationship I had ever had or was ever likely to have: This child I had rescued from motherlessness because I could not have my own, who was no relation to me, a foreign being, instinctively could not stand the sight of me. I couldn't blame our lack of genetic connection. I knew from clients with recalcitrant, snotty daughters of their own that it might have been exactly the same if she'd been my flesh and blood; and meanwhile, most of the other women I knew who had adopted daughters had relationships with them as complex and warm as biological mothers and daughters. They shared jokes with them, hugged and kissed them, shared a bond as deep as any blood tie. But for reasons I couldn't understand, Wendy and I had never managed anything more intimate or warm than a civil détente predicated on her knowledge that when she was finished with high school, she could go to college and be done with me. Her flat, pretty face was slammed permanently shut against me. I had no idea what this technically brilliant, mysteriously boring girl thought about, what she wanted besides the latest downloads of new albums by her favorite female singers and certain very particular items of clothing—pink leg warmers, faded skinny jeans, Juicy Couture hoodies, high-heeled boots. She seemed completely oblivious to her own intellectual potential, and, although she expended most of her energy on looking good, she didn't seem to direct her svelte, toned figure and glossy hair at any boys, either in the aggregate or the particular. She hung out with a group of similarly self-involved girls who seemed to dress solely, identically, for one another. Her grades were no better than adequate. Given her IQ, I could not fathom why she wasn't aiming her trajectory toward a physics lab at Bronx Science or a violin studio at Juilliard or at least a library. Instead, the only ambition she ever revealed, besides trying to be as pretty as possible, was to get away from me. To this end, even though she was only in eighth grade, she pored over college Web sites and gave herself (and scored unsurprisingly high on) sample SAT tests she found online. I knew this only because I regularly and secretly checked her laptop's E-mail and Internet history just in case she was being preyed on by pedophiles. I was touched to discover that she seemed to have a fixation with UCLA, which I imagined appealed to her as a huge campus filled with palm trees and sunshine and photogenic, clean-cut kids as far away from home as possible. I was glad, because it was also, possibly but maybe not entirely coincidentally, academically challenging enough to wake up the slumbering giant in Wendy's brain. But her going anywhere at all was a long way off, and of course this was only hopeful speculation on my part.

It was astonishing to me to realize, as I did over and over, how little advantage my clinical education, training, expertise, and experience as a psychologist had ever given me as a mother.

Thank God for wine. I was already half-done with this new glass. I counted how many glasses I'd had that night—five—and concluded that I was drunk. The fact that I didn't even feel tipsy meant I had to be well into the manic zone of false bravado and foolish actions, which I knew all too well could lead to a night of sleepless, sheepish regret and a morning of pain both psychic and physical if I weren't careful. I had had a bit of a wine-drinking habit in my youth—until I'd adopted Wendy, in fact. I had never entirely conquered it, only subdued it with dull duty and domestic habit, and here it was, still with me, like an old, beloved, but unpredictable friend. Like Raquel. I chuckled then, remembering my ill-fated flirtation with Mick. That would make a funny story for Raquel. I'll call her tomorrow, I thought. I hadn't talked to her in a week or so.

I came to the end of my glass of wine and pondered my next move. Another one meant certain pain in the morning, whereas going home now in a cab to drink a big cold glass of water with two ibuprofens and put myself straight to bed might mean a reduced sentence. Fuck it, I thought, fuck everything, and I hailed the bartender. As I did so, I caught the eye of the guy who'd bought me the drink. He was still in his spot at the bar, still alone, and he was looking at me. I looked away, but it was too late; he was on his feet and making his way toward me. The bartender handed me another glass of wine. Did I ask her for one? I wondered. I offered her some money and she waved it away with a jerk of her thumb at my pal, who had arrived at my elbow.

"You looked thirsty," he said.

"I am thirsty," I admitted. What the hell. He looked twenty-five or thirty, young enough to be my . . . younger something. He was harmlessly eager for my company, and I didn't have anyone better to talk to at the moment. The wine I'd drunk since I'd arrived had mellowed me considerably, and the knowledge of what I was going to have to do about my marriage was pressing in on me from all sides like that shrinking room in the Poe story, or was it a Sherlock Holmes one? Anyway. The room was shrinking, and here was someone to distract me. "Thanks for the drink."

"Drinks, plural," he said.

"Of course," I said, "I didn't ask for them."

"Sure you did."

I shook my head at him, smiling.

"My name is Peter," he said.

"Josie," I told him.

We clinked glasses. I took a gulp.

"What do you do, Josie? Besides being someone's wife?" He pointed to my wedding ring.

"I'm a shrink," I said bluntly; I wouldn't lie about that again. "What about you?"

"Hold on," he said, "we'll get to me in a minute. What kind of shrink?"

He wasn't nearly as interesting-looking as Mick. He was skinny and his hair needed cutting. He wore a black sweatshirt that said DETROIT in white block letters on the front. His face was smooth and boyish; he had a small mouth with sharp teeth, eyes of indeterminate color set rather closely together, and a crooked nose. But he was appealing somehow, possibly just because he was so young and pushy, or maybe because I was so drunk and feeling reckless.

"No particular kind," I said. "I make it up as I go along."

"You what, just hung out a shingle or something?"

"I have a Ph.D."

He looked skeptical.

"I'm trained, all right. I know all the techniques. But I don't ascribe to any particular methodology or school—you know, like Jungian or behavioral or whatever. I don't do therapy by the book. I invent something new for every client, or at least I try to."

"How much do you charge?"

"A lot."

"Do you have a sliding scale?"

"Sometimes."

"Can I come and see you?"

"I'll give you my card."

"Actually, can I have a session right now? For another glass of wine?"

I laughed.

"I mean it," he said, but he was laughing, too. "I'm crazy. I need help."

"Okay," I said. "What can I do for you?"

"I'm trying to decide how to answer that," he said with a suggestive look at me. I looked blandly back at him; this was certainly my night for frank male sexual interest. Where was it coming from all of a sudden? Alcohol? No one had been sexually interested in me, to my knowledge, for a long time. Maybe I was emitting some sort of weird premenopausal pheromone. "Okay," he said after a beat. "I've been having nightmares. Horrible ones.

I mean I wake up sweating and screaming. That's why I'm here tonight, to stay awake. If I go home, I'll fall asleep."

"How old are you?" I blurted.

"Thirty-nine."

"You are?"

"Don't tell me I look younger than that; it's the fucking bane of my existence. Anyway, what does that have to do with my nightmares?"

"It doesn't. I just wondered. Most people would be happy to hear that."

"Well, not me. I'm a teacher."

"What do you teach?"

"Not much. So anyway, in these dreams, my father is alive again and he's fucking molesting me. He never touched me in real life. It's literally unbearable. I wake up yelling and freaked-out."

"How often does this happen?"

"Often! A couple times a week, lately."

"When did he die?"

"Thirteen years ago. I always liked him fine. I never had major problems with him. Now he's butt-fucking me in my sleep."

I laughed.

He laughed, too. "I know, it's funny, right?"

"No," I said, "but yes."

"Right," he said. "I feel so much better already, Doctor."

"Sorry," I said.

"No, I actually sort of do," he said, and leaned against me. I leaned back against him, because I liked him now, all of a sudden, and why the hell not, and we stood there, shoulder-to-shoulder. "And you know," he said, leaning in even closer to talk into my ear, "what's even weirder is that when I first saw you tonight, I thought, I have to talk to her. I don't know why; it was just something about you. You looked totally sane, but I had the feeling you could listen to my story and get it, and I was right."

"So what are you going to do? You have to sleep eventually."

"I need someone to come and sleep with me," he said.

I held up my left hand.

"I know," he said. "I wish I could just borrow you, though. It would calm me down a lot."

"There are plenty of girls in here."

"They're five years old. The only reason I'm in here is that basically I live upstairs."

For some reason, I found this very funny.

"Thank God you have a sense of humor," he said.

"My marriage is over," I announced cheerfully. "That's what I'm doing here."

"Really?"

"Really."

"So you're separated?"

"No," I said. "I just realized it tonight. I'm still living with my husband. He doesn't know yet. In fact, you're the only one who does."

"That's a nightmare of its own making, right there," he said sympathetically, and it was about then that I fell into temporary love with him.

An hour later, we were still standing there, still leaning against each other as if for warmth and stability in a terrible storm. Both of us had reached the state of drunkenness at which the identity dissolves and becomes so fluid, it merges with the identity of whoever else is around. We had become psychic twins, my new friend Peter and I. Every now and then I would recall with an unpleasant sharpness Anthony and Wendy and the next day's four clients, and then I would push all of that from my mind by saying something loudly and confidently that justified the very real and important reason why I was staying out till the wee hours getting shit-faced with a strange man.

"The more tightly a spring is coiled, the more violently it springs forth," I said.

"That's so true," said Peter, laughing. "Is that a quote from somewhere? Who said that?"

"Me, right now. Describing myself, right now."

"You're springing forth?"

"In a manner of speaking."

"Well, that's good news for me."

This man smelled like toast and jam; his shoulder felt young and strong against my older, bonier one. Thirty-nine was fair game; thirty-nine was a fine, adult age.

God, I was angry at Anthony. His sins were legion: He had not looked at me in years, had not expressed a bit of concern about the state of our marriage, had, in fact, refused repeatedly to go to therapy with me. Evidently, he expected me just to wait patiently for him to stop being depressed without medication or clinical help. And worse, I had fallen for it. I had waited. Well, no more. His time was up. I'm still young, I thought boozily, still viable, still beautiful, even. Whatever I'm doing now, it serves him right for ignoring me.

"I'm springing forth," I said, "with a vengeance."

"Come upstairs with me," Peter said, "please. Just to sleep, or whatever you want. It would be so nice. We could both use the company, it seems to me."

We climbed the stairs to the floor above the bar together and walked through the dark apartment to his bedroom. We lay together on his bed, fully clothed, kissing slowly with our arms around each other and our bodies pressed together. Peter kissed me probingly, as if he were asking me question after question, demanding answers from me, refusing to be deterred, exactly the way he had pursued me in the bar. When the room began to spin slowly, and then faster, I crawled down his body and unzipped his jeans, took his cock into my mouth, and sucked and licked and stroked it until he came all over my hand. Then I sat up, rapt with sudden cold horror, and said, "I have to go."

The next day, I remembered smeared lights jerking hazily out the cab window, then, when I got home, some difficulty finding the keys to my apartment door. I don't remember crawling into our bed and falling asleep next to Anthony. I woke up the next morning in bed alone.

CHAPTER TWO

I walked into the kitchen, wearing my bathrobe, my hair going in a hundred unflattering directions, reeking of stale wine and guilt, my skull crackling with pain.

"Hi," Wendy said, not looking at me, taking a granola bar out of the box and putting the box back into the cupboard and the granola bar into her backpack. She already had her coat and hat on. "I'm so late. I overslept. Oh my God. I missed first period."

"Oh no," I said. "Where's Daddy?"

"He had a morning radio thing. No one woke me up!"

"Sorry, Wendy," I said contritely. I began to make coffee, groping behind a mason jar of rice for a filter, standing at the sink while cold water ran from the faucet, forgetting momentarily what I was supposed to be doing with the glass carafe. "You want to go with me to Indrani's after school today? I told her I'd help her clean up the party. She said she'd love to see you."

"No thanks," she said. "I want to go over to Ariel's after school, if that's okay with you. Her mom will be there."

"Sure," I said. "Will you have dinner there or come home?"

"I don't know," she said. "I'll call you."

"Okay," I said. "Let me know by six."

"Okay," she said. "Bye, Mom," and she was out the door.

I wandered around the empty apartment with my coffee, looking into Anthony's study, into Wendy's room, irrationally searching for evidence of my own transgression, or at least some explanation for it. Anthony's cramped study off the kitchen, formerly a walk-in pantry, was littered with newspapers and magazines. Wendy's bedroom was a tangle of clothes. Crouched in his cage, her hamster, an animate wad of hair she'd named Melvin, ignored me. Neither room offered me anything of what I was looking for; the contents of both were at once dully familiar and wholly opaque in their unyielding, private loyalty to their proper occupants.

I wandered to the living room window and stood looking down at our quiet, unremarkable stretch of West Eighteenth Street. Behind me, our rather scraggly but jaunty Christmas tree gave off a faint piney smell. I thought I could almost hear the tinsel moving in the air currents with a glassy rustle. It was 8:30; I had to be at my office by 9:45. At two o'clock, I would be free for two weeks. I always took a two-week vacation this time of year, even though it was famously the darkest, most suicidal time for therapy patients. This year, I had no particular plans besides staying home and reading a couple of long nineteenth-century novels and maybe, if I felt inspired and enterprising, painting a little. I rarely went anywhere during my winter breaks; I just needed a vacation from helping people around the holidays. The rest of the year, I had no problem focusing on my work. Taking this vacation was the one act of selfishness I ever permitted myself, and I needed it. And it wasn't really so selfish, in the end. I had learned through the years that almost all of my clients did surprisingly well during my winter breaks; surprising to them, that is, not to me. Interestingly, most of them dreaded my absence and acted out in various ways beforehand, and then during their break they discovered unsuspected reserves of strength and self-reliance and came back renewed and purposeful and proud of themselves. Only one or two had ever had meltdowns while I was gone, and those had been handled just fine by the substitute therapist who was on call then, my colleague, Susan Berg, for whom I returned the favor in August.

I yawned. Oh my God. Last night. I had had roughly four hours of sleep and more wine than I cared to recall. The taste of Peter was excitingly strong in my mouth, and the visceral feeling of his mouth on mine was overwhelming. I took a mouthful of scalding coffee and forced myself to hold it there to make it burn away the sense memory from my tongue.

In the shower, I scrubbed myself all over, washed my hair twice, brushed my teeth till they squeaked. I had been too drunk the previous night to do anything but fall into bed half-clothed, reeking of God only knew what. I wondered now whether Anthony had somehow suspected anything. Sometimes he fell sound asleep in his study and roused himself at three o'clock, awakened by his bladder, and then he took a pee, brushed his teeth, and came to bed. If this had happened the night before, he would certainly have noticed my absence and wondered about it. And if he had awakened during my brief tenure in our bed, he would have smelled the booze on me, unless he was so boozed up himself he couldn't tell the difference between his alcoholic breath and my own.

But no matter what, he would never think, not in a thousand years, that I would do anything as foolish as what I'd done. I was the model of sober rationality. Thank God for my hobgoblin, small-minded consistency, I thought. It was useful camouflage, now that I had lapsed.

While I blow-dried my hair, I studied my face in the mirror, dismayed. I looked like shit. I had puffy bags under my eyes that did my crow's-feet no favors, folds by my mouth and nose, forehead creases. Staying out all night and getting drunk used to leave no mark whatsoever anywhere on me; now, especially at this time of year, I might as well have hung a sign around my neck that said I'M PAYING THE PRICE FOR NOT ACTING MY AGE. That beautiful woman I had seen in the mirror the night before must have been a wine and candlelight and lust–inspired mirage. I put on lipstick and mascara, which did nothing to help my plight, but it cheered me up a little. I dressed in a pair of tailored black wool trousers, low-heeled ankle boots, a cream-colored sweater, and a charcoal gray blazer. With a pair of earrings and a slender gold bracelet, as well as a black wool coat and cashmere scarf, my disguise was complete. In the unimpeachable persona of a successful middle-aged Manhattan clinical psychologist, I rode the elevator down to the street and walked to my office near Union Square.

The streets of Chelsea were filled with twinkling Christmas lights, grimy ice and snow, merchandise aggressively displayed in windows with boughs of holly and pine wreaths, decorated, lit-up trees. The Christian Advent was a dark, difficult time of year, a season of soul-searching, stress, and loneliness, short days, long nights, obligations, insomnia, family tensions, financial worries, longings and regrets, the ghosts of old fears and sorrows. I looked into the faces of the people I passed and felt compassion for all of them, no matter who they were—that fat old guy with bushy eyebrows who was wearing a quilted olive green jacket, those two young Latinas in tight jeans and down coats with fake fur trimming on the hoods, that mother with baby twins, pushing a double stroller and talking emphatically on her cell phone. All of them were struggling to get through their days as well as they could. All of them were faced with things they didn't want to deal with, people who didn't treat them kindly enough. I smiled warmly at anyone who met my eyes and silently wished the rest of them a Merry Christmas even if they celebrated something else. "Merry Christmas" was, to me, a coded catchall phrase that meant "I hope you get through this mess with as little pain as possible." The rest of the year, Jesus was a grown-up with a beard, but in this season, he was a needy, tender little baby just like the rest of us. To me, saying "Merry Christmas" just acknowledged this general vulnerable-newborn status. It struck me as nothing but good manners and common sense.

I stopped in at my favorite deli, then crossed Union Square and walked a block down Broadway to my office building. I let myself into the building, climbed one flight of stairs, unlocked the office door, and went in. It was dark and a little chilly in there. I placed the deli bag on my desk, turned on the lamps, turned up the thermostat, and took off my coat and hung it in the closet. I loved my office. It had a thick rug, two comfy club chairs, a long leather couch, a tiled coffee table, bookshelves, and a small cherrywood desk. The lamps cast a warm, flattering, cozy light. A translucent curtain hung like a scrim in front of the window to let in daylight but soften the harshness of the cityscape. The walls were thick, the window double-paned, so the only noises that filtered in were muted, almost unnoticeable. The room's atmosphere was intended to suggest hopeful possibility and nonthreatening comfort in equal measure.

I sat at my desk and unpacked a toasted everything bagel with melted Swiss cheese. I hit the play button on my answering machine, hoping everyone had canceled, but there were no new messages. I ate my bagel and drank hot black coffee while I reviewed my notes from the previous week's session with Sasha Delahunt, my first client that morning.

The taste of Peter remained through toothpaste, coffee, and food. The sensation of his cock in my mouth would not go away. It was a pleasurable, shocking memory. And before that, the excitement of my conversation with Mick remained, too, the heady triumph of being sexually alive again. I dreaded seeing Anthony later; I hoped Wendy would come home for dinner so I wouldn't have to eat alone with him. Maybe I'd stay at Indrani's and eat party leftovers with her. I was so relieved to be going over there that afternoon after work; thank God for Indrani. She was so easygoing, such a warm, familiar, comfortable friend. Even the thought of her gently plaintive neediness didn't bother me now. I felt grateful for it, in fact. Right now, I was very glad to be needed by someone who would listen, someone I could confess everything to.

The buzzer rang. I pressed the button that opened the door, then put Sasha's folder back into my desk drawer and cleaned up all evidence of my breakfast. I sat and stared into space for a few minutes, collecting myself. I fluffed my hair, checked my teeth for poppy seeds in a tiny mirror I kept in the top drawer, put the mirror away, and then, at exactly ten o'clock, I got up and opened my office door with a welcoming, reassuring smile.

"Hello, Sasha," I said. "Come on in."

Sasha was a pixieish, skittish fashion designer with a pathological fear of her boss, and, for that matter, anyone in a position of authority or power over her, including me. She had been terrorized by her two older sisters and her father, and meanwhile her mother had been meek and apologetic and no help at all. I had been working with Sasha for almost a year, and she was just beginning to be able to enter my office without visibly cringing. She reported similar progress at work; apparently, she was now able to make eye contact with her boss in meetings or when she met her in the hallway during the workday.

I not only empathized with Sasha's plight in a general way, but I secretly considered my work with her to be a kind of penance for terrorizing my baby sister Juliet with many of the very same techniques Sasha's own older sisters had used on her. These included telling her direly in a hushed voice, as if it were a terrible family secret, that she was retarded or adopted, or both; reading her diary and correcting her spelling and grammar and writing comments in the margins; enchanting all her friends at her slumber parties and stealing them away from her; and putting manufactured notes into her textbooks, ostensibly from whatever boy she currently had a crush on, telling her she smelled of BO. Even my parents' general outlines, domineering father and repressed mother, had been similar to Sasha's. Needless to say, Juliet lived in London now and was distant and wary at our rare family gatherings. I wasn't proud of my earlier incarnation as her tormentor. Nor was I proud of the fact that to this day, my sister Jane and I shrieked with horrified, guilty laughter when we remembered what we'd done to her. Such was, of course, the Darwinian way of sibling birth order. As the responsible firstborn, I was glad to have the chance to help a client who was grappling with such a strikingly similar family history.

"He doesn't seem to take me that seriously," Sasha was saying about her new boyfriend, whose name was Kent. "He's like, 'You can sleep in tomorrow, but I have to get up and work.' Like my work doesn't matter or something. You know? Like I'm lazy."

"What tone of voice does he use when he's saying this?"

"He's laughing, but I can tell he's pretending he's just joking as a cover for telling me I'm not serious or ambitious enough."

"Have you asked him what he means by making this joke?"

"Yeah, and he acted like I was overreacting and being hypersensitive, you know? Which just compounded it, right? I mean, it was like, Wait, you're making fun of me; that's bad enough, but then you make fun of me for noticing and being bothered by it? How can I win here? That's just not fair!" Sasha was near tears.

"Do you sleep later than Kent as a rule?"

"Well, yes, but I stay up later, working! I like to work at night.

He has this whole thing about getting up early, like it's somehow morally better to get work done in the morning than at night."

"Are you feeling defensive with me right now?" I asked her.

She looked surprised, started to answer, then thought for an instant and said, "Well, yes, a little."

"Can you be more specific?"

"Are you asking if I sleep later than he does as a general rule because you think I really am lazy, and you're judging me, just like he is?"

"Good for you for asking me that," I said. This was something we were working on: Whenever I said something that made her feel judged, she had agreed that she would ask me directly what I meant and check my answer, which she felt could be trusted to reflect reality, against her own perceptions. "I promise I wasn't judging you. As a matter of fact, I don't think you're lazy at all, I think you're extremely hardworking and ambitious, impressively so."

"Oh, thank you!" she said. "That is so nice to hear!"

It was always amazingly easy to reassure Sasha, who soaked up any word of approval or respect. I found it quite touching, really. Was Juliet at this moment in a British shrink's office, almost weeping with gratitude to be told that she didn't really smell of BO?

"I'm still curious to get to the root of what he means by teasing you for sleeping later than he does," I said. "I wonder whether he's feeling competitive with you in some way."

"You think?" she said, as if I had suggested she might have been nominated for a Nobel. Her whole body seemed to vibrate with joy.

"I can't know for sure, of course," I said. "But I can be more objective, possibly. I see before me a confident young professional woman who's got her life together. He might need reassurance from you on some level that you don't look down on him. Maybe he's not putting you down at all. He might be trying to right a balance in his own mind, trying to impress you, underneath."

After Sasha departed, burbling, "Happy holidays! See you in two weeks," I made a few comments in her folder, then reviewed my notes from Jacob Turner's session from the previous week. As I did so, I remembered the smell of Peter's apartment—it, like him, had smelled of toast and jam—and gently burped up some red wine–tasting gas. I was a little surprised to realize that I wasn't feeling guilty; I was feeling more psychically awake than I had felt in a long time and almost dazed with the force of my own suddenly freed, untrammeled anger. I had worked so hard with so many clients for so many years to get them to acknowledge and feel their own anger, and meanwhile I had been containing mine with every muscle and tendon and neuron. Now it was loosened, sparking freely, high-voltage and dangerous. God, it felt good.

The buzzer rang, and with a sigh I pushed the button to let Jacob in. I rubbed my hand over my face. Jacob had made very little identifiable progress in three years. In fact, at times I feared he was regressing. He was a forty-three-year-old Santa's elf of a man, with a manic, spritely, hectically charming manner that masked a stark and seemingly insurmountable terror of change. Jacob was one of those clients who caused me to question my therapeutic chops, although in the main I still believed we could get somewhere together, someday. His tactic was to keep any meaningful work at bay by erecting a shield of chatter the instant he arrived, which he kept impenetrably aloft for the entire session, every session. I had to force him to shut up and think about what he was saying by interrupting him, catching him off guard with an unexpected question or statement. Sometimes he was startled into a rare insight about himself, which led to a more substantive discussion between us, but this seemed to fade from his brain the instant he left my office and went back to the largely self-generated maelstrom of his emotional life.

Now, because I was going on vacation, he was frantic and babbling.

"And then, of course, I tried Macy's, but my God, the throngs, it was like trying to see the shit through the flies." He cackled.

"That must have been stressful," I said. "How did you—"

"So I gave up and went home and ordered a couple of sweaters for Manny on-line and said screw everyone else and got in a hot bath and had myself a merry little hot toddy or two. It was more like four."

"And how did you—"

"Dr. Dorvillier, I swear, one of these days I will join AA, but not now, not in the holiday season, please. Do you know I am the only person I know whose therapist goes away for the holidays?"

We went through this every year.

"How are you feeling about that today?" I asked.

"Not good! But not to worry, I'll survive, thanks in part to my dear friends Jim Beam, Jack Daniel's, and Johnnie Walker red and black, and Manny, when he bothers to come over. Damn it,

I bet he's going to break up with me before Christmas, the little cunt, and then he'll get out of giving me a present *and* get hot make-up sex at New Year's."

"Do you feel pressure from me to quit drinking?"

"I feel pressure from the whole frickin' universe! Like the universe cares what I do. Listen to me. But I absolutely do drink much, much, much too much. And I look like shit. Look at me. I'm a fucking crone. Vanity will make me quit eventually, if nothing else does. The liver regenerates, and I don't need to live forever, but I do want to be beautiful."

Jacob had been talking about wanting to quit drinking and join AA since he'd started therapy with me.

"Jacob," I said, leaning forward and giving him my most therapeutically direct look, trying to make us both believe that anything I said would have any effect on him whatsoever, "I think it would be a very good idea for you to try to drink less while I'm gone. I think it exacerbates your mania and panic attacks, and I feel strongly that you'd feel much, much calmer about things like Manny and holiday shopping if you eased up a little on the booze. It screws with your body chemistry. It affects your sleep patterns, your moods, and your ability to think clearly."

"I know," he said with a catch in his voice. "Thank you for saying that."

I held his gaze.

"Don't go," he said. He tried to make it sound like a joke, but his face crumpled a little. Jacob was a weeper; he wept openly, easily, like a kid. His face reminded me of a marionette's; he had pronounced nasolabial lines, a long, thin, comical mouth, glittering, merry eyes, and a preserved, wooden, boyish innocence.

He had grown up in a small and small-minded town in the Midwest, the oldest son of an evangelical preacher and his wife. He had been tormented with his terrible secret, feeling that his family would never love him or accept him, and, exactly as he had feared, his parents had cursed him and cut him off when he'd finally confessed, almost ten years before, that he was gay. He had been in constant, terrible emotional pain as long as he could remember, and I could not figure out how to get him to let me help him. I was feeling sweaty and impotent; my underarms prickled. I wished I hadn't turned the thermostat up so high. I wished he would shut up for one whole session and let me tell him exactly what he needed to do, and then do it. "I'm going to be so lonely without you," he told me.

"Why don't you try a meeting while I'm gone, if you feel like it?" I said. "Report back to me when we meet in January. I'd be very interested to hear your thoughts about what it's like. I think, if nothing else, it would give you a lot to think about. You'd hear a lot of stories that would resonate with you, and you would feel so much less alone."

"You're making me bawl, damn it," he said, bawling. He took a Kleenex from the box at his elbow and dabbed at his eyes.

"Let's make a deal, Jacob, that you'll go to one meeting while I'm gone, and meanwhile, you'll drink half as much as usual for a couple of nights. One meeting, fewer drinks. Do you think you can do that?"

After Jacob was gone, I let out a long breath. Of course he would not do a single thing I'd suggested. He would go to no meeting; he would have several nightcaps every night and fall asleep drunk and in tears and, more often than not, alone. He would let his unfaithful, selfish, sexy boyfriend treat him like shit, and he would buy him a lot of presents he couldn't afford, and then he would drink even more to drown his sadness, his loneliness, his belief that he was worthless. The answer was right there: Quit drinking, join AA, dump Manny, and be alone until you find someone who respects and loves you. But he didn't want it. He desperately did not want to change. He wanted to stay exactly as he was and have it all somehow magically made okay. A few times, I had suggested terminating therapy to stop wasting his money and time, but he had adamantly refused. He seemed to think merely showing up to these sessions ought to be enough: Why should he have to do anything beyond talk to me? The answer was that of course he didn't. It was his life and his decision. I was an instrument he could use, or not, at his own discretion, nothing more. As a therapist, I knew this, but as a person, I worried about him and, at the same time, I wanted to shake him hard.

Two down, two to go: halfway there. I looked at Jacob's file, holding my pen poised over the empty page dated December 21. What was there to say that I hadn't said already? "Agreed to go to a meeting," I wrote, feeling futile and disingenuous. I put his file away and took out Corinne Martin's. I had a feeling she wouldn't come; she had been "forgetting" sessions lately, but as I opened her file, the buzzer rang, and I let her in. "Wonder what she's not telling me," I had written after the previous week's session. "Skipped the session, no call."

I checked my teeth in the little mirror again, took a drink of water from the bottle in my desk, ate a breath mint, then got up and let her in.

She swept in, wearing some new perfume I had never smelled before. She took off her coat and fussed with folding it just so on the couch, then stripped off her scarf. "I'm sorry, Josephine," she said. "Something came up last week, and I didn't have my cell phone, and then afterward I just got so busy with everything. I'm really sorry! I know you're going to charge me, and that's okay. That's the deal."

I waited until she was sitting down and ready to start.

"What's going on?" I asked her.

She could not meet my eyes. "God, you know, the usual."

She was silent.

I waited. Normally, I did not purposefully create silence. I was active; I was involved and verbal and engaged. I was never the sort of shrink who presented a blank slate for everyone to project their nightmares and fears and paranoid fantasies onto, which had always seemed to me to be a perverse, inutile form of torture. But now, with Corinne, who happened to be a lapsed Catholic, I had the distinct feeling that I was serving as a stand-in for a priest, as some kind of confessor. I had the feeling she needed me to wait quietly and patiently until she was ready to tell me.

"I don't know how to say this," she said.

Corinne was a tall, dark-haired, beautiful but haggard, intellectually brilliant fifty-three-year-old surgeon with a Battery Park City three-bedroom condo, two kids, a lawyer husband who worked insane hours and did nothing to help around the house, virtually no sex life, a strong, healthy ego, an equally strong, healthy fear of intimacy, and various other interesting but fairly typical issues. I enjoyed working with her; she was highly motivated to fix her problems and get the hell out of my

office, and we had been making tremendous progress, or so I
had thought, until recently. She had sort of disappeared over the
past few weeks, either not showing up or showing up and eva-
sively presenting a kind of pseudostory, a narrative of problems
that I suspected ran parallel to the real thing she wasn't saying. I
had been guessing she was keeping an urgent secret, something
all-important that she could not say aloud to me and possibly,
but not necessarily, even to herself.

"I have something I need to tell you," she said finally.

I waited. Years ago, a client had complained about my goofy,
earnest, annoying expression. I had immediately checked in the
mirror after the session and discovered that where I had thought
I was smiling neutrally, interestedly, with concern and openness,
I was actually making exaggerated idiot faces. I had worked very
hard since on my shrink face.

"I met someone," said Corinne. "Met someone, hell, I work
with the guy. He's my colleague, and, yes, we're fucking, and,
yes, I know this is a bad idea, but Josephine, I can't go back to
what my life was like before. I cannot. I feel like I will die if I
do. This literally feels like a life-and-death decision to me. I was
dead before."

She gazed in my direction, but she was looking through me,
at the man she had fallen in love with. Her face looked naked,
her pupils huge. For the first time in weeks, she was letting me
see her.

"I am listening," I said.

"I know you're gonna tell me I'm making a horrible mistake,
I'm betraying Andrew, I'm crashing and burning everything
we've worked so hard for, what about my kids, whatever. I know

it, believe me. It's like this feels like a catastrophe waiting to happen, but are catastrophes really so bad? Maybe sometimes we need them. You think I'm rationalizing. This is why I couldn't tell you. I feel like I can't live without him."

Our gazes met and held for a moment. Something vibrated in the air between us.

"I'm not judging you in any way," I said. "I'm not thinking anything at all. I am here for you, for whatever you need. I promise you, Corinne, I have absolutely no agenda at all, none whatsoever."

She took a deep breath. "Okay," she said. Then she began to cry, hollow, racking sobs that shook her shoulders hard.

"He seems to be someone you feel very deeply about," I said. Corinne's marriage had always reminded me a lot of my own. I was frankly envious of what she was doing; I wished I could do something like that myself. In fact, I was burning to know what it felt like to be alive again, what it felt like to fuck someone you were madly in love with, what it felt like to be willing to throw away everything for that, because I had no idea. I couldn't say all that, of course. But still, I felt it. "It must feel very strange to be saying all of this here to me," I added, greedy for details, hoping she would tell me more, tell me all of it.

Instead of rolling her eyes at my clueless flat-footedness, she blew her nose and laughed. "Oh my God," she said shakily, "you have no idea. I've never, ever opened myself like this to another person before. I've never exposed myself so fully and felt so adored. I can't believe he loves me as much as I love him. It almost has no place being talked about here in therapy because it's so . . . Anyway, we're very discreet and no one suspects, but that can't go on much longer. He's married, too, of course, and of course he has kids, too. We're fully aware of the damage this could cause. We're trying so hard to stay grounded, but we both feel like we're on massive amounts of crack. It's not exactly conducive to rational thought. And don't worry, we're able to do our jobs as well as ever; we do not let this affect our patients. The Hippocratic oath is alive and well in our minds. Our kids, too. Our spouses, on the other hand . . ."

She was flushed and laughing now, giddy, exalted. She had lost weight; she had always been skinny, but now she was gaunt. But she looked healthy. She looked vibrant, in fact. As it often did in my sessions with her, the Dylan song was running through my head: "Corrina, Corrina/Gal, where you been so long?"

"You're both angry at your spouses?" I asked.

"Sure," she said impatiently. "I knew you'd get into that. Yeah, I'm furious at Andrew. Yeah, Pablo is new and unknown and forbidden. Yeah, he's mad at his wife. Yeah, adultery is like drug addiction with a person instead of a substance. Okay, got it. Listen, I know. I know. I am fully aware. But I don't give a flying fuck about any by-the-book facts about affairs."

"Okay," I said.

"I want to leave Andrew and be with Pablo. It's been less than a month since I first had sex with him and I know. I'm fifty-three, not fifteen. Although I feel fifteen in some ways."

"Okay," I said.

"You're worried about me. I can hear it in your voice."

"Not necessarily," I said, smiling.

"Well, you should be!"

I laughed. "You're a big girl," I said.

"Thank you for not expelling me from therapy," she said.

"Why would I expel you? I promise you, I'm not here either to punish or to absolve. My job is to help you figure it all out, not tell you what to do."

"In a way, it would be easier if you just gave me ten thousand Hail Marys."

"If you really wanted that, you'd be back in church."

"Yeah," she said. "Whew." She subsided back against the couch pillows and closed her eyes. "What a relief. I finally told you. Now what? What do I do now? How do I protect my kids and get what I want? How do I get out of this without giving up my own happiness and without everyone hating me?"

"Objectively, I'm not sure," I said. "I think that's something we need to look at."

"Ya think?"

I laughed. "I think."

By the time Corinne's session was over, I was wrung out from vicarious panicky excitement. She left after promising me that in my absence she would keep the affair a secret from everyone; she would not tell Andrew about it or take any steps to change any aspect of her life; and she would encourage Pablo to do the same. Off she went into the cold, her coat flapping against her bony ankles, cheeks aflame, eyes feverishly glassy as a Victorian consumptive's or laudanum addict's.

I had a lot to write in her folder. The minutes ticked by as I scribbled, trying to remain detached, not entirely succeeding. I finished and took out Amy Margolis's folder and went over the previous week's notes, waiting for the buzzer. Almost fifteen minutes past the start of her session, it finally rang.

"Fuck!" Amy said, entering my office in a long down parka and wool stocking cap. She peeled them off and threw them on the couch. I had a coatrack in the waiting area, but not everyone liked using it. "Fuck! I missed my train by two seconds 'cause my MetroCard ran out, and then the next train took like forever to come and was so slow I thought I was gonna scream. I am so sorry!"

"Subway trouble is the worst," I said.

"The worst," she echoed. "Except, like, cancer, global warming, world war."

I laughed. Amy sat down and blew her nose. She was a Barnard sophomore who'd grown up in the Hollywood Hills in an Italianate villa and had gone to elite private schools. Her mother had died of cancer when she was six, and her father, a studio executive, had rarely been home, so his not too bright, leggy, blond, much younger second wife had raised Amy, if *raised* was really the word. Melanie, the stepmother, had never forgiven Amy for not looking exactly like her. Amy, who loved to eat and was naturally "zaftig"—her own word for her body—was forced to go on every diet that came down the pike and was sent away every summer to fat camp; every fall, Melanie had taken her shopping for school clothes and ridiculed her in front of the other shoppers and salesclerks.

I could almost, summoning all the empathy I possessed, imagine how Melanie must have felt, faced with the task of raising an imperfect girl in a world of didactic, almost-medieval physical requirements and constraints for women. But I still secretly wanted to throttle her. Amy was healthy and sexy. Her hair was glossy black, her skin like porcelain, her lips cherry-red, like

Snow White's; she was beautiful, but it would take a long time before she would be able to know that. Her self-loathing was so profound, she often considered killing herself. She was also intermittently bulimic and given to disastrous relationships with distant but needy men and critical, demanding female friends.

I smiled at her and immediately felt my face make that annoying furrowed-brow shrink-empathy expression I had worked so hard to eradicate from my repertoire. I hastily tried to smooth my features.

"Quit it," said Amy. "Don't fucking feel sorry for me."

"Sorry," I said. "I sometimes make that expression without meaning to. I don't feel sorry for you."

She laughed. "Thanks for validating my experience."

"That's what I'm here for."

"I was being sarcastic, dude."

"I can take it."

"Do you ever lose your shit in here, like yell at someone or have a meltdown or just, you know, totally lose control of yourself?"

"Do you wish I would lose control of myself?"

"It's weird how you have all the power in here. You sit there like you have it all together, and I'm the fucked-up loser on the couch. And then I pay you. Something is wrong with this picture."

"What do you wish I would say to equalize things?"

She thought about this and then laughed self-consciously. "Probably I'd be horrified. I need you to be perfect and have your shit together."

"You think I'm perfect?"

"Well," she said. "Let's see. You're thin, you have a Ph.D., and you're married. You make a good living, and you're really pretty. How bad can your life ever be?"

I laughed. "You're right: We're not here to discuss my problems," I said.

"Right, 'cause then you'd have to pay me, and I'm totally unqualified to help you. But you know what I mean, right?"

"You mean it's a different kind of relationship. Not like any other one you have."

"Yeah," she said.

I nodded and waited to see whether she had more to say. When she didn't say anything, I said, "How are you feeling about going home for the holidays?"

"Like slitting my wrists," she said.

"You remember you promised to call me if you ever seriously think you might try that?"

"I meant it figuratively."

"Good," I said.

"This time," she added.

"Okay. Let's see if we can figure out a way to get you through the visit so you don't even think about slitting your wrists."

"Xanax?"

"I'm thinking more like survival strategies. How you can take your stepmother's power to hurt you away from her."

"Xanax?"

I laughed. "We'll keep working on how you feel, but for the purpose of this visit, let's try to give you new ways to react outwardly to the things she says that hurt you."

"Like, 'Oh my God, Amy, that freshman fifteen looks like it

turned into the sophomore thirty! I will juice you some organic pomegranates right this minute.' I hate her so fucking much. I miss my mother. She loved me."

She cried gutturally for a while, then wiped her tear-smeared face and sighed, then laughed. "That fucking cunt bitch. I want to pop her boobs with a chopstick."

"A knitting needle might work better."

"I want to tie her up and force-feed her Cheetos. You know, I've fantasized about putting weight-gain powder in her stupid flaxseed, like the mean girls in that movie. I wish my father would dump her for a younger woman. Or, like, 'Hey, Melanie, your neck looks like shit! Maybe you ought to get it Botoxed!' All fake concerned. Old crone." She looked at me. "Sorry. She's not that old."

"No need to apologize," I said. "She's probably much younger than I am, but your point is well taken. Fight fire with fire."

"You have any better ideas?"

"Let's take that statement. 'That freshman fifteen looks like it turned into the sophomore thirty.' You could look her right in the eye and say, 'You may not insult me like that ever again as long as we live. I am your husband's daughter, and I deserve respect and kindness from you.'"

Amy giggled. "Yeah, right, as if," she said.

"It's a thought," I said.

"Like I'm gonna say that to her? A lightning bolt would probably strike me in the head."

"I will bet you'd be surprised," I said.

"How do you think she'd react?"

"I'll bet it won't be anything you'd expect."

"Of course, it's not really that simple," she said. "Or that easy."

"But it's a start," I said.

"Yeah, well, it's all very fun to think about that here with you, where I'm nice and safe," she said, "but I still have to lug these thirty pounds back to L.A. and face that witch, while you get to stay here all perfect in your perfect life."

"You seem," I said mildly, "a little angry about that."

"I know I'm a total fucking spoiled brat, poor little rich girl, but that just makes it *worse*! I have no right to complain, and I'm so miserable, I could fucking die! Why is there no comfort? Why is everything so hard?"

"Amy," I said. "You're not a spoiled brat. You're in a lot of pain for some very good reasons. I promise it will lessen, and there will be comfort. I know it seems like it will take forever, but it will happen faster than you think."

"I wish I could believe you!" she said.

I wanted to take her into my arms and hold her close, the way her mother would have, but instead I said with as much conviction as I could muster without sounding annoyingly patronizing, "You'll just have to trust me."

"Right," she said, "I have to. I've got no better options."

And that, I thought, was a great description of the therapeutic process.

CHAPTER THREE

I stepped out of the elevator into Indrani's hallway just before three o'clock. Her building was lavishly appointed, as they used to say in some bygone era. The corridor was paved with a plush gold-and-black patterned carpet; gilt mirrors and sconces decorated the black-and-cream flocked-wallpaper walls. The hallway was silent and odorless, as if all sensory information were scrubbed from the air by some invisible, powerful machine. I walked without making a sound down to 11F and knocked. Indrani came to the door in a bathrobe, cradling a mug in both hands.

"Sorry, I forgot you were coming. The party is still going on, sort of." She whispered as I came in, and she closed the door behind me. "My damned brother. They're all doing crystal meth."

"Who's still here?"

"Ravi and his pals are out on the terrace doing God knows

what, blowing bubbles and telling one another's fortune, for all I know. I rudely told them to go home at seven in the morning, but they wouldn't leave, so I went to bed. I just got up, and they're still here, drinking all the leftover wine. Want some coffee?"

We hugged and kissed. She was very warm and smelled like coffee, shampoo, and sleep.

"I feel like shit. Look at me," I said. "I could barely function at work today, but I hope at least I did no harm."

"You look gorgeous," she lied. "And you left early last night! Why did you—oh, right, you had a headache. Are you feeling better?"

"No," I said. "But yes, so much better, in another way. I'll tell you the whole story after I've had some coffee. And maybe something stronger. I have a lot to get off my chest here."

We went into her kitchen. I looked into her liquor cupboard and extracted a bottle of rum. I poured some into the cup of hot coffee she handed me and stirred it with my finger, licked my finger, and said, "Aaah."

"I started cleaning up last night when they wouldn't leave," she said, adding some rum to her own coffee. "I put all the food away, loaded the dishwasher and ran it, wiped all the surfaces, and bagged the recycling. I thought they would take the hint, but they were still here, so I unloaded the clean dishes and ran another load and then I put away all the booze and picked up some of the trash. Crystal meth! Like he's twenty-five? I think it was that English guy who was so hot for you—I think he brought it."

"Mick," I said. "He's still here? Oh God. What else did I miss?"

"Not one thing," she said. "I was wishing I could go home and go to bed, too. Which is rather inconvenient when it's your own party."

We went into the salonlike living room with our cups and curled up across from each other on the two long, white, downy couches. There was a silver bowl of unshelled walnuts and clementines on the coffee table between us. Through the enormous thick-paned windows to my left, the sky was white and still and heavy, as if it were about to snow. Indrani's Christmas tree was festooned with old-fashioned popcorn-and-cranberry strings, gilt balls, handmade wooden ornaments, and colored nonblinking bulbs. A fire burned in the deep fireplace to my right, which was set into built-in mahogany shelves and cupboards and had a marble hearthstone, a Victorian screen, a basket of kindling and logs next to it. Over the mantel hung the prophetic gilt-edged mirror that had informed me the night before that I had to leave Anthony and change the entire structure of my life.

"God, your apartment is nice," I said.

"Thanks," she said warily. Indrani was a little touchy about having a trust fund and then, to gild the lily, having inherited a buttload of money from a doting great-uncle when she was thirty, something like eight million dollars. She did everything in her power to deflect any whiff of envy or resentment from the people she was close to, so I tried to mute my lust for her apartment, not to mention her Montauk beachfront house and her furniture, wardrobe, and art collection. She was almost embarrassingly generous with everything she had, and the irony, of course, was that all she really wanted was a husband and a kid or, ideally, two. I would have traded places with her in a heartbeat, but that evidently wasn't an option. Why someone hadn't come along and married her, I could not begin to imagine. She wasn't especially picky. Her last boyfriend had been Vince, a sweet-talking but shifty-eyed much younger man who said he was a "music producer" and thereby justified his many late nights out without Indrani. That relationship had finally ended, after nearly two years, when Indrani had come home unexpectedly early one day, having cut her office hours short. She had caught him in her own bed with, of course, a younger woman. One of the few things Indrani didn't have was common sense about men, probably because her father and three brothers were all ne'er-do-well charmers and her mother was an insecure doormat.

Vince had shattered her trust and her heart. She'd been alone ever since, and, according to her, she now had not one husband-like prospect in sight. She was beginning to resign herself to more or less permanent singleness, and she was forty-five, so unless she adopted pretty soon, she was probably not going to have any kids, either. Indrani and I talked a lot about aging, trying to figure out how to accept it with as much dignity and as little Botox and embarrassing attempts to cling to youth as possible. So far, we were doing all right, but we were aware that pretty soon everything on our faces and bodies was going to slide into tragicomic ruination, and we'd start feeling desperate, and then God only knew what we'd resort to. However, implicit in these conversations was the unspoken but ever-present fact that, unlike Indrani, I had a husband, and so presumably didn't need to panic about losing my looks, whereas she needed them to catch a man.

"So?" she said.

"So," I said. "Hang on, sweetheart, it's going to be a bumpy ride."

"Is Anthony having an affair?" she asked.

I looked at her, so shocked I laughed. "Not that I know of," I said. "But you never know. I wish he would, in a way; it would mean he was still alive."

"Really?"

And then I told her everything, all about my realization the night before that I was still youngish and fairly vital and, most important, sexually functioning, that my marriage was a dead duck floating in pond scum, that I needed to get out while I still could, and that I had behaved extremely foolishly with a nice young man I had picked up in a bar, but that was a symptom of a larger problem, not a problem in and of itself. I couldn't help allowing a kind of giddy hilarity to creep into my voice, even though I knew this was serious, knew things were very bad. Still, when I talked about Peter, the blow job, I described the whole thing airily, a little sardonically, as if it were akin to shoplifting or sneaking through a subway turnstile, a prank, a madcap adventure on the wrong side of the law. My voice bubbled with excitement, fear, adrenaline. Meanwhile, Indrani listened raptly, without blinking or moving or drinking her coffee. I took big gulps of my own, and when I was pretty much finished with the rough outline of the story, I went into the kitchen for more coffee, but especially more rum. When I came back, she was watching me, her face as still as a cat's.

"Go on," she said. "What are you going to do now?"

"I guess," I said, "I'll talk to Anthony tonight, which I'm dreading, tell him I want a separation, and figure out where to go. It's his apartment, or at least it was all those years ago when I moved in. And I'm the one who wants to leave, so I should be the one who mostly deals with the upheaval."

"You sound so calm about it all," she said.

"I'm scared and sad, but mostly it's a relief. I realized last night that I've felt dead for so long."

"You know," she said, "it's strange; I never had the slightest idea you felt this way. You always said things were going well."

"I don't think I could admit it even to myself. I think this has been brewing a long time, underneath, the way things do when you try to avoid them."

She hesitated, as if she had something to say and was trying to think of the best way to put it. "You and Anthony have been married a very long time."

"Fifteen years. The first five were good."

"My grandmother would say to you, 'Does he beat you? Is he a drunk? Is he in prison? No? Then why are you leaving him?' That's what she said to my mother when she left my father."

"He ignores me," I said. "I'm so bored by him, I could throw up. He won't do anything to improve matters. He thinks this is just the way marriage is."

"He's a catch," said Indrani. "Seriously. You're lucky to have him. He's brilliant and good-looking, and he makes a good living and comes home every night and is a good father."

"All true," I said. "But that's not enough. I realized last night that I am withering on the vine, so to speak. Anthony is like the perfect shell of a husband. All the insides are missing."

"So you picked up a guy in a bar?"

"He didn't matter," I said. "He was just a symptom."

"Anthony doesn't know any of this yet, right?"

"That's right," I said.

She waited for me to go on.

"It was a stupid thing, what I did last night," I said, "but like I said, it's a symptom, not a cause. It wasn't the point. Anthony refuses to go to marital therapy. He refuses to address our problems. He does not see me anymore. He might not even notice I'm gone; that's how indifferent he's become to me."

"I hope he surprises you," said Indrani.

"He won't surprise me," I said.

"Are you willing to give him the chance?"

I laughed. "Anthony? I've given him nothing but chances."

"Oh, Josie," she said. "This whole thing makes me sad. If you guys can't make it, then who can?"

"Don't worry about me," I said. "Please. That isn't what I need right now."

"Are you sure?" she said, watching me closely. "I feel like maybe you haven't thought this through entirely. It feels a little hasty to me, a little extreme."

"Maybe so," I replied. "But I'm not asking for advice, I promise."

"I believe," she said, "that friends have to question each other. We have to be sounding boards for each other. We can't just take everything the other one says and does at face value and accept it blindly. I would feel like I wasn't being a good friend if I didn't say these things."

"I agree that friends should be honest," I said. "And I appreciate your concern. But I can't help feeling a little judged, or something."

"Well," she said, "maybe no one can be totally nonjudgmental about anything. I'm sure you think I was a fool about Vince. How could you not? You were very understanding and supportive, it's true, and maybe I'm not as good a listener as you are; maybe I'm not as tactful. But you must have secretly thought I was an idiot for letting Vince live with me for so long, for spending all that money on him, and you were right."

I had a sudden clear memory of sitting with her in this living room after she'd caught him cheating and kicked him out, my arms around her, handing her Kleenex and assuring her over and over that she would be all right, that she would get over this.

"I didn't judge you," I said.

"I was a fool, and you know it."

"We're all fools, Indrani."

"I don't want you to end up alone, like I am," she said.

"I would rather be alone than lonely in a bad marriage," I said. "It's the worst kind of loneliness. It's like a deadweight. Actually, I feel sort of excited about leaving. Sad, too, but mostly relieved. I feel like I just woke up from a coma."

"What about Wendy?" Indrani asked.

I looked searchingly at her for a moment. Her lips were pursed; she was squinting at me. Cruelly, I noticed that the skin around her eyes seemed to have softened and melted slightly. I always tried not to see signs of aging in my friends; the fact that I was allowing myself to notice Indrani's meant that I must have been angry at her, no matter how hard I was trying not to be.

"It will be hard for Wendy at first, I imagine," I said. "She can choose whom she wants to stay with. Maybe it's best for her to stay with Anthony, but that is up to her."

The French doors to the terrace opened and Mick tumbled in with Indrani's younger brother, Ravi, and three gorgeous young women, one of whom was Indrani's teaching assistant. The five of them were laughing and windblown and pink-cheeked, manic. A cloud of cigarette smoke had blown in with the fresh air. They all wore their coats and hats. They all carried empty wineglasses. "More wine!" Mick said. "Indrani, come and join us! Oh, hello there, Shrink; it's snowing out there."

The three young women giggled. Indrani and I exchanged a look, immediately united in our resistance against their debauchery, no matter what deeper differences we had.

"No, thanks," said Indrani. "I think it's time for you all to go home to bed."

"No way," said Ravi. "We're in the prime of our lives now."

"Dr. Dressler," said the teaching assistant, whose glittering, zany eyes made her look not only high as a loon but sexually jacked up, as if she'd been hotly making out with someone for hours, "sorry. We really can leave now if you'd like."

"I would like, very much," said Indrani crisply. "And Elissa, in general, like I said last night, I advise you strongly against hanging out with my brother."

"She's hanging out with me," said Mick, putting a jovial, proprietary arm around her.

"Even worse," I said darkly.

"What have you got against me?" Ravi said indignantly.

"I could ask the same thing," said Mick, as if he didn't much care what I thought of him. He disappeared briefly into the kitchen and reemerged with two fresh bottles of wine. He put them on the table behind the couch Indrani was sitting on and deftly removed the corks with a corkscrew he took from his pocket, the same antique silver corkscrew, I was interested to note, that I had given Indrani for Christmas just the night before.

"Nice corkscrew," I said. "Don't you guys have any respect for the wishes of your hostess?"

Mick didn't seem to hear. "I've been wondering about the origin of the phrase 'Go soak your head,' " he said. "Soak your head in what? Why your head? Why not 'Go shave your balls?' " He refilled everyone's wineglasses.

"Also," said the loveliest of the three ravishing girls, "soak your head in what? Hot oil? Dishwater? Piss?"

"Out," said Indrani, "all of you. If you won't leave, then at least go back outside."

They all traipsed back out onto the terrace and the French doors slammed shut.

"Oh my God," I said. "They're on crystal meth?"

"They'll be out there till tomorrow morning. With any luck, they'll all fall off the terrace and splat on the sidewalk."

"Doesn't your TA worry about losing her job if she acts like this in your apartment?"

"Apparently not," said Indrani. "She doesn't need to; she's indispensable to me and she knows it. Why does Mick call you 'Shrink'?"

"I lied to him last night and told him I was a painter," I said. "You blew my cover. That's why."

"You said you were a painter?"

"He was hitting on me, and I was flattered."

"He's a sleazeball. I think he's a meth dealer, actually. It's a good thing you didn't go home with *him*."

I chose to ignore this little dig, hoping our prior conversation was just a hiccup and we'd naturally fall back into sync.

"Aha!" I said. "I wondered how he supported himself. It certainly isn't by writing operas. He was the boyfriend of an old client of mine. I let on to him last night that I knew her, and then I had to pretend not to be a shrink, so he wouldn't realize that I was the one who convinced her to dump him."

When Indrani laughed, I laughed too, mostly with relief. "Oh my God," she said. "What a weird coincidence."

"I know. You should have heard the things my client told me about him. The minute I realized who he was, I should have excused myself and walked away."

"How often does this kind of thing happen to you?" she asked.

"Sometimes I see clients on the subway or in line for a movie. But something like this? Almost never."

Indrani reached forward, took a clementine from the bowl, and began to peel it. "Have you told Raquel yet that you're leaving Anthony?"

"You're the only person I've talked to so far." Peter was a stranger; he didn't count.

"I feel like a broken record, I know, but I'm worried about

you. I can't help it. And I'm worried about Anthony and Wendy, too."

"Thanks," I said, but I didn't feel grateful; I felt a bit insulted and nettled, although I wasn't sure why. Had I really hoped she'd be excited for me? I must have, somehow.

"Look at us," she said, turning the peeled clementine in her hands like a tiny, naked orange brain, "you and me and Raquel. Remember we used to predict our lives and how we'd all end up? We had all those big ideas. I never thought I'd end up a single middle-aged professor, not in a million years. I was going to live in the country and write novels and have a bunch of kids with my perfect husband, remember? Did you ever think you'd end up a divorced middle-aged shrink?"

"I'm not ending up just yet," I said. "I don't really see your point."

"And Raquel," she said. "Sleeping with a twenty-whatever-year-old."

"Yeah?" I said. "So what?"

"So," said Indrani. "Maybe these are our so-called midlife crises. You leaving your husband, Raquel with a guy half her age . . ."

"What about you?" I asked, trying to turn this into light banter instead of what it actually felt like, which was an unwelcome confrontation of some kind. "You've been alone since Vince. Isn't it time for you to realize you're gay and fall in love with a woman? Or maybe go to Jamaica and meet a native and—"

"I think we're all pretty pathetic," said Indrani.

"Indrani," I said. "Come on."

"We are," she said. "All three of us. What happened to us?"

"Are you serious?"

"Yeah," she said.

"But Indrani, we're all doing just fine."

"Are we? Raquel is fucking someone who's young enough to be her own kid, you just picked up some strange guy in a bar and you're about to get a divorce, and I'm a lonely spinster with a terrace full of meth heads. I don't know who's a bigger loser here."

I laughed, relieved: she was kidding after all.

"I'm not kidding," she said, as if she were reprimanding all three of us, me, Raquel, and herself.

I stared at her; I had seen this stern and somewhat puritanical side of Indrani before, of course, but not for a long time, not since we were in our early thirties. Back then, Raquel had just admitted to Indrani and me that she was a junkie; she had been taken to the emergency room by her boyfriend after her second overdose. She had survived, and in the aftermath of this brush with death, she had contacted Indrani and me, her two oldest, closest friends, and told us she was going to get clean, for real. Meanwhile, I was having problems for the first time with Anthony and freaking out about being a new mother, and Indrani had just been cheated on and dumped by another hot, seductive asshole. Raquel flew to New York, and the three of us camped out in Indrani's living room for a three-day powwow, during which Indrani had turned into some kind of hands-on tough-love life coach and told Raquel and me she was horribly disappointed in all three of us, and what were we all thinking? Raquel and I had uncharacteristically lost our usual stoic, self-reliant tough-mindedness and agreed with her; at one very raw low point, we'd all cried together. In the end, after relapsing again, and more than one stint in rehab, Raquel had finally gotten clean and made a new album, I'd mothered Wendy as well as I could and stayed in my marriage, but Indrani had remained alone and preyed upon.

"Frankly, I don't feel pathetic at all, Indrani," I said. "I can't speak for Raquel, but I bet she doesn't, either."

"I know I do," said Indrani.

"And you think I am, too."

"Well," she said, then stopped, looking down at the little clementine, which she turned in her hands. "Maybe not pathetic. But I'm disappointed. I can't lie to you."

I looked into the fire. "Are you actually mad that I'm leaving Anthony?" I asked her cautiously. The caution was my effort to keep my anger at bay, to keep myself from telling her to stop projecting her own regrets and self-castigations onto her best friends.

"I'm not mad," she said. "I'm concerned. There's a difference."

"The thing is," I said, "I don't need concern at all right now. I am fine. I feel like I'm coming back to life. Like this is long overdue. I wish you could trust me. I wish you had more confidence in my ability to make a sane and rational decision, no matter how sudden it feels to you."

"I can't believe you want me to sit here and tell you it's all going to be fine," she said. "I can't do that; it wouldn't be honest."

"It's what I told you when Vince left," I said. "And I was right, wasn't I?"

"But he was a loser," she said. "And he didn't matter. This is a fifteen-year marriage we're talking about here. How could I not at least try to help you save it?"

"It's beyond saving," I said. "That's what I'm trying to tell you."

"But how can you know that when you haven't even told Anthony yet?"

"I know that because I've been married to him for so long. I know what's possible and what isn't." I stopped, too weary to repeat myself anymore. "Please stop lecturing me, Indrani."

We looked blankly at each other. I was so angry at her I was shaking.

"We're going in circles," she said.

"I know we are."

"I don't think I can talk about this anymore," she said.

"Me, neither."

I got up and went out to the foyer and took my coat and scarf off the coat tree, took my bag off the bench. Without another word between us, I left Indrani sitting there alone on her couch. Down on the street, I walked fast, glad for the cold air on my face. I passed the bar where I'd met Peter. In daylight, the neon was muted, the facade sordidly inviting. It would be warm and cozy in there right now, and another hot coffee with rum would go down so nicely, I thought, but I passed by, the entire memory of the previous night resurging in my brain, whole, unmitigated. Still, I felt no guilt, only exhilarated disbelief that I had finally cracked open the carapace that had contained me for so long. Life was so much bigger, so much more interesting, than I had allowed myself to know.

I rode the subway downtown, slumped in my seat, rocking with the motion of the almost-empty train until I was nearly asleep. I got out at Twenty-third Street and walked the darkening early-evening blocks west and south to my building, my head full of spiderwebs, my eyes grainy with fatigue. The trees were bare, the sidewalks grimy. Tinkly Christmas carols assaulted me as I walked through a vendor's piney sidewalk grove of chopped-down, tied-up Christmas trees. He sat in a folding chair in a little jerry-rigged shelter, hunched into his coat and scarf, a small heater burning at his feet.

It amazed me how quickly my fight with Indrani, if that was what it was, had escalated. It felt as if this rupture had always been there, waiting to happen, inevitable in the differences between us, our circumstances and upbringings and personalities. She clung to consistency and stasis after a childhood of upsetting, confusing upheavals, whereas I, having been stuck in the small California town where I was born until I left for college, having been raised by quasi-devout Catholic parents who stayed together for life despite gross incompatibility and mutual boredom, eagerly embraced any kind of change as long as it was in a positive direction. Maybe Indrani and I had both overreacted, had both leapt too quickly to our respective corners, but I couldn't help feeling completely blindsided by her reaction. I had always empathized loyally with her and taken her side in everything, no matter what. I had somehow expected the same in return, and that had been a mistake. She seemed to need me to stay the same; I needed to change, so badly that I was willing to sacrifice a close, old friendship, if that was what it took.

I unlocked the front door of my building, climbed the stairs to the fourth floor, and let myself into our apartment. It was quiet, exactly as I had left it that morning. As always after I'd spent time at Indrani's, our perfectly nice two-bedroom apartment looked shabby and small and plain. The old brown chair in the living room had a dark stain on the headrest; the TV screen was dusty; the hall rug had a hole right by the bathroom doorsill; the Formica counters in the kitchen were covered with burn and scuff marks, stains, and dents; the whole place needed repainting, and the rooms felt close and cramped, the ceilings low.

No one was home yet. My sleepiness was overwhelming. I went into Anthony's and my bedroom, where I took off all my clothes and put them away, shivering even though the room was warm. I put on my pajamas, got into bed, and was asleep so fast, I wasn't aware of any time having passed when I awoke. The room was dark, and my head ached. I listened drowsily for sounds of someone home. I saw a light through the crack under the door, so someone was there. Gradually, I became aware of cooking smells, faint kitchen noises, water running from the sink faucet, a pot lid rattling. I curled up more deeply under the covers and closed my eyes again and fell into a waking doze. A while later, the bedroom door opened.

"Josie?" Anthony said in a low voice. "I made some spaghetti, if you want some."

"Ummph," I said. "Thanks. I'll be right out."

I got up and put on my bathrobe and wandered out to the kitchen, rubbing my eyes and yawning. Anthony was sitting at the kitchen table with a book propped in front of him, already eating. I took a plate from the cupboard and scooped some pasta onto my plate. I knew it wouldn't be cooked enough for my liking; Anthony, whose parents were both Italian, insisted on taking *al dente* literally, despite my frequently pointing out that the pasta was not nearly as good that way. I glopped some tomato sauce on top of the pasta; this, at least, would be palatable, because I'd bought it ready-made at Whole Foods for Anthony and Wendy to eat when I wasn't home to cook for them.

"More wine?" I said, pouring myself a glass from the bottle on the counter.

"Sure," he said, pushing his wineglass forward on the table without looking up from his book.

Sixteen years earlier, I had gone one night, alone, out of sheer curiosity, to hear Anthony Bianchi lecture at The New School. He was a political scientist who specialized in international environmental policies; I had recently discovered a sudden, unprecedented urge in myself to become more informed about such things. I sat in the back of the auditorium and was instantly smitten when he began to speak. I could hardly follow a word of what he said, I was so busy admiring his forthright, easy, confident, irreverent delivery, his profound erudition, and his ability to make the audience, which was made up mostly of college-age and graduate-school kids, laugh. He was not especially handsome or tall, but he was strikingly charismatic in the way of all men who love what they do and are very good at it.

I was single at the time. My private practice was just beginning to flourish; I was twenty-nine and, although I wouldn't have articulated it to myself in quite this way back then, I was in the frame of mind to find a husband. When the lecture was over, I made my way to the front of the room and waited my turn, then introduced myself to Anthony Bianchi. I admitted to him that I hadn't understood much of his lecture, and said I would like to invite him out for a drink and interrogate him.

He looked me over with the careful, acquisitive scrutiny of a customer being offered a bargain that might be too good to be true but too good to pass up, and said he'd love to, that he had no other plans.

Once he'd freed himself from the remainder of his admirers, off we went to a picturesque basement bistro on East Ninth Street. We sat knee-to-knee at a little table and drank wine. I found him seductively abstracted, even brusque; he was amused but impatient at my absolute ignorance about the things that most concerned him. But I was very pretty in those days, and young and bright enough, which didn't hurt. I think I must have disarmed him with my frank, open curiosity about him; I got him talking about his childhood in the New Jersey Pine Barrens, his college years in Providence, at Brown. He was eight years older than I was; I loved the fact that he was a grown-up, a successful writer and professor. I loved the naïve, brash way he made me feel and act, and I loved the challenge of having to win him.

It turned out not to be all that hard after all: I went home with him that night and tumbled with him into his bed. We did not sleep much that night, or many of the nights that followed. Our sex was so urgent, we sometimes bit or scratched each other; it was always mutual and to the point, since Anthony didn't trouble himself much with foreplay, and I didn't need it, I was so turned on by him already. I proceeded to fall so passionately in love with him, I felt as if all the skin had been flayed from my body. This caused me to behave in ways I never had before. I wrote vital, hot, urgent love letters to him and sent them through the mail; they delighted him, he claimed, although he never wrote any back to me. All the corny, cheesy love songs I'd sung along to in junior high made startling sense to me for the first time in my life, so much so that they seemed to have been written expressly for the way I felt about him: "The Twelfth of Never," "Top of the World," "You Light Up My Life," "I Can't Live If Living Is Without You." I could not get enough of his stocky, compact, willing body, could not believe how lucky I was to know his erudite, curious, cynical, funny mind. Watching his face over a restaurant table as he talked could cause me to lose my appetite from love. The smell of the back of his neck could make me swoon. Misunderstandings and missteps and painful fights had been there all along, and he had been condescending and fatalistic from the start, but instead of seeing these as warning signs, I allowed whatever feelings of frustration and doubt I had to be swept away with sex. That had possibly been my biggest mistake with him.

Now, I stood at the kitchen counter looking at his well-shaped head, watching him eat spaghetti that hadn't been cooked enough, remembering how much I had adored him. I felt like crying, but I couldn't cry. On his face was an expression of deep engagement in whatever he was reading.

He had squandered my love. That was what it came down to. I had no more to give him, and therefore it was over.

"Anthony," I said.

"My sweet," he said, turning a page.

"Hello," I said.

"Hello," he repeated. His voice held a certain amount of warmth, but he did not look up from his book. His reading glasses had slid halfway down his nose. His hairline had receded high up on his scalp; his graying hair spiraled down his neck in discrete, handsome curls. Under his V-necked blue sweater, his stomach had gone a bit soft. He wore black trousers and sneakers. He was beginning to look like Benjamin Franklin, with that firm, well-shaped mouth, those weary, intelligent eyes with pouches underneath, those incipient jowls. He was fifty-three years old, and he looked it, but he still had whatever quality it was that had originally attracted me to him. I could easily imagine, without a single pang of regret, some other woman scooping him up as soon as I had extricated myself from him. She was welcome to him; I had outgrown him. It was her turn now, whoever she was.

I looked at him, jangling with wakefulness and nerves. "Where's Wendy?" I asked, my leg jittering up and down. I took a gulp of wine.

"She stayed for dinner at her friend's house."

"What are you reading?"

"A book about post-Communist capitalism in Eastern Europe." He held his book up briefly to show me the dark, scholarly-looking cover; then he found his place in it again. "He's a Marxist," said Anthony as he continued to read, "who can't accept the fact that Communism failed because of its inherent flaws, not because of history. He actually skewers certain of his fellow Marxist sociologists for failing to demonstrate the proper optimism." Anthony said the word *optimism* with ironic emphasis. It was a quality he had little patience for.

"How did your radio interview go this morning? I had clients; I missed it."

"All the NPR announcers are doped up on Xanax. Cozy little world we live in, cozy little people."

"What are they supposed to do, scream with horror? They're just reporting the news." He had no response to this. "Sounds like it went well, actually," I said.

"All I was doing," he said, his eyes in his book, "was preaching to the choir. The Prius-driving, recycling, low-carbon-footprint choir."

Anthony could talk and read at the same time. But his eyes trumped his ears: He usually remembered what he'd read while talking, but he never remembered conversations he'd had while reading. He was like a sleepwalker who grocery-shopped and paid bills in his sleep and forgot it all the next morning. Most of our conversations were now conducted with a book between us— his book, of course. When I read, I shushed him ferociously, for all the good it did me; he had never accepted the fact that other people didn't possess his unique facility for ingesting words with his eyes while spewing them from his mouth.

He turned a page, scratched his forehead. He had barely looked at me since I had entered the kitchen. Normally, I wouldn't have noticed, but now that I had been awakened to the fact that this marriage was dead, I took it as confirmation. I sat across from him with my plate of spaghetti. I began to eat, because I was hungry, but I had to force the food in, chew the undercooked strands hard and swallow hard to get them past the tight constriction in my throat. The wine tasted like life's blood to me; I took another acidic, thick red gulp. The wine and spaghetti roiled in my stomach. I forced more of everything down.

I didn't know how to say it. I couldn't even begin. I had helped and guided so many clients through moments just like this one.

In fact, I thought of myself as an advocate for and expert in how to leave your partner, a sort of breakup maven. But this expertise was couched in the context of my being a happily married therapist. Like the frog in a pot of tap water on the stove, I had thought things were still room temperature between Anthony and me even as I was being cooked alive.

I imagined returning from my office to some quiet new apartment, shedding my work clothes, rummaging through the fridge, all alone. Wendy was somewhere in the background in this fantasy; it didn't exclude her, but the point of it was that Anthony was nowhere to be found in it.

"I have to hop out of the pot," I said absurdly.

"Ha-ha," he said automatically, not listening.

"I mean it, Anthony," I said.

"Mean what, my love," he said. This wasn't a question; it was a soothing pat on the head, meant to appease me while he stayed happily submerged.

"I mean I want a separation," I said.

He looked sharply at me.

"I want a separation," I said. "From you. From our marriage."

He put his fork down on his plate and coughed. He continued to stare at me, blinking.

"You heard me right," I said.

It was out; I had said it. I had broken the hymen of this virgin topic, and now everything would take its own natural course from here. I took another gulp of wine. I watched Anthony's face as he absorbed what I had said and formulated his response to it. I knew his expressions so well, knew his very thoughts, even. This conversation might as well have already been scripted, I thought, for all the surprises I'm going to find in it.

"I have to ask the obvious question," said Anthony. He blinked, took a sharp breath. "Have you met someone else?"

"There is no other man involved here," I said, and then I waited for his next question.

"Are you sure about this?"

"I am absolutely sure," I responded promptly, right on cue.

"Is there anything I can say to change your mind?"

"No," I said. "There isn't. I want to move out. We can talk about what to do about Wendy. In the immediate future, I want to find myself a place. You can have this apartment; it was yours to begin with."

He took off his reading glasses and set them down next to his book. A fugitive vapor of old, old passion crossed his face like a tissue-thin wisp of cloud being blown across a clear sky by a rogue wind. The planes of his face contracted slightly with the impact of its passing, and then it was gone, as quickly as it had appeared.

"Yes," he said. "The apartment was mine to begin with. And you're much more adaptable than I am to new places. I'll help you in any way I can, of course. But I suppose you've figured it all out already, down to the last stick of furniture." He gave me a sad smile. "I always loved that expression, 'stick of furniture.' So Victorian."

I began to cry, racking heaving sobs that made me gasp and hiccup. I cried and cried. He sat with me while I wept, didn't say a word or move to comfort me, as if he had already realized that all our sorrows and joys would now be experienced apart rather than together.

"You're not even going to fight for me," I yelled through streams of mucus, my mouth contorting with weeping so absurdly I could hardly get the words out. "You're just going to let me go."

"Here," he said, handing me a Kleenex.

I blew my nose, but I could not stop crying.

"Josie," he said. "I think you're being a little ridiculous, but I know better than to try to talk you out of something you want to do."

"I would hardly use the word *want*," I said hotly. "*Need*, maybe. You never even look at me anymore. We haven't had sex since last spring, and that was just because I got drunk and threw myself at you. You don't see me. I feel like a ghost to you, like I'm dead. Like we both are." I lost control of my face then and had to struggle with my cheek muscles for a moment. "You would never go to therapy with me," I added.

Anthony closed his book. "You know why, Josie," he said tightly. "I was this way when you met me. I haven't changed. You've changed, and I accept that, although I would vastly prefer you didn't leave me, and that's an understatement. Of course you deserve a man who's more compatible with you. I am so sorry I've failed you." He said this last sentence as if it were a line in a school play he was mocking. I hated it when he did this, couched something that ought to have been genuine and touching in ironic glibness. It seemed cowardly; it was nothing but a sign of how limited he was.

"I think I should move out as soon as possible," I said. I gave a small vestigial hiccup, which annoyed me; it undercut my righteous anger at him. "We should tell Wendy tonight, when she gets home. You've made this very easy for me, Anthony. There doesn't seem to be anything left to say."

"You'll be back," he said.

"Not until you stop being condescending and impervious," I told him, my anger suddenly gone, just like that—poof—replaced by something like giddy relief. I was leaving; I was free. I began to eat my spaghetti again. "You make the worst spaghetti," I said, laughing.

I noticed that he had not reopened his book. I had his full attention, it seemed. "All of us Italians know how to make spaghetti," he said. "It's in our blood."

"Well, yours is horrible," I said. "Undercooked and glutinous."

"I follow the directions!"

"The directions are fallible."

He shook his head. This was by no means the first time I had pointed this out to him. "I like it like this," he said.

"That's very sad."

"Maybe I just have different taste in pasta doneness than you do."

"Maybe you're totally out of touch with the sensory world."

"Maybe not entirely," he said, looking fondly at me.

Now it was my turn to feel the old, old pull of passion for him.

"You know, if you would agree to just a few therapy sessions, I might be able to stay," I said. "What's the harm in just trying?"

"If we can't work it out on our own, we can't work it out."

"That makes no sense whatsoever," I said.

"Nevertheless," he said.

"You think if you use a word like *nevertheless,* it makes your argument viable?"

He rubbed his hands over his face and blinked a few times. "Listen," he said. "I can't say I'm totally surprised here. So you want to go? Go. I predict you'll come back eventually. I feel like you need to do this. I am not going to fight you, but that's only because I believe that you will come back in the end."

"You're kicking me out?" I said.

"Not exactly," he replied.

"You're just being preemptive," I said. "You macho guido."

We both laughed.

"If I thought therapy would do a thing, I would go," he said. "No offense to your profession."

He had always mocked my profession; I had never been the least bit offended. Now I wondered why the hell not.

"If I were our marital therapist," I said briskly, "I would force you to exercise regularly, cut down on the booze, and take vitamin B supplements."

"Right there, you've lost me," said Anthony. His tone was predictably laconic.

"And then," I said, "I would send you and me on a weeklong vacation to somewhere like Glacier National Park to stay in the lodge and hike all day and canoe on the lake, then come in and take a hot shower, have cocktails, eat a big dinner, and go to bed early and have sex every night."

He watched me, half-smiling skeptically, waiting for me to go on. His book lay on the table, ignored.

"And then we could start to talk about the reasons why we've both shut down over the past ten or so years. You know, clean up the marital ecosystem. Try to get everyone thinking more collectively, with more foresight."

He reached across the table to take my hand. "Optimist," he said with a small smile.

"You know, fatalism isn't the answer to everything," I said. I paused, remembering. "Oh God, I had a horrible fight with Indrani today."

"About what?" he said.

Just in time, I realized that the subject of my fight with Indrani wasn't necessarily germane or appropriate to reveal to Anthony just now. "You know I love her," I said. "But she can be a little judgmental and myopic sometimes."

We were still holding hands, but the meaning had gone out of the contact, and now our hands were inert and disconnected in each other's grasp. I pulled mine away and picked up my wineglass.

"Sometimes," Anthony said, his eyebrows raised.

"Well," I said, "no one's perfect."

"Except for you," he said.

"Sure," I replied.

"You are," he said. "You're perfect. I have never had the slightest complaint about you."

I laughed bitterly. "Ecch, shut up. That's of no use to me at all. You say that, but you won't do one goddamned thing to help me stay with you. That's manipulative and cruel."

He inhaled sharply through his nose. His nostrils flared a little; his eyes bulged. He blinked.

"Are you crying?" I asked him.

Instead of answering, he took my hand again and led me into our bedroom, where he stripped off my pajamas. I helped him off with his clothes, and then we lay in our bed naked together and held each other. His body still felt so good against mine.

"I forgot about this," he said. "You feel so good."

He put his face in my neck and breathed.

"You do, too," I said. I kissed his head, the smooth part high on his forehead where he was losing his hair. It smelled of him.

CHAPTER FOUR

FOUR

Anthony and I were wearing our pajamas and robes, sitting in the living room with glasses of wine, by the time Wendy got home at 9:27. Her curfew was nine o'clock, but we were prepared to overlook her lateness, given the news we were about to spring on her.

"Hello, Wendy," I called when I heard her in the entryway. "We're in here."

She took her time taking off her coat, hanging it in the closet, going into the kitchen, going to her room to leave her backpack. Anthony and I waited for her, occasionally exchanging a look but not speaking. I heard her cooing to her hamster, Melvin, as she fed him.

I could smell the musk of sex wafting up from my pajama shirt, the smell of Anthony's skin and semen, and my own smells. It had been a short and emotional fuck just now, possibly, but not necessarily, our last. Immediately afterward, he had sat up. "Well," he had said, "I think we needed that."

Wendy sidled into the living room, not looking at either of us, holding a glass of cranberry juice. "Hey," she said, perching as far as she could get from me on the far end of the couch, tucking a leg under her, putting her juice down on the table next to the couch. She looked like a stork poised for flight, bony and awkward, contained. She was formidably pretty. Her cheeks were flushed from the cold night air and what had, no doubt, been a mad dash to get home as close to her curfew as possible. Her shiny black hair, which she wore long and layered, so she looked, unfortunately and totally misleadingly, like an Asian call girl, was as perfectly in place as ever. She wore a pair of narrow-legged jeans and a rather elegant rose-pink cardigan sweater with appliquéd sequins that I hadn't seen before; where had she gotten it? It made her tiny breasts look rounded and bigger, or maybe they had grown recently when I wasn't looking.

"How was Indrani's, Mom?" she asked.

Wendy worshipped Indrani's taste in clothes and furniture, her apartment, her blondeness, her composure and sweetness. She allowed Indrani to take her shopping; maybe Indrani had bought her that sweater. I had never been jealous at all of Indrani's sway over my daughter. In fact, I had bestowed on her the unofficial title of godmother and written into my will her official legal guardianship of Wendy if Anthony and I were both killed in a freak bus accident. But now, I felt a new, unaccustomed sharpness when Wendy said her name.

"She was hungover and tired," I said disloyally. "I didn't stay long."

Wendy sniffed and rubbed her nose. "Was the party fun?"

"It was okay," I said. "How was it at Ariel's?"

"Okay. We sang karaoke with this new program her mom got her. Mostly Shakira and Christina Aguilera, and also some Rihanna songs. The only problem is that Ariel seriously thinks Ashley Tisdale is, like, really talented and she always wants to do *High School Musical* stuff. Anyway, we recorded me and I sounded really good."

Wendy planned to go to the High School of Music and Art to study acting and singing in hopes, of course, of becoming a star as soon as possible, which also explained her interest in UCLA. She had an unfortunate passion, currently, for what Anthony called "tuneless ghetto singing," the highly ornamented, emotionally overwrought style called "melisma," which allowed today's kids to drive today's parents up the same wall their own parents—that is, mine—had been driven up by the likes of Blondie, Pink Floyd, and Led Zeppelin. Lately, Wendy had been adopting the nasal, loud, vibrato-y, equally emotionally overwrought Broadway-musical style, which was, in my opinion, worse than melisma, whereas Anthony thought nothing was worse than melisma. In any case, Wendy affected a blithe, serene indifference to her parents' unspoken but barely hidden loathing of the activity she felt most passionately about.

"We've been waiting for you," I said.

"Sorry I was late! I lost track of time. I practically ran the whole way home."

"It's okay," I said. "There's something serious your dad and I need to discuss with you."

Her karaoke-inspired animation faded and her face went blank and closed off. "What is it?" she asked cautiously.

"Dad and I have been having a lot of problems in recent years," I said.

"I haven't noticed anything," said Wendy too quickly.

"I'm so sorry that this is coming out of the blue for you," I said. "But your father and I don't feel that this marriage is working for either one of us anymore, and we agree that these are issues that can't be resolved."

"So you're getting divorced?"

"No, not yet," I said. "We're separating for now. But we want you to know that this has nothing to do with you at all. We both love you so much. This is totally and completely between Dad and me; it's our failure."

She was silent for a moment, watching me expressionlessly, as if she was waiting for me to say more. I was ready for tears, a tantrum, something dramatic and out of character. I would have welcomed a display of emotion from her, I realized. It would have been a relief.

"Um, Mom?"

"Yeah."

"You don't have to do the whole shrink thing. I know it's not my fault. How could it be? It's your marriage, and I'm just a kid."

I smiled at her. "Maybe it's obvious to you, but I really wanted you to know that."

"Thanks," she said. "I guess I sort of figured that."

"You never fail to impress me," I said.

"So where am I going to live? Can I stay here? Are you moving out, or is Dad? I think I want to stay here."

"Dad is staying here," I said. "I'll move somewhere nearby for now. If you want to stay here with Dad, that is absolutely your decision and fine with both of us."

"Are you sure, Dad?" she asked Anthony.

"Of course!" said Anthony, but I could tell he was slightly faking his jovial delight at the thought of single-handedly having to keep a close, first-line-of-defense monitoring parental eye on an adolescent girl. Still, it might do him good to have to try, and meanwhile, although I didn't necessarily want to bring this up just then, I already knew I would be doing a lot of cell-phone mothering during the day; Wendy could get herself to school just fine, but maybe, especially at the beginning, I would come home most evenings, cook dinner, and be there for anything she needed. Then we would see how to separate our lives in the best way for her. We'd play it by ear, as a family, until she went to college.

"For now, then, that's what we'll do," I said. "You can always change your mind and come live with me, Wendy."

"Okay," she said formally. "Thanks, Mom."

"And Dad and I will always be friends," I added.

"I figured," she said. "You never even, like, fight or anything."

"Sometimes that can be as much of an indication of trouble as anything," I said.

A strange silence fell among the three of us. We all sat there, looking and feeling a little forlorn. For nearly thirteen years, since Wendy had come home with us from China, we had been a disconnected, odd family unit, but we were all we had, and now

I was busting us up. It would be awkward at first for my husband and daughter, just the two of them there, without me.

With some effort, I forced myself to wait for one of them to break the silence, unwilling to be the workhorse for another minute. Let Anthony say something sensitive and loving to his daughter, who had just received what any normal kid would consider rather shattering, life-changing, possibly traumatic news. Wendy rarely revealed much of anything, but of course that didn't mean she had no feelings; it just indicated a deeply reserved nature that might hide latent or delayed reactions to things that would later come around and bite her in the ass in the form of adult-onset mental disorders of varying degrees of severity, from garden-variety neuroses to full-blown suicidal depression. Or maybe, I thought, Wendy sensed my probing motherly and psychological inquiries into her personality and withdrew all evidence from my appropriating, hypothesizing, curious grasp, and who could blame her? Having a shrink for a mother was, no doubt, a great motivator for trying to fly under the radar. When she got her first period, she had hidden all traces of it from me; I had learned she was menstruating when her friend Ariel had referred casually to the fact that the two of them always got their periods on the same day.

Anthony rested his ankle on his knee and waggled his suspended foot. He was dying to get back to his book now that the domestic crisis had hit and we'd all survived, but he knew he had to put in at least another ten minutes with us before he could get away without appearing cold-blooded.

"So guess what," Wendy said, hunching her skinny shoulders and hugging herself. "I heard this stuff today about Raquel."

"What stuff?" I asked.

"Okay, like, so Ariel's mother lets her go on all those sites, so I was just watching over her shoulder. I didn't go on them myself."

Wendy was not permitted to read gossip Web logs.

"And?" I said, my expression conveying that I just wanted to know the story about Raquel; Wendy wasn't going to get in trouble, at least not this time.

"So today there was this story everywhere. Mina Boriqua was the worst. She's this big fat dyke with blue hair who lives in L.A. and does nothing all day but write gossip on her blog. Ariel and I usually think she's funny, but this was really, really mean and awful."

" 'Dyke'?" I said pointedly.

"Whatever, lesbian," she said. "Anyway, she hates most rock-star girls except for Madonna, Amy Winehouse, and Posh Spice, and most of the Latina ones because she's Puerto Rican. So you would think she would like Raquel, because she's Mexican, right? But today she called her 'a horny senior citizen on the prowl' and 'a cougar gone wild' and drew wrinkles on the face of her photo and droopy boobs on her front. She draws on people's pictures. She's such a three-year-old."

Anthony snorted gently.

"Dad," said Wendy patiently, "a cougar means a sexy older woman. She didn't literally mean a large wildcat."

"I know what *cougar* means," said Anthony. "I was just envisioning Raquel's reaction to being called 'a horny senior citizen.' "

"Oh God," I said. "That'll mean five more Botox appointments and a week at a spa on a detox fast, with three colonics and five hours of yoga a day."

Anthony shook his head. "What did she do to deserve this treatment?" he asked.

"She supposedly had an affair with Jimmy Black," said Wendy.

"Well," said Anthony dryly. "Serves her right, then."

"The actor?" Wendy said with patient condescention. "From *Endless Pool*? That new show on HBO? That *very popular and famous* new show on HBO, which I'm not allowed to watch but all of my friends get to?"

We did not have cable in our family, a sore topic for Wendy.

"He's a big TV star," I said. "Indrani was telling me earlier."

"A big TV star with a pregnant girlfriend!" said Wendy. "The paparazzi caught Raquel coming out of the Four Seasons with him at four in the morning! He's, like, twenty-three, and she's . . ." She looked at me. "Your age," she said.

"A senior citizen," I said.

Wendy said sheepishly, "Okay, not *that* old. But a lot older than he is."

"Maybe they were just sitting in the hotel bar, having a meeting," I said.

"I don't know," said Wendy. "It said Raquel can't be reached for comment. Anyway, his girlfriend is about to have a baby."

"I believe I'll get back to work now," said Anthony.

He got up and left the room. We heard him in his little study off the kitchen, giving a little groan of relief as he sank into his armchair. Wendy giggled softly. I didn't make a move to get up, and neither did she. We sat at either end of the couch, looking at each other.

"I hope you're going to be okay, Mom," said Wendy.

"This won't be easy for any of us," I said. "But just so you know, I'll still be around. You might wish I would be around less, but that's okay; that's better than not enough."

She hesitated, seeming to be about to say something joking and deflecting, and then she said, "I'm glad. At least at first."

"It's going to be okay. We'll get through this. Daddy and I both love you so much."

She looked away, smiling slyly. "Daddy loves reading so much."

I laughed.

"I heard that," Anthony called from his study.

"You're not denying it, Daddy," Wendy called back.

"I deny it!" Anthony said.

"Anyway," said Wendy, "I think it's lame for people to stay together just for the kids."

"You do?" I said.

"Parents have needs. Kids shouldn't run the universe."

I shook my head. "Where did you get this?"

"My own independent thought."

I burst out laughing. She looked hurt. I stopped laughing and said, "Wendy, you're allowed to be upset about this. You're not required to be mature and accepting. You can get mad at me and tell me I'm a selfish bitch, if you want to. I can take it, I promise."

"Well, thanks," she said. "I'll keep that in mind, but I'm just saying, I think it's probably for the best that you and Daddy are splitting up, Mom. I think it will benefit you both to be independent of each other if the marriage isn't really working for you."

"She was a sage in her past life," Anthony called.

"Shut up, Daddy," said Wendy, looking pleased.

"With a Fu Manchu beard and yellow teeth," he added.

"Shut up, Daddy," Wendy said again. "Anyway, Ariel's parents got divorced three years ago, and she says they're both much happier, and she and her little brother are, too. It means everyone is nicer to them and they get more stuff. Dad, can we get cable after Mom moves out? I'll bother you so much less if we get it. Think about it."

I heard Anthony laughing. Now that we were coming apart, Anthony and Wendy were suddenly bantering like one of those 1970s TV families I'd grown up envying. All it took to turn us into Sonny and Cher and Chastity was for me to decide to leave.

Wendy picked up her glass of juice. "Maybe you should go call Raquel, Mom. I want to know the story from her point of view, so I can tell Ariel tomorrow."

"You can't gossip about Raquel. This is private. Anyway, you're too young to know about this, aren't you?"

"Probably," said Wendy. "But—"

"Right," I said. "I'm not going to tell you a thing. But I am going to go and call her now. I've been planning to call her all day."

I leaned over and kissed her forehead. She accepted this without flinching, which under any other circumstances might have made me wonder whether she had been taken over by an alien. I got up and went into Anthony's and my bedroom and closed the door. I sat on the bed, fished my cell phone out of my bag, and punched in the speed-dial number for Raquel's cell phone.

"Jo," she said in my ear before the phone even rang. Her low, husky, very slightly Spanish-accented voice was loud in my ear. "I was about to call you."

"Wendy just told me she read something about you on the Internet gossip—"

"Yeah," she said. "Goddamn it. They were lying in wait. He tipped them off, the little bastard."

"Who did?" I slid my legs under the covers. With one hand, I arranged all the pillows behind me and leaned against them.

"Jimmy Black," she said. "He wanted to get away from that girl. He told me he hates her, and he's freaked-out about the kid. I see it all now. He used me. Now he gets off scot-free, gets rid of both of us, and she's up shit creek and I'm collateral damage."

"Raq," I said, "so what? You slept with a guy half your age. That's good, if anything, right? I mean, all publicity is good publicity, first of all, and second, it means you're hot."

"It means I'm an evil bitch stealing a father away from a pregnant woman," she said. "He's a spineless asshole who didn't have the nerve to just end it with her; he had to drag me down with him. And now I'm the one who's painted with the tarred brush. This country is full of puritans, and nothing makes them more puritanical than pregnancy, and nothing makes them more vengeful than a home wrecker. 'Home wrecker'—that's what they're calling me! In addition to some other horrible things. All publicity is not good publicity. Some publicity can screw up your entire life forever. I'm being burned at the stake, metaphorically. Sorry, do I sound overdramatic? Sorry. I know. It sounds absurd."

"It'll blow over in five minutes, won't it?"

"No," she said. "My name has hardly been in the news much lately, so now this is all they'll think about when they think about me, if they do. So this is basically the end of the world for me. In a manner of speaking. I'm at the airport right now. My flight boards in about ten minutes. Anyway, I was going to call you just now to beg you to come down to meet me."

My cell phone was getting hot against my ear. I always wondered whether it was cooking my brains when it did that. "Meet you where?"

"I'm going down to Mexico City for a while. I speak the language and it's a quick flight, but it's far away from all this. My publicist, which is a word that I still can't say with a straight face, told me to get out of town and say nothing and that she'll handle the press. I said, okay, whatever, so I'm getting on this plane and leaving. I got to the airport without being followed."

"I just can't believe this is really all that bad," I said.

"I'm going to stay in the Centro in a cheap backpackers' hotel. It's nothing fancy, to put it mildly, but no one will look for me there, and it's where I used to stay in the old days, so it has good memories, and I really need the good memories right now. And Josie, I also really need you to come down and hold my hand and cheer me up and have fun with me. I'm begging you. Please? When have I ever begged you for anything before?"

"You haven't," I said. "And I will seriously think about coming. I promise. But I know you'll be all right. Something like this can't hurt you. Think how brilliant your new album is. It'll speak for itself. That's all that matters. By tomorrow, everyone will have moved on to the next scandal."

"You're speaking logically," she said. "And I'm sure you have a point. It's just that I'm freaking out. I'm a complete irrational mess. So you're on vacation now, right?"

"Right," I said, thinking fast. Raquel was one of the few people in the world I would drop everything for, do anything for, anytime. Could I go? I wondered.

"So come down! Come the day after Christmas. I can get you a ticket, my treat. You can have your own room, also my treat, but I really want you to stay in my room; there're two beds and it's more fun that way. Don't you need a trip somewhere warm right now?"

"Mexico City is not warm right now."

"Warmer than New York!"

"Actually," I said, "I have some news for you, too."

"What?"

"I'm leaving Anthony," I said. "We're separating. I was planning to spend my vacation finding a place to live. We just decided tonight; we just told Wendy."

"Holy shit," said Raquel. "Are you okay?"

"Yeah," I said. "Well, sort of. I guess. I will be."

"You sure?"

"I have to admit that I'm relieved," I said, "and, yes, a little sad, but also excited."

"Well then," said Raquel, "I have to admit that I'm not all that surprised."

"Really? Indrani was."

"Indrani would be."

"I'm kind of upset with her, Raq. She was a little hard on me."

"She would be. She takes everything very personally. Never mind that your whole life is in upheaval. I'm sure she made it all about herself, right? I love the girl, but she is a bit of a narcissist."

This was funny, actually, coming from Raquel, who was

amazingly self-involved, albeit charmingly, self-deprecatingly so, but I chose not to point this out. Anyway, I was happy to hear Raquel bad-mouth Indrani, because for the first time, I agreed with her. Now that Indrani had judged me, I was free to judge her right back. The floodgates were open. She could be a bit of a narcissist, come to think of it.

"She told me she thought I was pathetic," I said.

"Please," said Raquel. "I think you know exactly what you need; you've always been that way. But I think you need to get away. Come down! We'll drink tequila and go dancing and breathe pollution. And eat chorizo tacos. They're so good, you'll die; they're like crack. Come down, Jo, please? We'll be Thelmita and Luisa!"

"I'll think about it," I said.

"That means no. Don't say no. Come on, Luisa!"

"I get to be Thelmita," I said.

"No way. I'm shorter than you. You're the tall sexy one; I'm the short crazy one."

"Thelma was the *tall* crazy one. Anyway, they were both sexy. Whatever; the point is, I can't come down; I need to do battle with Manhattan real estate."

"Shit, they're calling my flight. I'm going to call you again tomorrow night, and you'll tell me what time your flight lands on December twenty-sixth and I'll tell you how to get to the Hotel Isabel. *¿Comprendes, chica?* It's on me, my treat. Wish me a safe flight. I love you, Jo. You're gonna be okay, I promise." She made kissing noises into the receiver, and then the line went dead.

I sat alone in the darkened bedroom for a while, thinking. The apartment had gone quiet again. Anthony had sunk back into his little fiefdom; no doubt Wendy was listening to her CD player on headphones and figuring out what to wear to the birthday party she had been invited to the following night. I had nothing to do. I figured I could go into the kitchen and clean up the remnants of dinner, then take a shower, then check on Wendy and make sure she wasn't on her laptop, being lured to a Burger King by a predatory middle-aged man posing as Zac Efron, and then I could come back to bed and read *The New Yorker* until I fell asleep. I was so sick of *The New Yorker*, I couldn't bear it. I had read just about every issue for the past twenty years, and for a long time now, I had suspected that they recycled their articles and stories and cartoons in five-year loops; the poems were all just rearranged jumbles of the same words over and over: *land, sky, light, death, love, cabin, hand, deer, cedar, lake, face, dark, kitchen table, skin, you.* It made me want to try my hand at a *New Yorker* poem myself. How hard could it be?

My fight with Indrani still rankled; my stomach was in knots from everything that had happened in the past twenty-four hours, but somehow this unexpected schism with my old, close friend was foremost in my tangle of thoughts. I looked over at the phone, tempted to call her. I was surprised, in fact, that she hadn't called me to apologize and ask how I was doing. That she hadn't implied that she felt justified in acting the way she had, which was unforgivable. An apology, now, would have made everything better; merely to feel understood, that she had listened to me, would have made all the difference.

I lay back against the pillows and looked up at the dim ceiling and ran my hands over my body—hips, breasts, waist, thighs, neck, face—then crossed my arms over my chest and closed my eyes and lay there like a dead person. I would be dead soon enough. But I felt sparks of light shooting through my veins, electric sparks, hot white light that meant I needed to do exactly what I had just set in motion. I knew that of course I would be hit soon enough by terrible pain and sadness about the end of my marriage, but right then I felt nothing but curiosity about what would happen next. It had been so simple, really, to extricate myself from my cage. Indrani had been right about one thing: Wendy would suffer because of our split. But I would do everything I could to help her through it. Including, I decided, getting cable so she could watch Raquel's erstwhile boyfriend's show and talk about it with all her friends.

Thank God for Raquel.

It was Friday night. Christmas was on Tuesday. If I left Wednesday morning, I thought, I'd have time to set things in motion with Realtors that weekend.

Of course I couldn't go to Mexico. What was I thinking? I had to take care of Wendy. I had to deal with my impending move.

I got out of bed and went to the little desk in the corner where my computer was. As it booted up, I stuck my head out of my bedroom door. "Wendy," I called to her closed bedroom door.

Her door opened. "Yeah?"

"What was that Web site called?"

"Mina Boriqua dot com," she said. "Mina with an *i* and Boriqua, like Puerto Rican Day Parade signs. Are you going on? Can I look?"

I hesitated. "You already looked at it today."

"But she might have added new stuff since then."

"All right," I said.

I sat at my desk; she stood looking over my shoulder, breathing into my ear. I typed in the address and hit the return key, and there it was, a picture of Raquel looking uncharacteristically haggard, her dark red hair up in a messy ponytail, her skin white and parchmentlike in the harsh California sun and dry air. HAS SHE SKIPPED TOWN? said the headline.

"She always does that," said Wendy. "Puts up really ugly pictures of stars she's mad at and then makes fun of them. She is so, so mean. But sometimes really funny, and she makes fun of herself just as much."

"How does she know Raquel left?" I said. "I talked to her just now and she said no one saw her leave."

"Mina has spies everywhere," said Wendy. "So where did she go?"

"I'm not telling," I said.

"Come on, Mom!"

"If I tell you, you'll tell Ariel," I said. "Then Ariel will send this Mina Boriqua person an E-mail, tipping her off, and then the whole world will know."

"I promise. She would never do that."

"I was a thirteen-year-old girl once, don't forget, Wendy, hard as it may be to believe. It would be too much of a burden for you and Ariel to keep such juicy information to yourselves. And Raquel doesn't want anyone but me to know." I paused, then added skeptically, "She also wants me to meet her there."

"You have to go!" Wendy said immediately.

"I can't go, Wendy."

"Why not?"

"For one thing, I have to find an apartment. For another, I

want to spend time with you while we adjust to this whole idea of the separation."

"I don't need you to do that," she said. "Really, I'm totally okay about this. Parents split up. It happens to everyone. It's, like, part of life. Anyway, you're not really going anywhere. I know you. You'll be over here all the time to keep an eye on me because you don't think Daddy will be strict enough. It'll be like you never even moved out."

"My God," I said, scrolling down to read the gossip about Raquel. "She *is* mean. No wonder Raquel is so freaked-out. This is unbelievable. Did she draw these horns on her head? And what's that stuff that's supposed to be coming out of her crotch?"

"She draws that stuff all the time. The crotch stuff is supposed to mean she has an STD or something. I know. And everyone reads her, like, everyone in the entire world."

" 'My sources tell me,' " I read out loud, in horror for Raquel, " 'that Rock-hell Dominguez has slithered out of town since we broke the story of her home-wrecker activities this morning. Good riddance to a poisonous snake. Meanwhile, we hear that Jimmy Black is available now, for all you homo horndogs!' "

" 'Rock-hell,' " echoed Wendy admiringly. "So totally stupid. Mom, I am serious; you have to go meet her. She's probably really, really upset. I command you to go. We'll be fine without you. We'll eat takeout."

I laughed as I turned off the computer. "You 'command' me?"

Wendy laughed, too. "Ariel and I always say that."

She had started bantering with her father a few minutes ago, and now she was including me in her and Ariel's private world. Maybe I should have left Anthony years ago. Maybe Wendy had been shut down and closed off because daughters learned how to behave from their mothers. I wasn't naïve enough to think that this heralded a whole new change in our relationship; once the shock of this new development wore off, she'd probably slam the door again. But for now, this was an unexpected joy.

"Can you keep a secret from Ariel?" I asked.

"I never have before," said Wendy. "But maybe I could keep this one, for Raquel."

"Tell me tomorrow if you think you really and truly can keep what I'm going to tell you between us."

"Okay," she said. "I'll think about it." To her credit, she neither tried to wheedle it out of me nor promised glibly. Such a good girl.

Later that night, when Anthony came to bed, I was lying awake, waiting for him. He got into bed quietly, easing himself onto the mattress so he wouldn't jostle me, sliding under the covers so he wouldn't steal them from me. I had trained him to do this early in our marriage; it was one of my major (and only) triumphs as his wife, at least in terms of positively affecting his behavior.

"I'm awake," I said as he carefully laid his head on his pillow.

"Oh!" He jumped. "God, I almost had a heart attack."

"Sorry."

He settled himself more comfortably on the mattress.

"You okay?" I asked.

"Considering that my wife is leaving me," he said.

"That's what I meant."

"Never been better," he said. I scooched over and found his

nearest arm, moved it so it was around me, and fitted myself to him, my own arm draped over his stomach. He smelled very strongly of toothpaste and, underneath that, whiskey. "I've gained some weight," he said, resting his head against mine. "I hadn't really noticed till tonight."

His stomach was warm and fairly firm under my hand; he hadn't gained much weight, but he did need to exercise. "Till someone saw you naked for the first time in months?"

"Well," he said. "Yes. It was sobering."

"All you need," I said, "is exercise."

"What kind?"

I wasn't falling for this. He tended to grill me about what I thought he needed to do to improve himself, all of which advice he would proceed to ignore and then use against me, somehow, in our next argument about why he was such a lousy husband, as evidence that I nagged and pushed him too much. "You figure it out," I said. "You're a big boy."

"You won't tell me?"

"I've resigned as your life coach, effective immediately."

He readjusted his leg so it fit better between mine. "I guess I'll have to learn how to cook something besides horrible spaghetti."

Here we were again, Sonny and Cher, our jaunty new personae.

"I talked to Raquel," I said. "She's in deep trouble. She's going down to Mexico City tonight, and she asked me to meet her there on Wednesday."

"Are you going?"

"Wendy commanded me to."

He gave a small groan. "You're leaving us," he said.

"I didn't say I was going," I replied.

"No, you're leaving us in a larger sense. You're really going to move out, aren't you?"

"Yes," I said.

He groaned again. "It's very sad," he said.

"I know."

"Why Mexico City?" he asked. "The whole valley is caked with excrement and garbage and human remains. Every warm breeze that blows through the streets is filled with dried bits of shit and ash and decomposed bodies and chemicals and small particulate matter and chemicals and bacteria. New York is slightly cleaner, but not really by much."

I drummed my fingers on his stomach. He put his hand over mine to make it hold still.

"It's true," he said.

"Thank you, Santa Claus."

He laughed. "Now go to sleep."

We both sighed in unison and fell silent. A long time later, his body went lax as he slipped away into sleep. At some point, I must have followed, because the next thing I knew, it was morning again, and I was in bed alone, again.

I got up and put on my bathrobe. In the kitchen, Wendy sat at the table in pink pajamas, eating cereal and reading a book. Anthony sat across from her in his bathrobe, his hair spiraling out in odd directions, not eating, reading the *New York Times.* Neither of them looked up or said a word as I entered the kitchen and poured myself a cup of coffee. I didn't say anything, either. Their silence felt punitive and injured; my answering silence was stoic and resolved. It could not have escaped anyone's notice that I took the "Real Estate" section from its nest in the whole paper on the table. I tucked it under my arm and took it and my cup of coffee into the living room. I plugged in the Christmas tree lights and sat on the couch, sipping hot black coffee. All of the previous night's foxhole festivity had evaporated. The hard gray sky outside matched the apartment's inner weather in a grimly satisfying way.

It would have been so easy to change my mind and stay there. All I would have had to do was go into the kitchen and announce that I had decided not to go, and Anthony and Wendy would have looked up, expressed something—gladness, I imagined, but maybe not—and then we would have all gone on in exactly the way we always had. In another four or five years, Wendy would be gone, and then Anthony and I could settle into stolid, companionable lives lived parallel to each other, without really touching, until death did us part. Or I could leave then, once Wendy was safely settled in college.

I found three apartments that looked possible, but of course you never knew. I finished my coffee, went into the bedroom, and called the numbers listed on the ads. I got three Realtors' voice mails in a row, and left three identical messages, leaving my cell number and fervently avowing my excitement about the description of the place and my absolute availability anytime that weekend to go and take a look at it. I had already decided that if any one of the three turned out to be acceptably livable, I would take it. I didn't need much, just a simple one-bedroom with enough space in the living room for a foldout couch for Wendy if she ever cared to stay over. I could afford to pay the going rate. Eventually, when the divorce was final, I would find a place I wanted to settle into long-term. I would use as my down payment some of the money my parents had left me, part of which had been earmarked for Wendy's college education. We would figure out how to augment her tuition in the meantime, assuming she could get in anywhere in this brutally competitive climate.

God, this was sad. No one and nothing was forcing me to do this. It felt at once artificial, monumentally difficult, urgent, and exhausting. The thought of packing, dividing up all the books and dishes, the little things we'd accumulated over so many years, made me want to go back to bed and pull the covers over my head. But goading me was the sense that this would not always be the case. I was going toward life, away from numbed stasis and paralyzed discontent. Now things would begin to change, inevitably, probably in ways I hadn't anticipated, but certainly in ways I was desperately starving for. In my chest, a bubble of excitement was encased in an obdurate shell of dread. This nugget of fizzy, energetic hope would be all that I would have to draw on for a while in the way of sustenance and comfort.

Okay, I thought. I got dressed in jeans, a sweater, and boots. I went out to the foyer, put on my coat, and slung my bag across my body.

"I'm going out," I called. "Anyone want anything?"

"No," Wendy said curtly.

"World peace," came Anthony's rote response; I doubted he even heard the question anymore.

As I walked to a diner on Eighth Avenue, I got out my cell phone and checked my office machine. "Three new messages," the robotic male voice announced. No surprise there; a few clients always generated crises to keep me involved with them during the break. I listened to all three, which were predictably urgent, saved them all to deal with after I'd eaten, and went into the diner. I ordered fried eggs, toast, potatoes, bacon, coffee, and grapefruit juice and, covertly, watched all the other people in the diner in the mirror over the long counter. My breakfast came, greasy and piping hot. I ate it all, wiping the egg yolk from the plate with buttered rye toast, then got the check.

Outside on the street again, I made my way through the crowds of people thronging the stores, trying to find the right things for their kids and spouses on the last Saturday before Christmas. With my usual efficient forethought, I had bought Wendy's and Anthony's presents already: a new iPod with vast amounts of memory for Wendy, three very handsome new sweaters for Anthony, plus the usual books and CDs and socks and other things. I had mailed presents to my sisters' kids the week before. I had been planning to shop that weekend for Indrani, who always came over for brunch and present opening on Christmas Day, but now I wasn't sure I wanted to buy her anything or have her come over. I couldn't disinvite her, of course, but I felt like it. And I had already given her that wine opener, which had been expensive. The memory of the fight the day before was acrid in my brain.

It would be so good to see Raquel and explore an exotic new city and have an adventure and be autonomous, neither mother nor wife, for the first time in so many years.

I realized then that I must have decided at some point to go, because instead of walking down to the West Village boutiques,

I seemed to be heading toward the luggage store on Seventh Avenue to buy a wheeled suitcase. I had evidently begun to allow my guts to start making my decisions without consulting my brain; it was like turning the piloting of a ship over to the guy down in the engine room, bypassing the captain entirely, the charts and binoculars and compass. Well, my brain hadn't steered me anywhere too good lately, so I figured I might as well take a chance on the engineer. "I am the mechanic of my ship," I muttered to myself. "I am the grease monkey of my soul." Finally, that B.A. in English was earning its keep.

I carried my new empty suitcase back to my building, hauled it upstairs, and wheeled it into the bedroom. I called each of the three clients back, talked them all off whatever ledge they'd put themselves on, reassured them that I would be back in two weeks, and had them promise to call my substitute shrink if they needed help in the meantime.

When I came out of the shower, there were messages from two Realtors. They both sounded skeptical of me and annoyed at having to call me back. This real estate market was as cutthroat as the college-application process. There were too many people now, and the systems weren't keeping pace, as Anthony loved to point out.

Soon, with any luck, I'd live in a place that didn't contain a man who insisted on pointing out such things all the time, I thought as I dialed the first Realtor's number. And so it went, the dismantling of a marriage: step by instinctive step, fumblingly, sadly, with none of the heady delight that had fueled its beginning.

PART TWO

CHAPTER FIVE

*T*he plane lowered itself into a gigantic valley crammed absolutely full of concrete buildings, a valley so huge and so crowded it lived up to all my expectations, as did the air, which was yellow-gray and thick. The plane landed; I got off, disoriented. Down there on the ground, the air had a sharp but hazy quality; everything looked a little darker but also a little larger and clearer than normal. This airport smelled totally different from the ones in New York, some kind of harsh disinfectant, exotic food, different particulate matter blowing around. I wheeled my suitcase behind me to customs, my passport and filled-out forms in hand. I got in line behind all the other non-Mexicans, waited my turn, yawning, and then they stamped everything and waved me through.

I struck off down a long, wide hallway, following signs that said TAXI, armed with a sheet of instructions I had scribbled as

Raquel had dictated them over the phone: Withdraw a hundred dollars' worth of pesos from any bank machine. At the taxi stand, I would see two different companies side by side: I should use the one on the left. She had told me the amount the cab would be in pesos, the amount to tip, the address of the hotel in Spanish. Also, I should never get into a roving taxi cab in Mexico City because some drivers held you up, stole your debit card, demanded your password, and withdrew your daily limit until your bank account was empty, and meanwhile they held you hostage in a cheap, filthy hotel. Also, I should never be too friendly to Mexican men; they would get the wrong idea. They thought from TV and movies all American women were easy lays. I should act formal and distant and respectable. "Unleash your inner Catholic," she had said.

And when I got to the hotel, I was to ask for her by the fake name she'd registered under, an alias she'd chosen in honor of Wilde and Eliot, or rather, in honor of me, because we'd read and loved *The Importance of Being Earnest* and "Sweeney Among the Nightingales" together in college.

I waited at the curb with my taxi chit until a car pulled up. It was surprisingly chilly, although the sun was shining. I was glad I was wearing my jacket. I let the driver take my suitcase and put it into the trunk, got in, read the address carefully off the sheet of paper, and tried to give my reflection in his rearview mirror a respectable, formal expression. We drove off, bouncing gently on shot shocks, into a chaotic city made of concrete. Signs and business names were painted directly onto the front walls of buildings in bright bird-plumage colors—electric blue, pink, purple, magenta, acid yellow, bright green. We whizzed down an avenue with palm trees growing out of the divider, then plunged into old streets lined with grand colonial buildings, sidewalks massed with street vendors selling CDs, snacks, and piles of things on tables. Every ground-level entryway was the gaping mouth of a store hung and stuffed with bags or clothes or electronics for sale, or a taco stand with people sitting at a small counter eating, or a bright, shiny convenience store. The sidewalks were crammed with people trundling along as if they had somewhere to go and something to do—chop chop, gotta go, gotta go—exactly the way people walked in New York. Everyone was short. A lot of people were shaped like gnomes. Old Indian women in shapeless dresses, buttoned cardigans, and house slippers carried huge, bulging plastic sacks as if they weighed nothing. Dapper men in suits bustled along with cell phones. It was all exactly as I had expected, down to the guy on a bike with boxes strapped onto the back, towering over his head as he wobbled through traffic without capsizing or dropping anything.

In front of the hotel, I offered money to the driver and was deposited with my bag on the sidewalk. I went in past a uniformed guard and a small dank-looking hotel bar into a big lobby with couches, chairs, and tables everywhere. Overhead was a ceiling made of glass blocks glowing with daylight. A big fish tank sat on a high credenza under a painting of Queen Isabella. Looking off to the right, through an archway, I saw a homey-looking restaurant. The young man behind the front desk had a cheerful brown face, just like one of the photogenic, friendly natives whose pictures you always saw in the Lonely Planet guides.

"Hello," I said brightly to him. Raquel had told me they all spoke English. "I'm looking for Cecily Sweeney in room two oh three. I'm her friend from uh, New York City. Nueva York?"

"Dumbass," came Raquel's voice from behind me. "I'm right here." She laughed as she came forward to hug me. " 'Nueva York,' " she chortled into my ear. She was so tiny; I always forgot when I went without seeing her for a while. "Come on," she said. "I'll take you up to the room. God, it's so good to see you."

She led me past the front desk to a mirrored hallway, then up two very long, winding flights of stairs. We came into an upstairs courtyard, three stories high, lined with balconies with balustrades. She led me around the courtyard, past one set of doors after another, then ducked into a small alcove. She unlocked the tall double doors, flung them open, and gestured for me to go in. "Welcome to Casa Home Wrecker," she said. "It's not much, but it's ours."

I wheeled my silly little suitcase over an old gray carpet through an empty foyer and into a large room with a ridiculously high ceiling. French doors opened to a small balcony. Glancing through them, I saw a domed churchlike building across the street. The room was done in sixties drab—two beds with plain wooden headboards and a nightstand between them, an imitation Eames-era armchair, a huge armoire with a mirror, and a long vanity table of fake blond wood.

"No frills," I said. "But I like it." I felt dizzy and out of breath from the fast climb up the stairs, and my leg muscles were tight. I was in okay shape, so this was no doubt due to oxygen deprivation from being a mile high, breathing poor-quality air.

"I know, it's no palace," she said. She seemed perversely happy to be in this bare-bones hotel, which was what I had expected of her—she had always preferred unpretentious hotels and restaurants to tony, fancy ones. "Sorry. No matter how rich I get, I can't stand the luxury shit. It's totally removed from real life. Comes from having a Marxist father, maybe."

"And from rebelling against your mother, maybe," I said. Raquel's mother, Suzie Weinstein, was a Realtor who lived alone on the Upper East Side in a ritzy apartment in a doorman building; she loved to give the place an overhaul every few years, upping the chintz and brocade quotient with every redecoration. I had met her a few times through the years and liked her; she was warm and direct and funny. But Raquel, an only child, adored her father and couldn't stand her mother.

"This hotel used to be a whorehouse," said Raquel. "In the sixteenth or seventeenth century. Across the street, that building was a nunnery filled with cats. Two cathouses, facing off."

I set my suitcase on the bed that was clearly not Raquel's, since it was crisply made with an ugly bedspread, and the other one was rumpled, as if a wild animal had fought a lesser creature to its death at some point in its covers. But her stuff was all neatly organized, her toiletries on the vanity, her clothes all unpacked and out of sight. Raquel had oddly incompatible habits: In matters having to do with her own personal upkeep and wardrobe, she was obsessively fastidious, and in others, such as anything pertaining to housekeeping, she was like a sloppy ten-year-old boy. Her bungalow in Silver Lake was a study in this split personality, but luckily, she had a maid.

"Let me get a look at you," I said. I turned and studied her.

"I look like sheer crap," she said. "I'm a wreck. Ask me if I've slept one minute. Last night, I got drunk downstairs in the hotel bar and sang along to Bob Dylan songs with two dorky industrial engineers till the bar closed and they threw us out. What did I tell you about acting formal and not too friendly, right?"

"So did you bring them up here with you?"

"Thank God, no. I made it safely home alone."

Raquel looked gorgeous. Her hair was dyed its usual dark red, and she'd added a blond streak by her right ear. Her dark, exotic face, with its high cheekbones, sexy beak of a nose, deep-set dark eyes, and full mouth, which she'd been blessed with via a craggy-faced Mexican father and Jewish blood on her mother's side, had become even more beautiful with age and experience— and dermatological intervention, and obsessive health habits, although those seemed to have gone out the window down in Mexico. She was just lighting up a cigarette. She wore a fitted long-sleeved dark red wool dress that came demurely down to her bare knees, and black Frye motorcycle boots. She looked glamorously, almost painfully thin.

"How much do you weigh right now?" I asked her.

"Eighty-nine pounds," she said. "I know, I'm barely human. I'm like a bag of bird bones."

"You've never looked better," I said. "I mean it. Scandal becomes you."

She threw her arms around me. I felt like a huge, hulking oak tree being embraced by a wood nymph. "You look good yourself," she said, looking up at me. "Divorce becomes *you*." Smoke from her cigarette wafted past my nose. It smelled so good, I suddenly craved one. I was tremendously glad to be there. "Let's go get a drink," I said.

"Let's start at the fancy place and work our way down to the dives," she said.

Outside in the bracingly chilly air, we turned left and headed along Avenida Isabel la Católica. Raquel led me along several blocks, past a vendor with multiple stacked baskets of luridly colored nuts and seeds and candies for sale, past a wee dark-eyed beggar woman sitting on the sidewalk with a baby, past an organ-grinder in an ersatz army uniform. The sidewalks were about a foot higher than I was used to and very narrow. It was like walking on a tricky platform; every time we crossed the street, I had to remember to step down far enough. Sexy young women in tight police uniforms blew whistles madly at every intersection and made emphatic arm gestures at the onrushing cars.

We turned right onto Avenida Cinco de Mayo. The shop windows were fancier here, more upscale, a lot of jewelry stores, expensive-looking clothing emporia whose windows were hung with leather jackets and silk dresses that had been au courant in New York circa 1983; this was evidently the Madison Avenue of Mexico City.

"This is where we get our coffee in the morning," said Raquel, gesturing at El Café Popular. "Across the street, we get our fresh juice. We'll take them to the Zócalo. We'll be there in a minute. You can see it up ahead."

We came out onto an open square, so big that it was like a flat, paved plain. A curving snake of one-way traffic streamed around its perimeter. An ice rink took up a large portion of the square; skaters in street clothes, no coats or hats, were gliding around in groups, falling, laughing, clutching one another. A huge crowd stood watching. Several groups of Indians in head-dresses were dancing and drumming while other Indians waved burning herbs at people. Blankets on the ground were heaped with things for sale.

I wanted to stop and gawk and take it all in, but Raquel kept going, making a beeline for the other side of the square. Beyond the dancers, near the courtyard of the cathedral, were vendors with their wares spread out on blankets. A few artists had set up easels and were making portraits of tourists. A young one-armed man sat in a chair under an umbrella, working with his one hand, making something that looked like a landscape painting, but he was weaving, rather than painting, out of some material I couldn't identify because Raquel rushed me by so fast.

"We'll go into the cathedral later, after lunch," she called over her shoulder, "and honor our ancestors." Raquel had always proudly pretended to be a lapsed Catholic; although she had been raised agnostic, she had always identified more with her Catholic forebears than her Jewish ones, but she had never gone to church until we were in college and went together to an Easter Mass.

Behind the cathedral, she turned onto a small street, at the end of which, near some ancient ruins in some stage of excavation, was a small café called Las Sirenas. This was evidently our destination, because Raquel plunked herself down at one of the outside tables. I sat across from her. A waiter in a uniform brought big leather-bound menus, but Raquel waved him away and unleashed a cloud of Spanish. He smiled at her, nodded, and went off to fetch whatever she'd asked for.

She leaned back in her chair and lit a cigarette.

"Give me one of those," I said. "It doesn't count when you smoke on vacation; everyone knows that."

"Let's kill ourselves," she said, and handed me the pack and a lighter.

"What did you order?" I asked her.

"Tequila with sangrita, and some food. You'll like it."

"You're not supposed to eat any raw vegetables and fruits down here, right?" I asked anxiously.

She laughed. "Bullshit. They wash everything in purified water now. They're not stupid. They don't want all the gringos to be too sick to eat and drink. You can eat anything in restaurants. Just be careful of street food, because sometimes they have no place to wash their hands after they shit. But if they can, they do. And if you get sick, there's an antibiotic you can buy over the counter at the drugstore. Tourists don't know about it; it's sort of a Mexican secret."

The waiter returned with four tall shot glasses on a tray, two filled with amber tequila, two filled with tomato juice. He set them down ceremoniously along with a dish of roasted, salted peanuts, then went off again with a little flourish of his empty tray.

Raquel picked up her tequila glass. "To our fucked-up lives," she said.

"To our totally fucked-up lives," I replied. We clacked our tequila glasses, sipped, then sipped the other stuff. "Yum!" I said. "What is this?"

"Tomato juice, chili powder, cayenne, lime juice, other fruit juices, whatever they feel like throwing in. I know, it's good, right?"

Her eyes were filled with tears.

"Raquel," I said.

In the hotel lobby, on our way out, she had stopped so she could feed a ten-peso coin into one of the computers (she hadn't bothered to bring her laptop, since the hotel had no Wi-Fi). She had made me sit down and go online to check a couple of gossip sites to see what they were saying about her. I had had to read aloud to her their mean, unsavory speculations concerning her whereabouts, but since she hadn't been able to look at the screen herself, I was spared having to witness her reaction to the shockingly unflattering photos of her they'd managed to find. Surely they'd been altered on Photoshop, there was no way Raquel had ever looked so gaunt and wrinkled. No way.

"I am a wreck," she said. "I can't sleep. All I can do is smoke and drink. I feel better now that you're here." She smeared a tear across her cheek. "Thanks for coming," she said.

"Raquel," I said again. "It's only feelings." This was something we had started saying to each other back in college when one of us was heartbroken, furious at someone, or otherwise emotionally wrought up. By now, saying this had become a ritual so familiar, the words had all but lost their original meaning. She didn't react, possibly because I couldn't muster much conviction; I had been shaken by the vitriol of these Hollywood gossip columnists, these cyber-Heddas. It was as if Raquel had stepped into a nest of adders and was being repeatedly, venomously fanged; why was she drawing so much poison? She was right: Jimmy Black was getting off without even a slap on the wrist, and she was being vilified. "And you're a rock star. Relax."

"I'm a washed-up former rock star whose last album came out years ago."

This was technically true, but she was still famous. "You're still famous."

"Anyway," she said, waving the topic of herself away. "How about you? What happened with Anthony after you told him you were leaving?"

"I rented a one-bedroom apartment on West Twenty-fourth Street," I said.

"Wow," she said. "You work fast."

"It's basically the physical embodiment of the phrase 'expensive dump.' Wendy and Anthony are all alone now. I'm so sad, I can't believe it, but it's what I have to do."

"Yeah," she said. "I know, baby. But you're going to be okay."

"We're both going to be okay," I replied.

"I might be okay again someday," she said, "but for now, it's just bad. It just is what it is. You know what? I was really in love with him. Can you believe it?" She laughed shakily. She was still crying. "I was a fool. I want to hate him now, but I haven't been able to force myself to, so my heart is broken now, along with everything else. That kid. He has everyone in the world rooting for him, and I'm the evil seductress. They're all so hard on women in Hollywood."

"So move to New York," I said. "What are you doing in L.A.? You're a musician. What do you need to be there for?"

"I'm a California girl," she said. "I hate winter. I grew up in L.A. My dad lives there. If I move to New York, I'm afraid I'll turn into a horrible JAP like my mother. Also, it's just as puritanical as Hollywood, let's face it. On the plus side, some great musicians live there. Maybe I could get Jim White as my drummer."

"Who's he?" I asked.

"To your health," she said.

We sipped our tequilas. I was starting to feel a slight buzz; oxygen deprivation and airplane travel had made me a lightweight. The waiter came with fragrant bowls of thick green soup with golden squash blossoms floating on top. We ate the soup, drank more tequila, and then ate salads, beautiful and huge and fresh. After the waiter had cleared away all the dishes, we smoked another cigarette each and ordered a third round of tequila. I was feeling a little drunk. Raquel was cheering up now that I was asking her about the new album, which she hadn't let anyone hear yet.

"It's basically old-school rock," she said. "Not as jazz-influenced as my earlier albums. Kind of like if Mick Jagger and Chrissie Hynde gave birth to PJ Harvey."

The big blond Northern Europeans at the next table began loudly consulting each other about the menu in some goofy Scandinavian language. Raquel's eyes went very wide at me, and I grinned at her.

"Let's get the check and go pay our respects to Jesus," she said.

When the bill came, I let Raquel pay it; I would get the next one. We wandered off, more slowly now that we had eaten and drunk, and made our way around the other side of the cathedral through a crowd of people crouching on the concrete on blankets piled with stuff. "Oyster shells," she said. "They grind them up to make face lotion—right there, look." She nudged me and pointed to boxes of gleaming pure white creams. A kid of about ten was feeding shells into a grinder. "Jehovah's Witnesses are like flies here," she said to me then, waving off a smiling fresh-faced man who approached us with a pamphlet. "Oh, look, fermented pineapple juice. Want some?" She bought two plastic bags heavy-bellied with yellow-brown liquid, straws poking out of their tied-off tops. She handed me one and I took a sip of the tart, odd stuff; I hadn't realized how thirsty I was, and this was surprisingly quenching.

We wandered out onto the Zócalo and watched the Indian dancers while we drank our pineapple juice. They hopped and twirled and bounced in unison to heavy beats that reminded me of the hippies drumming in Tompkins Square Park, that same insistent, resonant pounding that got into your head. "Now let us pray," said Raquel. We threw our empty nectar sacs away and went through the wrought-iron gates, across the cathedral's courtyard to a massive stone sill that led through doors that were like the giant wooden portals to a medieval castle. Inside the cathedral, it was chilly and suddenly dark and quiet. It was like being inside a massive, lustrous, magical cavern in a fairy tale, with shafts of light shooting down through empty air, golden beams that struck the stone floor, stained glass glowing jewel-like in windows. Glassed-in coffins in side chapels held lifelike replicas of saints in various poses of suffering and supplication. Some of them were reliquaries, with parts of the actual saints' bodies set into little boxes in their chests, bits of hair and bone. Banks of thin white tapers burned with bright, hard tips of fire in front of them.

"I went to confession the other day," said Raquel. "I told the priest in that little booth everything. Saying it in Spanish made it all seem both more sinful and more human, somehow."

"You did?" I said.

"Yeah," she replied. "I was crying afterward. It felt really good."

"That's because you weren't raised with it. There's nothing traumatic attached to it for you."

"Probably," she said.

"Lucky you."

Raquel and I walked together to the middle of the cathedral to an open chapel where a Mass was being said. The priest with the censer was in full swing, releasing spicy clouds of incense smoke. We both genuflected automatically and slid into a pew and sat there listening to the ritual in Spanish. I was seized with a sudden need to sneeze, which I stifled. Once as a little kid, taking Communion, I had sneezed the wafer straight out of my mouth, and I never got over the horror of ejecting the body of Christ so violently in front of everyone. Although I was no longer a believer of any kind, and there was no injunction against sneezing during Mass that I knew of, I reflexively squeezed my eyes shut until the urge passed. Being in a church was complicated for me. I felt right at home in a chafing, itchy, but weirdly comforting way.

When the Mass had finished, I walked with Raquel over to a cordoned-off area behind red velvet ropes. What looked like a fairy-tale giant's plumb bob hung from a long cable from the cathedral's ceiling; its point had traced a pattern in the sandbox it hung over, a sort of record of the cathedral's shifting movement. "The cathedral is falling down," said Raquel. "The ground is sinking underneath. They just finished a massive renovation to shore it up, and it's still shifting." She pointed to the far-off rear wall, which looked lopsided and off-true. "Someday it'll all tumble down," she said. "You ready to go?"

We emerged into daylight, blinking. The Mexican flag on a pole over the Zócalo snapped and fluttered. The skaters were thick on the ice.

"Now what?" said Raquel. "Should we go and take our siestas? It's four-thirty."

The idea of a nap made me yawn fiercely. "Okay," I said. "Then we can stay up late tonight."

"Maybe we'll take a taxi to Roma and hear some music," said Raquel.

As we came out of the cathedral's courtyard, I saw the one-armed man I'd tried to watch earlier, when Raquel was hurrying me along.

"I want to see what that guy is doing," I said.

We went over to where the one-armed artist sat in his folding chair under a big umbrella. He was working on a small frame, making a replica of a steep mountainous landscape with a farmer pushing a plow behind two oxen, making furrows in a plot of earth on the extreme slope. Next to the weaver were piles of short colored straws. With his one hand, he pushed a green one deftly through a grid of string. He ignored us, as I imagined he ignored everyone who stopped just to ogle the cripple and not to buy his work.

"*¿Es Chiapas?*" Raquel asked the top of his bent head.

"*Sí,*" came the curt answer.

"I want to buy it," I said, not caring that I sounded like a stupid tourist. "It's beautiful. Ask him when it'll be done."

"Come back in twenty minutes," he replied in perfect American-accented English. "These don't take that long."

"You're American?" I asked.

He looked up at us finally. He had a thin, very dark face with high cheekbones and thick eyebrows. His eyes were black. He looked about thirty, but you could never tell. "Do I look North American to you?" he asked, unsmiling.

"Who knows?" I said. "What does a North American look like?"

One side of his mouth lifted in a ghostly echo of a smile, but the rest of his face remained impassive. "Not like me," he said.

"How much do you want for it?" I asked.

"For you," he said, squinting at me, "one hundred pesos."

That was about ten bucks, which seemed cheap enough to me, but I had read in a guidebook that if you didn't try to talk vendors down, you looked like a gullible rube.

"Do you bargain, or is that fixed?" I asked.

"What do you think a couple hours of my time is worth?" he asked. "I'm curious."

"We'll think about that," said Raquel firmly. "Come on, Jo."

She set off along the pavement, and without another word to the weaver, I followed her. "Did I do something wrong?" I asked her when we were out of earshot.

"No, you didn't," she said. "But his work isn't all that good. I've seen better. I bet he does great business because he lost his arm. I don't mean to be a bitch; it's just how it goes."

I had a feeling she was showing off for me, demonstrating her knowledge of the local artisans. "I could use a bathroom," I said.

"Should we go to El Café Popular? The hotel is about fifteen minutes from here. Or, wait, I know, we can go to the Gran Hotel. I haven't been there in years. Come on, it's just right over here, and the lobby is full of birdcages. It's cool."

We crossed the avenue that encircled the Zócalo and walked along the sidewalk past rows of jewelry stores, then took an abrupt right and headed off down a side street. Raquel led me up a set of red-carpeted steps and into the hotel lobby. At the top of the stairs, we were stopped by two guards in uniform and a red velvet rope. She jibber-jabbered in Spanish with them for a while; she seemed to be arguing with them, and they appeared to win.

Raquel turned to me and said, "You can't just go in anymore to look at the birds; you have to have a drink in their restaurant. We'll get a coffee. Come on." The guards, who obviously didn't recognize Raquel, who didn't seem to mind, escorted us across the lobby—which was loud with high chirping birdsong, and painted with murals under a Tiffany glass ceiling—and left us at the entrance to the restaurant. I ducked into the bathroom, then joined Raquel at one of the tables. The place was fancy in an upscale Denny's sort of way, with booths and white cloth–draped tables. It was completely empty. Glancing through the plate-glass window, we could see people walking along the sidewalk across from the Zócalo, where we had just been.

A waitress materialized from somewhere; she was stout and middle-aged and wore a yellow nylon dress with a white apron, thick panty hose, and black heeled shoes. She gave us big thick menus, which we ignored. Raquel ordered, and the woman nodded in resignation and went away.

After we'd finished our Nescafé, Raquel paid and then we went out to the lobby and duly admired the two big bamboo cages filled with small yellow birds. The lobby was as *gran* and ornate and balconied as the hotel's name suggested, with an old-fashioned wooden, glass-windowed elevator rising straight up through the soaring courtyard, but I would have liked it much more if we hadn't been shanghaied into paying to see it.

"I want to go and buy that thing now," I said to Raquel. I had the feeling I had insulted the artist somehow by trying to bargain with him, and I wanted to show him I had been sincere in wanting to buy his work and was willing to pay what he felt it was worth. Somehow, I couldn't admit to Raquel that I wanted to right some balance I had upset with that one-armed guy; I didn't want her to think I was a sucker, and I was feeling a bit vulnerable, newly arrived in this strange city, tired, tipsy, and sad. I hadn't seen Raquel in more than a year, and she was so brittle right now herself; I would have to be clear about my own state of mind. She could lean on me, of course, but I wasn't unbreakable, and I needed something from her at the moment, too. "I thought it was beautiful," I added.

She glanced at me and said with brusque amusement, "It's your money. Come on."

We went back to the Zócalo and found his umbrella again. The guy was still working on the same weaving, his head bent. He didn't look up as we approached. As soon as we were within earshot, Raquel called something quickly in Spanish to him. When he saw us, his face was blank and careless. "I'll handle this," I muttered, annoyed at Raquel for intervening, especially in Spanish, when he spoke perfect English and this was my thing.

"It's almost finished," he said directly to me, which made me glad I had insisted that we return. "You still want it?"

"Yes," I said. "I do." I handed him one hundred pesos. He set his work on his thigh and took it, set it on his other thigh, extracted a leather billfold from the breast pocket of his blue denim work shirt, and deftly stuffed the money inside. He had a muscular, veiny forearm, I noticed, and his hand was square and strong, with flat, clean nails. He went back to work matter-of-factly. Raquel and I stood in the chilly, dry air, squinting out into the Zócalo, waiting for him to finish. A glossy dark red curl of Raquel's hair lodged in her mouth; she freed it.

"So what happened with Indrani?" she asked me. "Did you make up with her?"

"She came for Christmas," I said. "It was stilted and weird."

I had managed to pretty much ignore Indrani the entire day and evening; we had focused energetically on Anthony and Wendy as we all ate coffee cake, opened presents, walked to the movie theater in the cold, quiet city. Indrani had given me a cashmere sweater. I hadn't given her anything, but Wendy had given her a CD by a band called Tokio Hotel, which she was fanatically passionate about. Anthony had begged off the movie; the three of us "girls," as Indrani always referred to us, had seen two movies in a row, emerged from the theater, and said good night; Indrani had gone uptown alone in a cab. Since that time, Indrani and I had not spoken.

"What does she know about any of it, anyway?" said Raquel.

She lifted her writhing mass of hair with both hands and tossed it down her back. "Has she ever separated from a husband or been set up by a villainous asshole and had gossip bloggers smear her name all over the world?"

I took an elastic hair band from my bag, bunched Raquel's hair with both my hands while keeping the band around my right palm, slipped the band around her hair, and gave her a high ponytail. While I ministered to her hair, she leaned against me like a little kid or a dog.

"Does she know about what happened with me and Jimmy Black?" Raquel asked.

"Yeah," I said reluctantly.

Raquel gave me a sharp, inquisitive look. "And?"

"Of course she's worried about you. To put it mildly."

"You mean she's judging me," said Raquel. "I feel bad for her that she's still single and that it upsets her so much, but maybe there's a reason why no man can stay with her. Maybe it's because she's so stuck and afraid to come unstuck. She can't bend to anyone else, ever. Even though she's overly accommodating, she's strangely rigid underneath that. You know what I mean?"

"I do," I said, and I meant it. "But I don't know why I can't just let this go. I feel silly, staying mad at her over this. We've been friends forever."

Raquel looked me dead in the eye. "What did she say about the whole thing with me?"

I looked away. "Do I have to tell you?"

"Of course you have to tell me."

I cleared my throat. "She said . . . Raquel, I don't want to get in the middle of this, I really don't. You can probably imagine what she said."

"Probably," Raquel said in a hard voice. "I'm sure she said it's pathetic, at my age, and what was I thinking? And how could I be such a bitch to that poor pregnant girl, stealing her 'fiancé,' which he so was not, no matter what she's saying now. And what's wrong with me? Do I think I'm in my twenties?"

I laughed.

"I knew it," she said. Her eyes were narrowed. "She's judging both of us. Where does she get off?"

"Thank God you're not," I said.

"Why would I judge you? You're separating from your husband. So what? People do it all the time. And he's been kind of a jerk to you, let's face it."

"How did I stay with him for so long?"

" 'Cause you love the hell out of him, and it takes a while to notice that the reality isn't matching the idea."

"He just completely let me go," I said. "He said he understood why I needed to leave and he agreed that I should. Poor Anthony." A brief but intense memory of kissing Peter came back to me, the harsh taste of wine in my throat, his insistent, inquisitive mouth. "Oh my God, I forgot to tell you. I did something really incredibly weird, for me at least."

"What?"

"I gave this guy a blow job the other night, this guy I met in a bar. After Indrani's Christmas party, I went out for a nightcap and ended up getting picked up by him."

Raquel stared at me and then let out a whoop; the one-armed weaver guy continued to ignore us. "You did not!"

"I did!"

She cackled. "Jo-zee! You slut!"

"Who knew?" I said, laughing, too.

"Hey," said the guy. "Your weaving is finished." He wrapped the thing in a piece of newspaper and stuffed it into a plastic sack, then handed it to me. Of course he had heard every word we had just said, but he looked at us as if he had never seen us before in his life. He obviously had a lot more on his mind than the exploits of two middle-aged women. He had real problems. Who knew where he lived, how he got by?

"Thank you so much," I said.

We headed back to the hotel. I felt as if I had grains of grit and sand behind my eyelids, and my limbs were so heavy, I could hardly move them. My head was pounding. "I don't feel well," I said as we walked along Avenida Cinco de Mayo.

"It's the altitude," said Raquel sympathetically. "You'll adjust, but it's hell at first. How long can you stay? Did you decide?"

"I have an open ticket."

"Be still my heart," she said.

Back in our hotel room, we lay on our beds, with the balcony doors shut to block out the noise of traffic and organ-grinders and the CD stand around the corner. I couldn't fall asleep right away. My narrow bed was too hard, and I wasn't used to these new sounds: different traffic noises, voices out in the hotel, Raquel's breathing, so different from Anthony's—lighter, more irregular. My head was fizzing from fatigue and stress, like static on a TV set.

When I woke up, it was dark, and I smelled cigarette smoke.

The balcony doors were open. Raquel's bed was empty. "Raquel," I called.

"I'm out here," she said, and stuck her head in from the balcony. "How'd you sleep?"

"What time is it?"

"Almost eight."

"I'm starving."

"Good, because I'm taking you to my favorite cantina right around the corner for tacos as soon as you're ready."

I sat up. I felt like shit. My mouth tasted like a rodent had died in it weeks before. My head was pounding, and my eyes were grainier than ever. "Damn," I said.

"Headache?"

"Yeah."

"You'll get used to it. I promise."

She led me around the block and over to a street that was lit up and filled with loud music. Outside the cantina was a guy at a stand heaped with piles of odd-looking meat, which he pulled from a bubbling drum of oily water, chopped, and threw onto a hot grill, then scooped up into two oily corn tortillas and sprinkled with radish, cilantro, and onion and slid onto a plastic plate, then handed them over to the next customer, who doused them with a green sauce from a dish on the counter. As we stood in line, Raquel said, "I'm ordering you two chorizo tacos. Trust me."

"What else is there?"

"Tongue, eye, tripe, foot, brain."

I made a dramatically disgusted face. "Isn't chorizo basically all that stuff in a sausage casing anyway?"

"With chorizo, you don't think about it; it's just spicy sausage. All that other stuff, you have to think about."

We took our plates into the cantina and got a table. I took a bite of a taco. Raquel watched me as I chewed and swallowed. "It's really good," I said, and this was an understatement.

A tall, angelic-faced waiter in a suit approached.

"*Tequila con sangrita, por favor,*" I said before Raquel could order for me.

"*Dos Herraduras blancos,*" said Raquel. "*Con sangrita para mi también.*"

When he had gone away, we wolfed our tacos. Our drinks arrived. We clacked glasses. "To your health," she said to me. "Which is really all that matters in life, when you get right down to it."

Two boys went up to the jukebox and put in money and punched in numbers. Mexican pop music blared out of the speakers. The boys sat down at their table and sang along with the song in loud, passionate voices. I looked over at them. They were tough-looking guys in jeans and leather jackets, but they sang without any irony or self-consciousness, looking at each other as if they were having a conversation.

"Want more tacos?" Raquel asked. "Or should we smoke now? This is great. I've been good for so long, and suddenly I don't give a fuck."

I took two cigarettes from the pack she'd set on the table and handed her one. We lit up and smoked and finished our tequilas. Then we ordered more, and at a certain point, Raquel got up and fetched another round of tacos.

Much later, we were drunk, full of grease and booze. My altitude sickness was gone. I felt fantastic. I had begun to fervently wish I knew the words to the songs on the jukebox so I could sing along, too.

"How did you meet him?" I asked Raquel, shouting over the music and loud conversations. We were analyzing what had happened with Jimmy Black, how Raquel could have been naïve enough to get involved with him—her word, of course, not mine. There was no point in saying anything that might make her feel worse than she already felt, and if she wanted my advice, she would ask for it. Until then, I had nothing but empathy; that was the primary job of a friend. I was so mad at Indrani; it felt like a big bruise on my heart. "Let nothing human be foreign to me," the Roman playwright Terence had written, and that sounded good to me.

I picked up my tequila glass and had another sip, then a sip of sangrita. I felt like I never wanted to drink anything else but this for the rest of my life.

"We met at a club," said Raquel. "A stupid club in Hollywood. I don't even know why I was there. I was bored that night, and a friend asked if I wanted to go hear a famous deejay. Jimmy and I started talking. We hit it off. He was horny and drunk. I was horny and sober, so I don't even have the excuse of intoxication. We had a one-night stand, and it was incredible, but I thought that was it. Then he called me the next day and said he couldn't stop thinking about me. I guess I was flattered. I had been feeling pretty down, over-the-hill, lonely. And he's so young, so beautiful, I couldn't resist. So we started to see each other. I fell in love with him. Such an idiot."

"You weren't an idiot," I said. "People fall in love. It's what people do."

"He's an *actor*," she said. "They're like poodles, but stupid."

I laughed.

"He talked about 'the work,'" she said. "'The work,' as in, 'The work is very demanding.' And 'The work forces me to dig so deep.' And I listened like it was the most brilliant shit. No, seriously, Jo, I was an idiot. He's a TV actor."

I laughed again. "He's hot, right?"

"You've never seen his show?"

"I had never heard of him before."

"It's called *Endless Pool*," said Raquel. "He plays the son of a guy who owns a pool-supply store. His character makes house calls to service malfunctioning swimming pools in Scottsdale, Arizona, and, wouldn't you know, he gets seduced by all the bored Republican housewives while their husbands play golf. 'The work.' Give me a break. He's barely even acting." She signaled to the waiter, who came over. She said something in Spanish. "I'm getting the check," she told me. "Then we're going upstairs, next door. I want you to see the dancing ladies. It's a trip."

We finished our last round. Raquel left money on the table and waved me away violently when I tried to pay. We stumbled out onto the sidewalk. "Los Portales de what?" I said, reading the mat by the cantina's front door. "What the hell is that name?"

"Come on," she said. She led me up a staircase. We entered another cantina, this one smaller, with red-draped walls and tiny round tables. Music roared from overhead speakers. There was a small dance floor; several couples were doing some kind of Mexican polka. The women all wore red evening gowns. Most of them were stout and middle-aged, with neat coifs and hard faces.

Raquel and I sat near the back. "Do you want another tequila?" she asked me.

"I'd better switch to water," I said. "I'm sloshed."

"Oh, come on," she said. "You're on vacation."

She told the waitress what we wanted. We lit cigarettes and leaned back in our chairs. "What's the deal with this place?"

"They're called *ficheras*. They're dime-a-dance girls. Like taxi dancers."

"They all look like grandmothers," I said. "Like church ladies."

Raquel laughed and rolled her eyes at me. "Yeah, right. And thirty pesos gets you one dance."

"Hey," I said. "There's that one-armed guy from earlier, who made that thing I bought."

I nudged her and pointed. He was sitting alone at a table near the front. A woman had just approached him, which was why I had noticed him. She had bronze-colored hair, a round belly, and a flat face, and she looked about twenty years older than he was.

"Oh right," she said. "So this is where he hangs out."

After some negotiation, he got up to dance with the woman, taking her hand. Her body stayed with his as if his other, phantom arm were holding her, guiding her around the dance floor. He looked up and saw us watching him. If he recognized us, he didn't show it. His expression was stern and blank, the way it had been under his umbrella. The song ended, and he went back to his table without a word to his dance partner.

"Let's go over and talk to him," said Raquel.

"What?" She had done this ever since I'd first met her—act on a wild hair and drag me along.

"Let's go sit at his table," she said, nudging me. "Come on."

Raquel picked up her drink, got up, and headed toward the front of the room.

It seemed to me that I had no choice but to follow her, so I got up with my own drink. The one-armed guy looked up as we approached his table.

CHAPTER SIX

"Hey," said Raquel. "Do you mind if we join you?" Before he could answer, she sat down at one of the chairs at his table.

"Sorry," I said lamely as I sat down, but what I was sorry for, I didn't know. Most men drinking alone at a table and paying women to dance with them, it seemed to me, would have welcomed our sudden company as a pleasant diversion, if nothing else. But something about this guy provoked uneasy guilt in me, a sense of obligation.

"I'm Raquel and this is Josie," said Raquel.

"I'm David," he said. He pronounced it *Dah-veed.*

"I bought your picture earlier," I said.

"You sure did," he said. I saw the barest flick of a smile.

I remembered that he had overheard every word Raquel and I had exchanged about our personal lives.

"So you're from Chiapas?" Raquel asked.

"San Juan Chamula."

"Oh, the violent Indian village with the mysterious church," said Raquel. "I've been there. It's wild. That is the most beautiful church I have ever seen in my life." She turned to me and added, "They've got a huge bare chapel with no pews, and pine boughs all over the floor. They do these rituals on the floor with rows of lit candles lined up and soda pop and bones. The church is all lit up with candles, and there are people everywhere, chanting, pouring Coke and orange pop on the floor. They're perfectly friendly and happy to explain everything, but if you take pictures or even bring a camera into the church, they take you outside and beat the shit out of you."

"They sure do," said David.

"How did you learn such fluent English?" Raquel asked. "Not from the tourists."

"No," said David, amused. "Not from the tourists."

"Okay," said Raquel. "I'm interested. I want your story. I want to know how you learned to speak English like a *norteamericano*, what happened to your arm, and what you really do besides making those little pictures. Can I buy you a drink?"

David appeared to consider this quite earnestly for a moment, looking off at the dancers, weighing his options. "Okay," he said finally. "But you'll be disappointed, I promise you."

Raquel motioned to the waitress. "What are you drinking?"

"A beer," he said. "Negra Modelo. And a shot of Herradura, since you're buying."

"Okay, but your story had better be good," said Raquel.

He looked at her as if he were inspecting her, not looking for anything in particular, but searching for any bit of information there was to be gathered through the eyes. "My story," said David, "is only as good as its listener."

"You're on," said Raquel, hunkering down. "So talk."

"When I was very little," said David, "my father left Chiapas and moved to Chicago with me and my brothers and sisters and our mother, and that's where I grew up until I left home. He worked as a mechanic, and he did okay. We all did well in school because we were smart, and our mother pushed us like a madwoman to succeed, and that is almost the literal truth. I was one of the younger middle kids, so I didn't have to be a doctor or a lawyer; I was lucky. I went to art school on full scholarship and studied sculpture and painting. Eleven years ago, when I was lifting a piece of cast concrete with a crane to make a sculpture outside a barn, I was living in the middle of nowhere. I stupidly failed to attach it securely enough, and it fell and crushed my arm, and by the time I got to the hospital, it was lost. In other words, I'm not a colorful peasant boy with a tragic history; I'm a college-educated brat who came back to the motherland to pay his debts to his heritage, or whatever, drink a lot of good beer. Go ahead and yawn. I warned you. Where's my drink?"

"Not so fast," said Raquel.

"That's it," he said. "You've got everything. Show's over."

"Not so fast," she said again. "Come on. So your family did well in the States. But it's not so simple. My own father is Mexican, from D.F., but now he lives in L.A. He got his law degree; he works to help illegals get their citizenship. He always says, 'You never escape from Mexico if you're Mexican.' Why did you really come back?"

"I told you," he said. "Where's the waitress? I couldn't get rid of her before you guys showed up."

"So you came back with your college degree to sit on the Zócalo and sell landscapes?"

"I didn't say that."

The waitress came; David ordered in Spanish. Raquel gestured to our tequila glasses, impatiently overruling my hand, which was waving negatively over the top of mine. I was feeling decidedly peripheral to this conversation, but I didn't mind. I had had enough of being front and center for a while.

"So what, then?" Raquel was saying. "What are you doing, making those things?"

"I send all the money I make on the Zócalo to my village," he said.

"For what?"

"A political organization."

"Aha!" Raquel jabbed my arm with her elbow. "Hear that? We're getting somewhere now. What organization?"

Our drinks arrived. David lifted his bottle and tipped a little beer into his glass and drank it, then wiped his mouth. "You've heard of clear-cutting?"

"Of course I've heard of clear-cutting," said Raquel.

"Well, there are logging companies in Chiapas that are stealing the forests the people need to survive, trees that belong to the Indians. These people are actively opposing the clear-cutting. That means women with babies lying down in front of the bulldozers. The bulldozers will not run over a woman with a baby, not in Mexico. But then the evildoers get their guys to drag them off. Forcibly, in other words. So my uncle and his compadres have to think up other means of stopping them."

"So you send them money for what?"

"Whatever they need it for. Lawyers, cell phone bills, printings costs, whatever. I send it to my uncle, who's in charge, and he disperses it as he sees fit."

"Why aren't you down there in front of the bulldozers?" Raquel asked.

"Because I'm not a woman with a baby. They're the most effective. And I have other things to do up here. I help them in other ways."

"What do you think of Subcomandante Marcos?"

"Marcos? He's nothing but a pretty boy. Has he ever built roads, or schools, or one hospital? What's he really doing for the peasants? Nothing. He poses in his outfits and gets media attention and it's all a big front, him and his cigars and his balaclavas."

Raquel mulled all this over, turning her tequila glass on the table. I didn't like the sangrita here at this cantina. It was sweet and thin, a bright, synthetic red, and tasted like cough syrup. But I was drinking it anyway; what the hell. The woman who had danced with David earlier came by the table and leaned down and said something in his ear. He said something back to her, unsmiling. Raquel leaned in very obviously to eavesdrop, but I could tell she couldn't catch what they were saying. The woman went off to another table, where a middle-aged man with a droopy gray mustache was sitting alone. He got up to dance with her. She jogged along with him, businesslike, professional.

"Is she mad that we're sitting with you and stealing her tips?" Raquel asked out of the blue.

David looked at her.

Raquel laughed carelessly. "Or maybe she doesn't care; you're still fair game for a dance."

"She's my sister," said David without inflection.

"Your sister?" said Raquel. "What's she doing working here?"

"It's complicated," said David.

Raquel and I both waited for him to explain.

"Our mother died when I was eight," he said after a moment. "Maria was seventeen. She gave up any idea of college, marriage, traveling, anything, to raise me and my little sisters and brothers. Our youngest sister had just been born, and Maria stuck around and mothered her until she went off to college. A while ago, Maria moved down here and got into some trouble, so I came down to help her. She works here because she's too proud to let her baby brother support her. I drive her home at the end of the night when I can."

"I'm such an asshole," said Raquel. "Sorry. Does she live with you?"

"She lives with her boyfriend," said David. From the way he said it, I guessed that he didn't think much of this boyfriend, but I couldn't be sure; David had a way of revealing almost nothing in his face or tone, so his carefully controlled words themselves were the only things that gave any information about him. This, in itself, was telling: It made me think he was a man accustomed to watching people carefully and being constantly on his guard, most likely with good reason.

"Where do you live?" I asked him.

"In Roma," he said.

"Where's that?"

"A neighborhood not too far from here."

"Where a lot of artists live," said Raquel. "We'll go there to hear some music, Jo, maybe tomorrow."

"Tomorrow night," said David, "you can hear Jesus Morales at Pata Negra."

"Chuy!" said Raquel. "Chuy Morales is here? He's an old friend of mine."

"How do you know him?" David asked.

"I sang and played guitar on his last album," said Raquel. "We've known each other for twenty years or so."

"Oh, right," I said. "I went to a party at his house in L.A. last time I visited you." Jesus—nicknamed "Chuy"—Morales was a punk Tex-Mex musician who lived in a ranch house in the Hollywood Hills. The party had taken place around the swimming pool and had featured a live mariachi band, margaritas, shrimp burritos, and about twenty major rock stars, including Raquel. I had loved every minute of it.

"I've never met him," said David. "But he's friends with Miguel, who lives in my apartment building."

"Miguel," said Raquel, puzzled, tapping a tooth with a fingernail.

"What's your last name?" David asked Raquel suddenly.

"Dominguez," said Raquel.

"So that's who you are," said David. "I never forget a face or a way of talking, and I knew your face but not how you talked. That explains it. I have one of your albums. You're on vacation down here?"

"You could say that," said Raquel.

All along, I had been waiting for these two to become attracted to each other. They had been at a sort of standoff since we had sat down. I had felt them deadlocked in a struggle for top-dog status; now, subtly, I felt a shift. Raquel had trumped David, and both of them seemed to know and accept this. David, like a dog in a pack, seemed to accept his place unquestioningly once he knew how things stood. Likewise, Raquel seemed to take her throne without any diminished respect for the lesser dog: One dog had to be first; that was the way of the world. As a firstborn, I well knew the responsibility and weight of expectation that came along with being top dog, so therefore, in adulthood, I was relieved and even happy to be the beta every now and then. I tossed off my tequila, feeling much more at ease, now that this question between David and Raquel had evidently been settled in Raquel's favor.

"Let me guess," said Raquel. "The album of mine you own is *Big Bad*." This album, her one big hit, had gone platinum in 1992; she claimed to hate it.

"No," said David. "*Habanero*."

"Yeah," said Raquel, "you and three other people. It came out on September 10, 2001. I have a new one, almost done."

"That's good," said David.

"I hope," said Raquel. "So Chuy is in town, huh? That's great. Playing at Pata Negra. I know that place. That's so great. I am so cheered up to know I'll get to see him tomorrow."

Raquel looked as if she had been lit up from within, like a jack-o'-lantern, aglow. She signaled to the waitress for another round.

Late that night, or, rather, early the next morning, Raquel stood out on the balcony, smoking, and I lay awake in bed in the dark room, still drunk. I had called Wendy's cell phone earlier from the desk in the hotel lobby, but I had just gotten her voice mail. She must have known it was me; how many calls would come up "International" on her caller ID? Maybe she had been on the subway, or maybe she had been in the middle of something. Since she was never without her cell phone, even put it on the bathroom sink with the ringer turned to loud when she took a shower so she wouldn't miss a call, I could only surmise that she had screened me, which hurt my feelings a little. I had left her a message; that was all I could do, but I missed her, and I was worried about her. I had no desire to talk to Anthony. I was really angry at him now, finally, after years of pretending to myself that everything was just fine. What a Pollyanna I had been. It was my fault as much as anyone else's that things had come to this between us, but still, even so, it enraged me that Anthony had allowed our marriage to end like this. It made me want to punch him in the head. It made me feel that he had never really cared about me at all. Fifteen years of marriage had ended with a whimper, with a terrible sense of defeat. I felt annihilated, somehow, as if I hadn't existed since our wedding, when I was thirty, all those years ago. Who was I, apart from Anthony?

I heard Raquel singing to herself outside, something in Spanish. The sound of her voice comforted me, a long-familiar sound that had always been associated with good things. My parents were both dead; my sisters and I were about as different as three sisters could be and still share DNA. My marriage was over, and Wendy was emotionally distant and growing up and beginning to leave me. Raquel and Indrani were my real family, my real sisters.

I fell asleep and had dreams in which I was alone in one way or another; all of them were tense with the knowledge that I had nothing to protect me.

When I awoke, Raquel was snoring softly in the next bed. The light in the room was a bright gray. I checked my physical being for damages from the night before and was surprised to realize that I wasn't hungover, just a little muzzy around the edges. I took a long, hot shower, being careful not to swallow even a speck of water. As I washed my hair and skin, I imagined the water at the microscopic level, teeming with fecal microorganisms. It seemed ironic to be washing myself in this sewage-tainted stuff. All those years of living with Anthony's preoccupation with environmental rack and ruin had left their mark. I emerged from the shower, dried off, brushed my teeth using the bottled water Raquel had thoughtfully left on the shelf by the mirror, dressed in my usual jeans and sweater, combed my wet hair and tousled it so it would dry wavy, and then my low-maintenance morning regime was done.

"Ecch," Raquel said. She sat straight up. Her face was pale, her eyes little slits in puffy bags. "Fuck me," she added.

I laughed. She did, too.

"Morning, Jo," she said. "Oh my God. I beg of you, will you go down and get me a cup of hot water so I can stick a detox tea bag in it?"

"Sure, sweet cheeks," I said. I was feeling exceedingly cheerful. "Anything else?"

"How about some *chilaquiles* and fresh orange juice?"

Normally, I might very well have told her to get her own damn breakfast, but today, for some reason, I felt like acquiescing. "Whatever you like."

"Holy shit," she said. "You're a goddess. Thanks. I owe you." She rubbed her eyes and lay back down.

I waited; I was willing to make one trip out there, but only one. "Anything else?"

"Well," she said. "If you want to see the newspapers, you could get us a *Jornada* and a *Herald*. At Sanborn's, right down the street, on the corner, like two blocks from here. The newspapers are in the back, by the books."

"Okay," I said, getting my bag, putting on my jacket.

"I love your ass," said Raquel. "Seriously, this is so nice of you. And if you want to check that gossip blog for any updates, feel free."

I returned forty-two minutes later, laden like a burro, still feeling unnaturally cheerful. I put the tray of plates and cups down on top of the vanity table and handed over the newspapers to Raquel, who had showered in my absence and dressed in peg-leg black trousers and a white wifebeater under a moss green jacket that looked as if it were made out of a combination of felt and wild grasses. She took the cup of hot water I handed her and stuck a tea bag into it. Already, she looked more like herself, just from the shower and being upright instead of lying down. How does she do it? I wondered. I was going to look like shit from now till the end of my life if I kept smoking and drinking the way I had the night before, which I fully intended to do as long as I was down here.

"What are these?" I asked, picking up my own plate of *chilaquiles.*

"Just eat them. What did that cunt say about me?"

That cunt had said quite a lot, as it happened, but I was just going to stick to the bare bones. "She mentioned Jimmy Black's ex-girlfriend. Who is she, anyway? Is she some kind of starlet?"

"Yeah," said Raquel. "She's on some show about privileged teens having nervous breakdowns."

"Well, apparently she had a nervous breakdown herself just now and almost lost her baby. Allegedly."

"Oh my God," said Raquel avidly. "How horrible. And now they'll want my head on a stake. So what names did she call me?"

"Stop it," I said. "Just cut it out. You're a grown woman, not some high school kid. What do you care what she said? You're torturing yourself for nothing."

"I've seen the things she says about other people," said Raquel. "She is a mean and nasty girl. She has power. Whatever she writes, millions of people read. She serves us up to them, and they eat us like nothing, like we're potato chips. Someone should assassinate her."

I sat on my bed with my plate of food, shoveling it into my mouth, crisp-fried wedges of corn tortillas soaked in a thick, slightly spicy red sauce, layered with savory chunks of chicken and slices of sweet raw onion.

"Or maybe I mean someone should murder her," said Raquel. "Is it only *assassinate* if it's a political figure?"

"Gandhi was assassinated," I said. "But was John Lennon?"

"Was he? I can't remember."

"Remind me to Google it."

"The point is," she said, "it's terrible to have such things said about you."

"I know it is," I said. "I know. But they don't matter, Raquel. She's not really talking about you; she's just playing with voodoo dolls, trying to stir up trouble."

"Voodoo dolls," she repeated with a smile.

After breakfast, we went down to the lobby. As I was handing the room key over to the desk clerk, I heard someone say, "Hello, please, Raquel Dominguez."

I turned around, to see two smiling Japanese girls approaching Raquel, holding pieces of paper and pens in front of them, giggling, with their other hands over their mouths, as if to show that they meant no harm. Even so, Raquel met my eyes, a flick of a fearful glance, then smiled back at the girls and obligingly gave them her autograph. "Sorry to bother you," said one of them, her English strongly accented.

"It's no problem," she said politely.

The girls went off. "Rock star," I said to Raquel.

"Those people always scare me," she replied. "I have no idea why."

We made our way to the subway and took two swift, clean, silent, rubber-wheeled trains to Chapultepec, a huge green park nicknamed the "Lungs of Mexico City." We walked on paved roads under green trees for a while and finally climbed a steep hill high up to a grand castle, paid the admission fee, and went in. The castle had been built in 1785, apparently; I envisioned

Mexican workers and various beasts of burden dragging enormous slabs of marble and heavy timber up that same hill we had just struggled up empty-handed.

I read the little plaque and managed to understand much of the Spanish: The viceroys of Nueva Espana had lived here, and in the 1840s it became a military academy. When the French had invaded and briefly ruled Mexico, the emperor Maximilian had refurbished the place for himself and his wife, the empress Carlotta. It now housed the National History Museum.

The residential part of the castle contained room after room of fantastic, elaborately carved furniture, embroidered hangings, parquet floors inlaid with marble. These rooms were flanked on two sides by a deep, vast marble-floored balcony that looked out far into the hazy air over the city. We went up onto the upper floor and inspected the gorgeous rooms around a roof courtyard where the emperor and empress had lived and visiting dignitaries had stayed. The wallpaper was hand-painted; the snuffboxes were carved of ivory and inlaid with mother-of-pearl; the pillowcases were richly embroidered, white on white, the product of hours and hours of squinting, painstaking work that you could hardly even see.

"Can you imagine living like this?" I asked Raquel.

"Yeah," she said. "With servants watching your every move."

"It's pretty amazing, though, you have to admit," I said. "This whole place."

"Built with blood," she said tersely.

"Hey, they're your ancestors, not mine."

"Oh, please," said Raquel. "All my people on both sides were persecuted like nobody's business. Meanwhile, look at you, with all your French and English."

"Touché," I said. "No wonder I wish I lived here."

We wandered down the hill and struck out onto a wooded road. We stumbled eventually onto a gravel area where vendors had set up a row of food shacks. We bought some chicken tacos and bottles of tamarind pop and sat at a white plastic table in white plastic chairs and had lunch. Then we threw away our trash and went on to the anthropological museum.

We stayed until after dark, and left only because they were closing, emerging blinking and confused into the suddenly chilly wet air streaming with car headlights. My head was filled with life-size dioramas, riveting in their details, showing how little difference there was between long-ago and present-day Mexican Indian village life. Now the Indians had lamps and little tin saints and wooden crucifixes, but aside from the obvious additions of Catholicism and kerosene, the prehistoric Mayans might have felt right at home in the Yucatán now. I wondered how fundamentally the Mayan language had changed over the millennia. And the contrast between those elaborately amazing fairy-tale things in the castle and the Indians' simple and functional stuff—straw baskets, handwoven family sleeping hammocks, three-legged stools, clay cooking pots—was strong in my mind. The reconstructions of the thatch-roofed huts of the Yucatán had shown whole families living in places the size of our bathroom at the Isabel, yet it hadn't seemed crowded or forlorn; it seemed smart, shipshape, efficient, and solidly in keeping with the scale of things. Anthony would have had a lot to say about all of it, but he was far away, so I kept all of my thoughts to myself. I also wanted to discuss the brutal but alluring human-sacrifice tools and the ingenious gigantic stone Mayan sun-wheel calendars, but Raquel was hungry and a little crabby, and in any case, she had seen it all before; she had indulged me by playing tour guide, so I didn't want to try her patience with any earnest ruminations.

Raquel led me along a wide avenue out of the park to a sudden dizzying cluster of skyscrapers. We went down into the subway again; we took a train, passing several stops and then coming out into a quiet neighborhood of trees, modern apartment buildings, little cafés, and old houses. A family sat at a table on the sidewalk, cooking their dinner on an outdoor brazier and listening to the radio. A skinny dog skulked around them. They all ignored him, even the littlest kids.

"Where are we?" I asked, breaking a silence of almost an hour.

"This is Roma," she said. "We'll eat across Zona Rosa, then go hear Chuy."

She took me to a small upstairs Korean place.

"I cannot believe Chuy is here," Raquel said, lighting a cigarette when the dishes had been cleared away. "He's like my good angel. You and Chuy, and you're both here."

I sneakily paid the dinner check while Raquel was in the bathroom, and then we set off into the night. The rain had stopped, and the air was soft now and almost warm. This part of the city was very different from the Centro Histórico—not as old, of course, and not nearly as grandiose. The streets were narrower and lined with houses; every now and then, I caught a glimpse into a house through an open door and saw a jumble of rubber-plant fronds in a courtyard, TV screens, kids playing on the linoleum floor, clothes tumbling from an open bureau drawer, and heard birds squawking, smelled hot fat and spices. We walked along under trees with spreading branches, through yellow lights spilling from windows, past Jetsons-era apartment buildings with chrome flourishes and curved glass-block windows. Purebred dogs on leashes passed homeless mutts with matted fur sleeping in doorways, as if they were two different, mutually exclusive species.

Pata Negra was a new bar on a corner near a small park. Inside, it was all gleaming wood, airy, modern. Behind the bar were rows of different tequilas and mescals. The bar was about half-full; we got a table near the stage in the back. Raquel ordered us glasses of mescal and lit a cigarette, then offered me one, but I waved it away. She scanned the crowd, looking toward the door every time someone came in, jiggling one leg up and down. She looked like a jittery hummingbird.

"So how's your shrink business going?" she asked.

"Booming," I said.

"Got any good stories for me?"

"One of my clients is having an affair with another doctor she works with," I said. "They're both in their early fifties, married, with kids. They might bust up both their families while I'm down here, but I tried to get her not to do anything drastic."

"Big deal," said Raquel. "Come on. Something really interesting. Hey, there's David. Check out that shirt."

David was wearing a black cowboy shirt with embroidered red roses and mother-of-pearl buttons. His hair looked as if he'd just had it cut. He saw us and inclined his head by way of greeting, then turned to talk to someone else.

All day, we hadn't mentioned him. I felt a kind of barbed-wire fence around him as far as conversational topics went. Raquel and I rarely encountered such obstacles, and whenever we did, as soon as we realized this was the case, we broached them and trampled down the fence. This time, we were both cautiously and tacitly observing the barrier. It was very odd; I wasn't sure why this should be so. We had parted from him the night before, shouting, "*¡Hasta mañana!*" and stumbling off in different directions, David toward his car with his sister, Raquel and I back to the Isabel. Nothing had happened that I could recall that might have caused this unspoken agreement not to mention him, but there it was.

We ordered another round. The bar was now jam-packed and full of smoke. David appeared by our table. Without asking, he sat at the empty chair and nodded hello to both of us; it was almost too noisy to try to talk. I could see David's hair wasn't freshly cut; it was wet and combed against his head. I was surprised that he'd joined us, and a little flattered, strangely, even though I wasn't sure whether or not I liked him.

Someone tapped the mike and the house music was cut off abruptly. In rapid Spanish, a guy I couldn't see said something I took to be an introduction. He said a triumphant "Jesus Morales!" and Chuy appeared to cheers and applause. He carried a guitar slung around his neck on a black strap decorated with skulls, which I was beginning to think of as the symbol of Mexico. He looked solemn and diffident and unpretentious, as always. He strummed a chord.

"*¿Qué tal?*" he said into the mike, and then, almost without drawing a breath, he was singing in a high falsetto in Spanish, a capella. Raquel began to hum along in harmony, quietly, just so I could hear her. I turned to look at her and her face was burning with happiness, the way it had been the previous night, as if an actual fire had been lit in her skull. I had always been astounded by Raquel's capacity for both joy and torment, which seemed to exceed that of almost everyone else I knew; this seemed to make her life more rich and interesting, but also more complicated and painful, than most. She saw me watching her and reached over and pinched my arm. I pinched her back. I had always loved Raquel's voice; it was rich, crackly, and ballsy.

Jesus Morales was a razor-thin, six-foot-three self-proclaimed "wetback" who looked like an El Greco figure. He had been born in a village in northern Mexico and had crossed the border in Nogales with his family as a kid. His mother had died in the Arizona desert during the crossing, and one brother had been caught and deported. They never saw him again, and it turned out later that he had died in a knife fight in a bar near the border, trying to cross again. The rest of the family had gone first to Tucson and then ended up in Houston.

Chuy had buzz-cut gray hair bristling on his bony scalp, a thin beard and mustache, and soulful black eyes. He was sixty years old and looked it. The skin of his face and head hewed to the bones of his skull without any fat pads to cushion it; his cheek-bones were very sharp, his eyes sunken deep in their sockets. His nose was a misshapen lump of smashed-in flesh. He wore tight leather jeans and a crucifix, without a bit of irony. He was as badass and earnest as any righteous old punk-rock survivor.

Raquel worshipped him, and he treated her like an adored, scrappy, tomboyish little sister who occasionally crossed some invisible line, and then he slapped her down like a puppy, and she cried and howled for a while and then got over it and bounced back to him. She had asked him to play on her new album, but he had given her a vague excuse about not feeling up to it. Chuy had always been a little competitive with Raquel, probably because she was, when all was said and done, a bigger star than he was, or at least she had been once, and might be again, once this new album came out. Raquel had told me that she got the feeling that he thought she should have paid a few more dues before becoming so successful, and that he himself deserved more fame than he'd gotten. But he'd asked Raquel to play on his albums more than once; she had performed with him in L.A. at a benefit concert, and that had been one of the biggest thrills of her life. His refusal to play on her album had hurt her feelings, and she had been nursing some private wounds ever since; she didn't bounce back now as quickly as she used to. But the happiness of seeing him, in her present beleaguered straits, seemed to have wiped away her lingering sadness and hurt feelings.

I drank more mescal and hugged myself. David, I noticed, was watching Raquel. I didn't blame him. I leaned back in my chair. Chuy sang with total abandon. I had noticed this about both him and Raquel; when they sang, it was as if the song burned through them, ripping from their chests and throats, and they let it. They didn't resist; they turned themselves into slaves of the song. Sometimes it seemed as if it caused them physical pain they bore with a lack of ego, a willingness to be transformed, to be a fool, even ugly, for the song. Chuy's throat was wide open and from it came words in Spanish I didn't understand but was sure must have to do with longing and loss and other dark Latin emotions. His singing was ropy and abrasive. Raquel's harmony burred against the melody and made it vibrate.

Then Chuy saw her; he might have heard her singing, maybe not, but his eyes were on her suddenly and through his singing I could tell that he saw her. He walked to the edge of the small stage and reached his hand out to her. She hopped up onto the stage. He made room for her at the mike; they sang the final verse of the song together, in unison, in the same register, Raquel craning her neck upward, Chuy stooping, making up for their differences in height, so their mouths both hit the mike. Some people in the crowd must have recognized her, because there was a burst of applause. They ended the song; above the wild clapping, Chuy said something in Spanish into the mike about Raquel, and the room was full of stamps and whistles. Someone brought another mike, tapped it, adjusted it to Raquel's height.

Chuy said something briefly to her as he put his hands on the guitar. He played a few opening chords to a song, then accompanied her as she sang solo on Bob Marley's "Redemption Song."

I glanced at David. He was staring fixedly at Raquel; when he caught me watching him, he looked over to meet my eyes. His face seemed carved of wood. Why didn't he ever seem to make normal human expressions? Maybe his facial muscles had been damaged in the same accident that had taken his arm, but I doubted it; I suspected he was just preternaturally reserved as a matter of choice. Maybe it suited him to seem mysterious. He reminded me of a cigar-store Indian; this struck me as pretentious, somehow.

I smiled at him, not out of warmth, but testing him, hoping he would surprise me and smile back. He quirked an eyebrow at me very slightly—as if, I thought, to suggest that I could try all I wanted to get him to act like a regular person but that he was onto me and wasn't going to capitulate. A flash of attraction struck me out of nowhere, followed by an internal thunder boom of antipathy.

During the applause after the song ended, Chuy reached back and took his extra guitar from its stand and handed it to Raquel. She played rhythm and he played lead on the third song, something else in Spanish, a lilting, raucous song I leaned into as if it were a warm wind. Then they switched off for the next song, one of Raquel's from her third album, a kick-ass song in English called "Suck It Up," which she had written for me a long time ago when we were suffering through life together. She looked like a tough little cricket bouncing on her heels.

Their voices blended well together, and they seemed to be showing off for each other, resolving their differences by letting loose and giving each other room to shine. The audience was with them, singing along when they knew the words. Chuy sang a kind of rock-flamenco ballad and sobbed on the high notes, his face twisted and contorted, and Raquel kept a low sweet hum going in the harmony. Then she sang another one of her own songs, "Ojos Azules," which she'd written for the love of her life, Ivan, who'd left her and married someone else. He was a sexy, hard-faced Russian documentary filmmaker, and he had been with her and helped her through the end of her junkie days. He'd possibly saved her life, then had left her when she'd gotten clean. "You only loved my need," the song went; "you only loved my pain." The waitress brought me another mescal, which I didn't remember ordering but was very glad to see.

The set ended with Chuy's biggest hit, a Tex-Mex waltz called "Los Caballeros de Nogales," narrated in the voice of a self-loathing white guy crossing the border from Arizona to find a cheap Mexican prostitute. Raquel sang a plaintive harmony and strummed along with an easy rhythm. Chuy's vocal snarled into the final verse, Raquel deepened her harmony, and finally they finished the song on a sustained unison note, her voice rich, his hollowed-out.

The crowd, including me, all yelled and whooped, while David sat very still and sipped at his bottle of beer. Chuy and Raquel came offstage smiling and ducking their heads, both of them, as if the music had been the star and to claim any praise for themselves would have been conceited and unseemly. Raquel's stage persona, her whole being when she performed, was hot and vulnerable in an untouchable, impersonal way. After her shows, I could never quite reconcile the Raquel onstage with the Raquel I knew, and I had given up trying. Here she was, back again. I handed her the mescal the waitress had brought for her and she drained it in one gulp.

"Hey, Chuy!" I said, not sure whether or not he would remember me; we had met only once, all those years ago.

"Josie!" To my surprised pleasure, he put an arm around me and kissed my cheek. He smelled of smoke and sweat. Up close, his skin was gleaming and tightly stretched like a drum across his face.

"This is David," said Raquel. "We met him on the Zócalo yesterday."

"How about that ice-skating rink? Crazy, huh?" said Chuy.

"The mayor," said David. "Instead of fixing any of the real problems, he sends poor Mexicans ice-skating. Stupid."

"I love it," said Raquel.

"What the fuck you doing down here, Dominguez?" said Chuy.

"Running from the paparazzi," she said. "What about you?"

"I'm on a little tour of Mexico," said Chuy.

"David Perez," said David. Chuy leaned over and shook his hand. We ordered another round, drank more, watched people come up to talk to Chuy and Raquel, shake their hands, lean down and say things into their ears. When it was time for Chuy to get up and play again, he gestured to Raquel, inviting her up, but she demurred, waving her cigarette at him—no-no-no—so he got up and played the next set alone. He seemed galvanized; I had never heard him sing and play with so much fire. He kept grinning down at Raquel. *"Mi hermanita,"* he said between songs, tapping his heart and gesturing down to her, and everyone cheered again. This Mexican audience seemed to keep no distance from its performers, unlike audiences in New York; they listened with earnest and unfiltered feeling. Tears kept springing to my eyes while Chuy sang, and I let them.

CHAPTER SEVEN

CHAPTER SEVEN

We all left Pata Negra together at about 1:30 in the morning—Raquel, David, Chuy, and a crowd of people I had just met, including Miguel, who owned David's house, and his wife, Luz, and a group of artists named Felipe, Alfredo, and Eugenia, who apparently all lived in Miguel's apartment building, too. It appeared that we were all headed there together to look at Felipe's paintings and have a late supper. Also, apparently, Alfredo and Eugenia were having a two-person opening the next night at an art gallery, which we were all going to go to. I gleaned all of this somehow, by making out some of their Spanish and having Raquel turn to me when she remembered to hurriedly translate. The Mexicans didn't seem to realize I didn't speak Spanish. Every now and then, one of them turned to me to include me in the conversation. I found that if I smiled at whoever was talking, the person felt as if I

were part of things, and was reassured that he or she was doing a
good job as host. I didn't want them all to feel they had to switch
to English just for me, assuming they all spoke it.

I could tell a lot about them just from watching their gestures
and reading their inflections. I had often thought before about
how little our intuitive knowledge of other people has to do with
the actual content of their words. David, in a group, was charming but self-controlled. Eugenia evidently had a terrible crush on
him; she shot frequent shy looks at him as she talked to make
sure he was listening, and seemed to be slightly self-conscious
but happy when he looked at her. I guessed that Luz was the
alpha female of the group, a plump little woman with short curly
hair and a motherly manner and a quiet but commanding voice.
She had a full, pendulous lower lip that twisted slightly when she
talked in an ugly-sexy way and showed her large square teeth.

The women were mysterious to me. They had none of the af-
fectations or gestures I was used to in New York women. They
were softer, more rounded, less edgy, not at all competitive with
the men, more sure of their looks; they seemed grounded in a
sense of their own entitlement to beauty, no matter what their
shape or size. Latinas in New York were a little like that, but
here they were quieter, less flaunting of their plumage, more
sexually subdued, but no less confident or forthright.

We all hunched and hugged our jackets to us, shivering.
We walked quickly through a small park and then turned left
and headed down the same tree-lined street Raquel and I had
come along earlier. Raquel was in a goofy, punch-drunk mood;
she and Chuy were walking together, jabbering away in Spanish, laughing. Their building was one of the Jetson-era chrome

ones. Miguel unlocked the front door and led us all through a tile-floored hallway into an entryway, then past a staircase that led to an upper floor. He ushered us into his apartment, a large, nearly bare room, the walls hung with paintings in various stages of completion. A long table in the middle was crammed full of jars and brushes and tubes of paint. I saw a courtyard through French doors, lit by a bare lightbulb, with a flowering bougain-villea covering the far wall and potted rubber plants around a tiled patio.

Miguel was striding around, turning on lights, offering a bot-tle of mescal. He poured shots into little glasses and we passed them around and toasted. Then Felipe led us all through the courtyard to the back. He unlocked one of the doors off the courtyard and led us into his apartment. We all stood around looking at his work. His paintings were of jungle vines, imagi-nary animals—part jaguar, part parrot, part lizard—and hulk-ing futuristic machinery tangled in the leaves and branches as if it had either grown there or been overtaken by nature. Although it was extremely late and Raquel and I had been going all day, I wasn't at all tired. The mescal was peppery and robust; it had some cocainelike quality that inspired wakefulness, hyperver-balness, and heightened observational skills. I felt great. By now, I wished like hell I spoke Spanish and felt like a complete retard for never having learned it after all those years in New York.

Felipe was a healthy-looking muscular guy with a slight, sexy lisp. His lips were very full. His eyes gleamed with what I took to be some unusual degree of intelligence and liveliness. I won-dered which of these women was his girlfriend or wife; he didn't seem to be attached to anyone, or so I thought, possibly hopefully. Was I attracted to him? I wondered. I wasn't in the habit of being attracted to men anymore. With an electric tingle, I was aware of long-unused nerves and neurons shaking themselves awake, wide-awake, zingingly awake.

"You speak Spanish?" he said to me in English, as if he were sensing and responding to my interest in him. How old was he, anyway? How old was I? "Your name is Josefina, right?"

"No, and no," I said. "It's Josie. You speak really good English."

"Yeah, I lived in Brooklyn for a while," he said. "You're from New York?"

"Right," I said. "What were you doing in Brooklyn?"

"I lived in a loft with my friend Carlos," he replied. "We were up there installing our work in a gallery for a show and I ended up staying a year and a half. And then I went back again the next winter and ended up staying another year. I like it there. But I like the art community better down here. It's friendlier. Up there, you're really on your own. Down here, it's very small, we all know one another, and everyone goes to every show. You'll see tomorrow night."

"Right, the opening," I said, remembering. I licked my lips, wanting more mescal. Everyone else seemed to have drifted back to Miguel and Luz's apartment. "Are these meant to be political, these paintings?"

"All art is political," he said with a flirtatiously disingenuous smile.

"I mean expressly."

"Not really," he said. "They're more personal. I used to draw these types of weird things when I was a kid, these fantasy landscapes with made-up animals and strange machines in the plants. Then in art school and afterward, I got into video art and computer art for a long time. Then a little while ago, I realized that I was faking it. So I went back to what I did as a kid. I don't care if they're good or bad."

"They're good," I said honestly.

"Yeah," he said. "I know they're better than that other shit I was doing. You can't be trying to impress people. That never works. What do you do?"

"I'm a psychologist," I said. "A therapist."

He took a small step backward to appraise me anew. "What kind?"

"No method. I sort of make it up as I go."

"Really?"

"Well, no. I should rephrase that. I try not to approach any-one with a dogmatic agenda."

"So who are your patients?"

"Some couples, some families, but mostly individual people with all sorts of interesting problems."

"Like depression?"

"Some, yes."

"We hardly have any depression down here," said Felipe. He had picked up a large dry paintbrush and was running the soft bristles over his palm, as if he liked the feeling. "Everyone works all the time and then you have your family and you go to church. There are all these festivals all the time, celebrations, and you're not alone so much. You have people around you all the time. That can make you crazy in a different way, but not depressed."

"Right," I said. "That makes sense."

He reached over with the paintbrush and ran it over my nose and down my face. I was instantly turned on. "So you would probably be out of work if you lived down here."

"I bet I wouldn't," I said. "I bet I'd have plenty of business."

"Tell that to all the macho Mexican guys. All the devout Católicas. They would laugh at you."

"All right," I said. "You win."

He laughed. We were standing close together. I felt very, very awake.

"Want to see the apartment?" he said suddenly. "I'll give you a tour."

He led me around his place, which was small and airy, and had hardwood floors and sparse but solid and elegant furniture. Of course we ended up in his bedroom. He led me in and turned to me in the darkness without a word, and suddenly we were making out, first standing up, and then lying together on his bed. I was purely thrilled and delighted to be doing this. It was so unlike me, so not married and not professional and not mature and not sober. I seemed to be continuing what I had begun with Mick and then Peter the night of Indrani's party. He smelled and tasted so good; none of this made any sense, but I figured why the hell not. I was starving. He pulled back to laugh down at me, his eyes slitted and his lips wet. His hand snaked up my shirt and under my bra to feel my bare breast, and I put my hand on his hard-on and rubbed it through his jeans. He put his hands around my waist and hoisted me up so I was straddling him and looking down at him, and then he caught both my breasts in his hands and arched his back to press his cock against me. I fell onto my elbows and kissed him openmouthed as we undulated, our crotches pressing together hard. I was so aroused I was gasping and laughing a little with the pleasure of touching him and being touched like this.

Then came the inevitable moment when all of this foreplay either was or was not going to progress to sex. It was a real question between us, one we batted around for a few rounds of kissing and wrestling. He made it clear to me wordlessly that he was perfectly willing to mate right there and then like happy, mindless animals, and I was dying to fuck him, but after what had happened with Peter, I didn't want to feel like I was turning into a total slut. My inner Catholic forced me to pull back and look him in the eye. He got the message: We would postpone the inevitable, and meanwhile, it was time to disengage and join the others again and drink more mescal. We got up, grinning at each other, stretching, and brushed ourselves off, straightened our clothes and hair, and wandered across the courtyard and into Miguel and Luz's kitchen, where Raquel, David, Eugenia, and Miguel were leaning against counters, drinking and smoking and talking. Felipe poured us both some mescal. "There you are," said Raquel easily.

"Hi," I said. She narrowed her eyes laughingly at me before turning back to David. He was, I could feel, in the middle of some sort of monologue, and Felipe and I had just come in, burning with pheromones, and interrupted him. Slightly chastened, I tried to dim my facial wattage a bit, but Felipe was resting his hand at the small of my back, gently moving a knuckle right at the base of my spine, and I wanted to climb him like a savage animal. I took a sip of mescal.

"They need press," said David in English; I suspected he had been speaking Spanish but was switching for my benefit. "They need publicity and attention. It's so easy for these huge corporations to bury their local pillage under the avalanche of other news. No one hears about the Chiapas logging. No one knows how the people from my village are risking their lives to save their livelihoods. And of course it's happening everywhere; it's not isolated. There are so many tiny pockets of people all over the world fighting alone against the huge multinationals. And these people in San Juan Chamula, I'm telling you, they can't afford the time it takes away from their farming to try to save their forests. You know, in Chiapas they still farm with a pair of oxen hitched to plows on steep mountainsides, just the same way their ancestors did. Seriously, tilted on the hillside at a fifty-degree angle sometimes, it looks like insanity. They're trying to just maintain the little they have, and meanwhile companies are set up only to get richer. It's not enough to make the same amount they made last year; they have to make more every year, and that is the capitalist sickness. Everything has to expand, populations and annual profits, just like the universe, moving outward into nothingness, and why?"

Normally—for example, when delivered by Anthony—this sort of diatribe made me itch. I had been a little kid in the 1960s in California; as far as I was concerned, people could fling themselves in front of as many bulldozers as they wanted, stuff flowers into gun muzzles till they turned blue, and nothing would stop violence and greed. I had geared my whole life to helping make changes on a small, individual basis, but in no way did I imagine that doing so would combat any of the implacable forces of destructive ruin that David was talking about. David sounded determined and pissed off, the way I remembered the activists I'd listened to in the sixties had sounded, not my parents, of course, but a lot of the people around us.

Maybe it was the mescal, maybe it was David's clear, impassioned way of talking, maybe it was the Don Quixote–like image of a farmer tilting on such a steep hillside with his oxen, and maybe it was Felipe's hand insinuating itself under the waistband of my jeans, at the very top of my butt crack, but I found David's eager and unapologetic earnestness appealing. Up in New York, whenever someone got political or impassioned at a party filled with people of my generation, those of us who'd been born in the early 1960s, I frequently felt a kind of mass withdrawal from whoever was going out on the limb, a backing up and moving away psychologically, not out of cynicism, but out of a realistic unwillingness to think that way, having seen where all that had ended up when we were impressionable kids. We weren't going to stick our necks out the way our elders had. We knew better.

"Our government, they're all on the take; they're all corrupt," David was saying. Finally, his impassiveness had cracked. When he talked, he gestured with his one arm. I could feel his phantom arm, could almost see its ghostly outline making parallel gestures. I stared at where he'd pinned the empty shirtsleeve to itself, sensing those defunct nerve endings in his shoulder still sparking away. His dark angular face looked intent and alight under the harsh overhead bulb. Behind him on the counter was a litter of fish heads and scales and tails on a big piece of brown paper that was stained wet and pink with fish blood. On the stove was a big pot of rice. On the opposite counter were a pineapple, some avocados, and some sort of squash I didn't recognize, cut in half, its seeds and innards spilling out onto the Formica. Next to the still life of produce was an ashtray crammed full of cigarette butts.

"They want Mexico to be exactly like the United States," David was saying. "They want the corporations to come in and take over and get fat off our land, and make them rich, and screw all the people. We can barely afford our own mescal now. Even tortillas are getting expensive. Can't stay here. Can't leave. They don't want us to do anything but drink their Coke and get fat and watch our kids die of diarrhea. Up in the States, they're all watching TV, eating Burger King, and sitting on the computer all day. Mexico won't go that way."

"No," said Eugenia. She was tall and skinny, with very blue eyes, a long face, and a diffident, polite manner. Her soft brown hair was cut in a kind of pageboy; I hadn't seen one of those in a while. "In Mexico, we fight it."

"Of course Mexico will go that way," said Chuy. "Everyone wants TVs and computers and McDonald's; they're going right down the same tubes. Have you ever seen a country reject an advance of technology? Have you? No, and it's because everyone wants what the multinationals are selling. If those peasants in Chiapas were offered tractors and TV sets in exchange for their forests, you think they'd turn them down?"

"They would," said David. "They would turn them down. They're the people who beat the shit out of you for taking pictures of the inside of their church, don't forget. They just want to be left alone to live the way they've always lived, eat their traditional food and do their ancient ways of farming and the old handcrafts and dress in their traditional clothes. You go there. You'll see what I mean."

"They sound like the Amish," I said.

"Maybe," said David. "The point is that they need those forests. That's their firewood and cooking fuel. For thousands of years, they've managed the wood supply, and now these logging companies are just taking it away. And believe me, these people in Chiapas don't want to turn into *norteamericanos*. To them, that would be a nightmare."

"What about your father?" Raquel asked. "Was it a nightmare for him to go up there and get an education for his kids and escape that kind of poverty?"

David shot her a hard, careful look. "My father had certain ideas for what he wanted for his kids," he said. "But never did he let us forget who we were. We were Mexicans every minute of our lives, although we lived up there, learned English, could get around. We still ate the same food and spoke Tzotzil and Spanish at home, so we would know both. The idea was to take what we got up there and bring it back here. That's what he taught us to do. He was a great man, in his way. He had a vision, and he lived according to it."

"So how many of you moved back down here?" I asked.

"My brother Carlos is down in Chiapas. Maria and I are here. Everyone else is still up there. But three out of eight isn't so bad."

Raquel lit a cigarette. "So you're doing good things for them all," she said. "Helping them. So that's great, good for you."

"David is our superhero," said Miguel, clapping him on the shoulder.

"The one-armed bandit of the Zócalo," said Felipe, laughing also. "Us, we're just painters. We don't know anything; we just make pretty pictures."

"No one is stopping you from being a superhero," said David without rancor. "All you need is a cape."

"Well, making art is a little bit heroic in a way, isn't it?" I said. "To put all that stuff out there, create something beautiful and interesting out of nothing. That's something, I think."

"Josie is a splayed-out romantic about artists," said Raquel. "Watch out."

"Music, too," I said.

"Yeah," said Raquel, "we're so generous and noble, right, Chuy?"

"Sure," said Chuy. "I agree with Josie, I think it is a pretty good thing to perform or make something, whatever. You're staying out of trouble, at the very least; you're not adding to the bullshit in the world."

"Not so sure about either of those things," said Raquel.

"When I was younger," said Chuy, "I was fucked-up and angry at the world, and I could have gotten into all kinds of bad shit."

"So instead you wrote a bunch of pissed-off anthems," said Raquel, laughing. "To spread the feeling."

"For me," said Miguel in careful English, "I first hear Chuy's music when I am eighteen. I am very angry, and his angry music makes me feel better. So instead of blow shit up and make a lot of trouble for myself, I turn up this music so loud, my mother want to kill me. Much better to do that."

"The fish is ready," said Luz, looking into the oven.

"How do you all speak such good English?" I asked.

"I watch many American movies," said Eugenia.

"You study at university," said Miguel. "Like me."

Eugenia answered him in Spanish, something that made everyone laugh. She found a small sharp knife in a drawer and began slicing the avocados. We ate dinner in candlelight at a long table in the next room. The table had been covered with an embroidered cloth and set with plates, forks, and knives. It was chilly in this house; the food warmed us up. There was some kind of firm-fleshed, mild-tasting fish baked in a green sauce, along with rice and squash and salad and tortillas. There were nine of us. I sat between Felipe and Miguel, Raquel sat across from me between Chuy and David, and Eugenia, Luz, and Alfredo sat at the other end of the table. We drank some not bad red wine out of juice glasses. It was after three o'clock in the morning by the time we finished all the food. We cleaned up and washed the dishes together. At almost four, we were back in the kitchen again, standing around, finishing the second bottle of mescal.

"Okay," said Raquel, "I think it's time to go back to our hotel and go to sleep."

Felipe looked at me, asking me a question. I looked back at him.

"Where are you staying?" he asked me softly.

"The Isabel," I told him.

"I'll see you at the opening tomorrow night?"

"I think so," I said. "Raquel is my master, so if she wants to go, we'll go."

"She wants to go," said Raquel. A cigarette dangled from her mouth. She looked like a tiny female gangster in her child-size white wifebeater and black pants, her hair wild around her head. We took a cab back to the hotel; Miguel had called the cab company for us and had written down the taxi's number before we drove off. The driver was evidently drunk off his ass. He talked into his cell phone, driving with a herky-jerky urgency through almost-empty streets.

"David is an interesting character," I said. There. I had broached the topic of David. It hung there like a fragile butterfly I wanted to crush without knowing why.

Raquel seemed not to hear me. "So what's this thing with Felipe?"

"We're hot for each other for some reason," I said. "I don't know if it's a 'thing.' I think the point is that it's nothing. Why?"

She gave me a flash of a sideways smile. "It's cute," she said.

"Fuck you," I said. Raquel pretended to be shocked at my unaccustomed profanity, and we laughed.

In our room at the Isabel, Raquel walked around in her black babydoll nightgown, pacing like a panicky insect. I settled into my bed and tried, without any luck, to find a soft spot on the mattress. The overhead light glared down at us.

"What's going on with you?" I asked her. "Want an Ambien?"

"Josie," she said. She perched on the end of my bed like a bird briefly alighting. "I'm not doing very well. I'm really fucked-up. Thank God you're here and thank God for Chuy tonight. I can barely keep it together. My heart feels like it cracked in half, and it doesn't help that he's so unworthy. It makes it worse. But man, I am still in love with him. It's not something I can turn off like a faucet. My body still wants him and my stupid heart is still sending out signals to him. I feel like he got ripped out of my arms at the height of passion. I know it sounds melodramatic, and it feels like cheesy Romeo and Juliet melodrama to me, too, but I feel like I'm going insane a little. Whatever he feels, I will never know, because I will never speak to him again."

"You will be okay," I said. "It's only feelings!"

"I know," she said with a flash of a weak smile. "But I can't take it. It's in too many pieces. God, I am freezing! It's never this cold here."

"I know," I said. "I wonder if we have enough blankets. Raquel, you're going to recover from this."

"If I were young, I would believe you," she said. "But keep telling me these things. I really need you to hold my hand."

I reached over and took her hand.

"I didn't mean literally," she said, squeezing my hand, "but thanks."

"So tell me about Jimmy Black," I said.

"God, just hearing his name makes my heart hurt like you would not believe," she said. She closed her eyes. Her face contracted slightly. "My heart literally hurts."

"Oh Raquel," I said.

She leapt up, took two cigarettes from the pack she'd left on the vanity, lit both, sat back down, and handed one to me. I had just brushed my teeth, but I took a drag anyway.

"We didn't go to Mass today," Raquel said on an exhale. "I need to go to Mass every day we're here."

"What's this sudden Catholicism?" I asked, laughing.

"Maybe it's just that I need all the help I can get," she said.

"It's sort of like the NA meetings I went to when I was first getting clean. Everyone was so raw. It was comforting. Safety in numbers. All the cavemen huddled around the same fire."

"That makes sense," I said.

We smoked in silence. Raquel was shivering with cold. We snuffed the cigarette ends out in the ashtray on the nightstand and then Raquel climbed under the covers with me. "Pretend I'm Wendy," she said. "It's too cold to sleep over there."

"Wendy would rather die of cold than sleep in the same bed with me," I replied, spooning with her and resting my head against hers. She felt as tiny and fragile, but also as tough, as a wicker basket.

The next morning, Raquel and I dressed in our warmest clothes and our jackets and went out into the sunny, crisply cold morning and bought newspapers at Sanborn's and sweet rolls and take-out cups of very strong *café con leche* from El Café Popular, and fresh pineapple juice at the place across Avenida Cinco de Mayo, then hauled our picnic breakfast to the Zócalo, where there was no sign of David or his umbrella. We sat on a low wall and read the papers and watched the skaters, laughing at how funny the Mexicans all seemed to find their own unaccustomed efforts to skate. When we'd finished our breakfast, we went into the cathedral. It was slightly warmer in there than it was outside. We squinted in the sudden darkness as we made our way to the small chapel in the middle of the cathedral, genuflected, and slid into a pew. We sat there in silence for a long, long time, with the soaring weight of belief all around us. Gradually, people gathered, filling the small chapel where we sat in the middle of the cathedral. A Mass began. We stayed for the whole thing, then afterward walked out into the cold sunshine of the cathedral's fenced-in courtyard.

David still wasn't at his post in the Zócalo, I noticed. Maybe we were looking for him, maybe not. Raquel led me across the square to the enormous building called the Palacio Nacional, which took up the entire east side of the Zócalo. We went in and showed our identification to the uniformed guards and were immediately admitted to a huge courtyard with a double staircase rising on either side of us. Raquel started up the stairs; I followed. There was a mural painted on the huge wall at the first twist in the staircase: armies and workers, animals and women.

"Diego Rivera?" I asked Raquel.

She rolled her eyes at me and said, "Duh."

"What was he, a Commie or something?" I whispered, kidding. She rolled her eyes at me again.

The murals continued around the walls along the upper balcony. Slowly, like little kids looking at a picture book, we examined each one. One by one, going around the upper balcony, they depicted the history of Mexico from the height of Aztec culture to the conquistadores' takeover of the pre-Hispanic civilizations, the story of an ancient, violent, mysterious, complex culture being brutally dismantled and enslaved by invading bearded blue-eyed devils with better weapons, who swashbuckled violently in and wrecked Mexico without a clue about what they were ruining. The early murals, gorgeously drawn and detailed, showed the Aztecs thriving in all their weird and fascinating glory of human sacrifice and strange customs and intriguing decorative self-mutilation. One panel showed a marketplace in the foreground, people bartering and selling heaps of grains and vegetables and handmade goods, and beyond, a farm set in verdant fields, a close-up view of brilliant farming and irrigation methods, and beyond that, the grand pyramids of the city.

"All of these drawings? We're right here," said Raquel. "The Zócalo was built on the ruins of the city of Tenochtitlán. The cathedral was built right on top of the Templo Mayor, where human sacrifices took place. The Aztecs used to rip out their hearts and throw them onto the steps of the temple. And the Palacio, this building, used to be Moctezuma's castle. We're basically standing on heaps of buried skulls. Ghosts are everywhere."

Then, inevitably, in ensuing panels, Cortés and his men came, and everything went to hell as those ransacking, heedless, cruel, barbaric Hun-like creatures raped the women and brutalized the men like animals and burned the towns, wrecked the buildings, took over the land. In one of the murals, a dog barked at a tied-up dumb sheep angrily, as if to say, Look at you, all trussed up like a retard!

"The Aztecs ate dogs," said Raquel when I pointed to the dog. "So he got his, in the end, just as much as the sheep."

In another mural, an Indian woman carried a blue-eyed baby in a sling. I was totally enthralled with all of it. Raquel had to nudge me along a couple of times; otherwise, I might have stood for half an hour in front of each panel. It was like watching a silent movie unfolding.

By the time we got outside again, we were both hungry. Raquel led me along the Zócalo, where I noticed that there was no sign of David yet, to Avenida Cinco de Mayo, then hustled me several blocks to a plain-looking restaurant. We went in and sat at a table near the front plate-glass window so we could watch everyone walking by.

"At least I can eat," said Raquel when the dishes had been cleared. "So maybe I won't die of heartbreak and shame."

I laughed. "Are you feeling better today?" I asked her.

"I guess," she said. "I wish my father had brought me down here more when I was a kid. I've been here only a few times before; I don't really know the city that well."

"You do so."

"I don't! I speak Spanish like a Chilanga because I learned it from my father, so I can pass as a native. But really I'm faking it, just showing off the few tourist attractions I know." She inhaled sharply, suddenly serious, as if gearing up for battle. "Let's go," she said. "Let's check the Internet before our siesta."

We trundled along the high, narrow sidewalk of Avenida Isabel la Católica, back to the hotel. In the lobby, we sprawled in the big comfortable leather chairs, waiting for one of the two computers to become available. Drowsily, I watched the big fish drifting around their tank. Raquel tapped her teeth with a fingernail. I thought about calling Wendy again but then figured maybe sending an E-mail was a better way to communicate with her. She had screened me twice in the past couple of days when I'd tried to reach her cell, so obviously she was doing just fine without me, which surprised me. Recalling my idea to go over and cook for them every night, I realized that they might not, in the end, want me to. I felt a chill of impending loneliness and pushed it away. No way was I going to prove Indrani right.

"Here," said Raquel, handing me a ten-peso coin. "Go, go; it's free now."

I slid the coin into the slot. First, I checked my E-mail, and found three: one from Wendy, assuring me that no one missed me at all; one from Anthony, which I didn't open; and one from my younger sister, Juliet, who had, true to hypochondriacal form, forwarded me a link to a breast cancer Web site, which I didn't open. I typed quickly to Wendy: "I miss you and love you so much. There's a freak cold snap down here—I think it might be even colder than it is up there. Can you believe it? Love from Mom (and Raquel)."

"Come on," Raquel urged from her chair behind me, "get it over with."

I made a face at her over my shoulder, but when I saw the naked dread on her face, the tension, I turned back around and typed "minaboriqua.com" into the box on the search engine. Within seconds, I was reading the words "Rock-Hell is in Mexico City!" There was that same unbelievably unflattering photo of Raquel, with white stuff coming out of her nose this time, and, beneath it, the story that sources had tipped off Mina Boriqua that "Rock-Hell" had been seen in Mexico City, giving a surprise performance at "a music club" the night before.

"They know you're here," I said to Raquel. I turned around to look at her. She was curled in her chair like a larva. "Not the Isabel," I added quickly. "But Mexico City. Someone told them after your performance."

Her pupils dilated and she flinched, but she waved this news away as if she didn't care. "It's a big city," she said. "They don't know where I'm staying. They don't know how to find me; I registered under another name."

"True," I said, still watching her.

"Oh my God," she said, looking wild-eyed and haunted.

"I know," I said. "But they won't find you. They may not even really be looking for you."

"Oh my God," she repeated. "Those Japanese girls, yesterday."

"That doesn't mean they're going to send E-mails to the gossip blogs."

"They're Japanese. They're all obsessed with the Internet."

"Don't assume that."

"I should never have gotten up on that stage. If it had been anyone but Chuy . . ."

"It doesn't matter," I said, trying not to think about the fact that I had told Wendy where I was going. Despite her promise to keep her trap shut, I knew she might not have the fortitude to keep it to herself. "You can't hide forever. You have to go home at some point, first of all. And second, frankly, you're famous. Someone will always recognize you. That's what being famous means. Does it really matter if they find you?"

"They find everyone," she said. "They hunt all over the world; they track us. It's a human game."

"That is so creepy," I said.

"Let's go upstairs," she said, looking around the lobby as if she had just realized that someone might be listening.

In our room, Raquel turned on the shower and waited for the water to get hot. She stayed in the shower for a long time. She came out fully dressed again, her hair in a turban made of one of the stiff, thin hotel towels. I was sitting in bed with the blankets over my legs, reading the novel I had brought, *A Passage to India*. Raquel sat on the edge of my bed and tucked her knees under her chin.

"The thing is," she said, "I hate to seem like I'm being hysterical or overreacting. But you have to understand. I don't have a lot of time left in my career. In rock years, I'm geriatric. This is my one last shot, this new album, or so it feels to me now. It might be different if I were a man, but not necessarily. This isn't victimization; it's the truth."

"I wasn't arguing with you."

"I know."

"One of the reasons this bites me in the ass so hard is that all I want is respect. I want attention, but not like this. I'm thin-skinned, I know, but most of the other performers I know are just as hypersensitive and overly vulnerable as I am. People with leather hides don't tend to go into this line of work."

We looked at each other in silence for a moment. I put my book facedown on the bed next to me. Raquel's eyes looked very hollow and dark. Her face was pale and bare from the shower. She scooched her butt around so she was sitting next to me in my bed, with her legs under my covers.

"Seriously, this is my worst nightmare," she said, leaning her head on my shoulder. "I need a nap."

We lay down back to front, spooning the way we had the night before. I stroked her hair while she cried hard but silently for a while, and then we must have fallen asleep.

I awoke to darkness and lamplight. I had a slight headache and a sense of dread I couldn't understand until I realized that it was purely physiological: My stomach hurt. "I think I'm sick," I groaned.

Raquel was sitting in her own bed, reading. "You're not sick," she said. "You're just getting used to the altitude and the strange bacteria in the food. You might feel like shit, but that's because it's your third day. You'll be fine if you keep your alcohol level good and high all night, and eat plenty of fat."

"Is there an alternative?" I asked.

"By tomorrow, the altitude sickness will be gone and your own bacteria will have adapted to these foreign ones and they'll coexist in peace and happiness. Here, have a cigarette, and drink a lot of water. That'll help both your head and your stomach. Then we'll go down to the Isabel bar for a quick tequila, and then we'll take a taxi to the gallery."

I sat up and smoked a cigarette and read my E. M. Forster novel while I drank most of the liter bottle of water I had bought at the stand outside the hotel.

The Isabel bar was empty. We sat at the bar and sipped a shot each of Tres Generaciones tequila; the sangrita in this place was the same too-sweet cough syrup–like stuff they served at the cantina with the dime-a-dance women. I saw the bartender pouring it out of a big industrial plastic jug and decided I wasn't going to drink any more of that fake stuff, ever, as long as I lived, so I drank the tequila without a back.

"Your taxi is here," said the bartender, waving to someone just outside the door to the bar: our driver, come in search of us. We paid and left the bar and climbed into a minivan, whose driver was a very young, very dark-skinned boy with a shock of black coarse hair standing straight up.

"I married Isis on the fifth day of May," Raquel sang with a nasal twang.

I leaned against her while the taxi jounced its way toward wherever we were going.

"Another thing that kills me," she said with deceptive calmness, looking out the window at the reflections of car headlights flashing in plate-glass store windows, briefly illuminating a flock of mannequins tarted up in what looked like prom dresses, "is that I was the first woman he ever fell in love with, or so he said. He was an emotional virgin. He didn't realize what he had, because he'd never lost anything before. He threw me away because he didn't know any better."

"He'll get his someday," I said.

"Maybe not," she said. "Some people don't, ever."

"That's true," I said. "Some people just sail right through the whole thing."

"Not us," she said.

"Not us."

CHAPTER EIGHT

*T*hings started to move very fast when we got to the gallery, and I was separated from Raquel for a long time. The gallery was in a row of seventeenth-century houses in a little gated mews just off a wide boulevard. Going through a pair of French doors off the mews, we came into two open, large, well-lit rooms filled with people. Felipe was right there as I entered, as if he had been waiting for me. He immediately kissed me warmly on both cheeks, took my arm, and led me through the crowd to the makeshift bar at the back of the second room and procured me a tequila in a plastic cup. Then he led me around, introducing me to his friends proprietarily, proudly, as if I were his girlfriend. I found this pleasantly surreal, and I didn't mind, but I wondered what had become of Raquel and hoped she didn't think I had abandoned her. For a while, Felipe and I stood sipping our tequila in a little clump of people that included a pink-cheeked, mad-eyed Polish sculptor who talked at length about the mirrored crosses he was making, which sounded a little pretentious and silly, but what did I know; and Elfriede, a sweet, ox-faced young German ceramicist who was in Mexico to study pottery making in a village near Oaxaca and was just passing through; and Miguel, who didn't seem to remember ever having met me before, but of course, we had all been shit-faced the previous night.

After a while, I disengaged from the group and from Felipe and went off in search of *el baño,* which I found near the bar. I had myself a nice pee, successfully remembering to put my toilet paper into the trash basket and not the toilet, washed my hands right outside the bathroom at a long troughlike sink littered with scraps of pink soap, and then reemerged into the gallery and got another cup of tequila. Raquel had been right: The liquor seemed to be helping my stomachache and headache. I plunged into the crowd and skirted the gallery walls, examining Alfredo and Eugenia's work. They seemed to be a husband-and-wife artist team, since both of their names were on all the little white cards. Evidently together, they made masklike, dense, enormous, flat, colorful animal faces, rough and strange and beautiful, out of bits and scraps of things they might have picked up off the street. I especially liked a blue wolverinelike face with rakish bat ears and flickering, intelligent eyes made out of beads and bits of reflective paper. I checked the price, five thousand pesos, about five hundred dollars, which seemed totally arbitrary, like all prices for art. I wanted to buy it but wondered how I would get it home. Was it sturdy enough to ship? Probably not, but I liked the idea of hanging it on the bare white walls of my stark,

empty new apartment, which I had managed to avoid thinking about since I'd arrived in Mexico City. Anthony had always
curled his lip if I tried to brighten our apartment with anything
too colorful or, as he had contemptuously dubbed the embroidered pillows and wall hangings I liked, "folksy."

I banished all thoughts of Anthony and looked into the thick
blur of moving, talking, expression-filled, unfamiliar faces for
Raquel.

"There you are," said Felipe. Suddenly, we were kissing very
lightly and slowly, holding back like racehorses in the gate,
mouths open, tongues barely touching, staring into each other's
eyes as if to say, Later. He felt young and alive and electric with
muscular heat. I was trying not to picture him naked, over me,
inside me, because the jolt of lust I got from these images made
me feel faint with urgency. I could not wait to fuck him. I had
rarely felt this way about sex when I was younger; there had
always been an element of self-consciousness and fear in my lust
before now, but something had shifted as I got older, and now
I felt a pure carnal craving, exactly like what I imagined men
must feel for women, straightforward, uncluttered by any worries about whether or not we were compatible in the long run. I
wasn't looking for a husband, and as far as I knew, Felipe wasn't
looking for a wife; we didn't have to think about each other in
any sort of scary, long-term, pragmatic, socially relevant ways.
We were in total alignment here about what we both wanted.

I pulled away, finally, and said, laughing, "I need some air."

"Come outside," he said.

We went out into the courtyard of the mews and stood in the
light of the lamplit windows in the old stone row houses and

the glimmering air of the city overhead. It was even colder than it had been the night before. The tips of my ears began to burn with cold. Felipe handed me his cup of tequila to take a sip of; mine was finished. I was happily buzzed, happily aroused, but my fingertips were going numb, and I was hungry.

"I love their work," I said. "Those masks. I'm thinking about buying one if I can figure out how to ship it home."

"They can ship it for you," he said. "You should buy one! It's beautiful, isn't it?"

It was then that I caught a glimpse of Raquel. She was standing by the entrance to the mews, the two huge wrought-iron gates, talking to someone quietly and intently. I squinted to see whom she was talking to, and almost, but not quite, identified David. Then they slipped through the gates and disappeared, leaving me wondering whether that woman had really been Raquel at all.

"You think they really can?"

"Yes," he said. "I think so. I will ask. Wait here, unless you are too cold?"

"I'll wait right here," I said.

I stood alone in the mews, hugging my arms to my body. A few people drifted out to smoke. I watched them talking in clicking, velvety Spanish, observing their faces. They were very vehement and sure of themselves. Their words came out without hesitation. There seemed to be an argument afoot about something—I couldn't understand what, but I assumed it was about personal gossip, art, or politics, like most social arguments. The group consisted of three men and one woman. It was the woman who fascinated me most. She was small, with abundant glossy black hair and a lot of very red lipstick on an ugly-sexy mouth like Luz's, with a full, twisty lower lip and an overbite. She wore a fur coat, and I could smell her spicy, fresh perfume through the cigarette smoke. She spoke softly and clearly, looking directly at whomever she was talking to. She held herself erect so that even though she was shorter than the three men, she seemed of equal stature. I breathed quietly, in and out, feeling invisible and rapt. She reminded me of female Italian movie stars from the 1950s, feminine, confident, alluring, but very tough. She was probably about twenty-six; at that age, I had been a neurotic, self-conscious mess, simultaneously arrogant and shy, full of myself and racked by self-loathing. This woman seemed wholly integrated, fully herself. A wedding ring flashed on her hand; one of these men was probably her husband. She probably already had a couple of kids, asleep at home, watched over by some loyal old *abuela*. I pictured a stucco villa, a leafy, serene courtyard with a splashing fountain, a full staff, and loud, cozy, extended-family dinners at a long candlelit table in the courtyard with platters of fish and meat, like a magazine ad for wine or pasta. As I watched her listen to one of the men, holding her face perfectly still, seeming to focus her entire attention on what he was saying, I tried to imagine the inside of her heart and mind, her private pains and unresolved conflicts. I could only imagine that she lived her life in comfortable, secure public display, with very few internal struggles, but of course I had no clue what really went on behind such a smooth and glossy facade. Maybe her psyche was a seething lava bed.

Then Felipe was back. "It's no problem," he said, pronouncing it *prahleen*. "They can ship it; they do it all the time. Come on, let's talk to him about which one you want."

Inside, the air was warm and smelled of people's breath and skin and clothes and perfumes and that harsh disinfectant I smelled everywhere in Mexico. We found Alfredo near the bar, in the back. With Felipe translating, he and I agreed that I would buy the blue wolverine from the gallery, pay a premium for shipping and leave my address, and it would arrive in New York City before too long.

"I don't have enough cash with me," I told Felipe.

"It's no prahleen," he said. "You can give a credit card."

I laughed; why had I thought the gallery would be too primitive to accept plastic? How provincial of me. "Who's the person to give it to?" I asked.

The gallery person was, conveniently, standing right near us. He was a dapper, slight man about my age in a down vest, blue work shirt, and painter's pants. He had a rock star–like swoopy coif and a handlebar mustache that he somehow managed to sport, amazingly, without being comical. I handed over my MasterCard and pointed to the blue wolverine, wrote my address on a gallery card, and signed the slip he brought back to me after about five minutes. Apparently, I had officially bought some art, and now it was time to toast my purchase. Alfredo and Felipe and the gallery guy and I clinked our plastic glasses together and simultaneously drank. This was so exciting, to be able to buy something without imagining Anthony's disparaging complaints once it arrived. He would hate this wolverine, would think it was crude and childish, and that was part of the reason I was so happy to own it: He would never have to look at it; it was all mine.

But just underneath my happiness was a sense of something gone awry. At some point since I had said I wanted to buy the mask, I had felt a wall come up between Felipe and me. He had stopped touching me, and the heat between us had noticeably ebbed. I turned to tell him about how glad I was to have the wolverine and to thank him for helping me buy it. As I spoke, I saw a smiling, pleasant, distant stranger's face.

"You seem very excited about it," he said.

"I am," I said.

He shook his head at me, smiling oddly, as if he were put off, or disapproving, or puzzled. So he felt this wall between us, too. I could see in his face the same retreating confusion I felt in myself, as if we would have both vastly preferred to feel the way we had just moments ago, but a gulf had opened, and we couldn't cross it. I had felt until then that we were playmates in a verdant garden of sex, the membrane between us open and slippery with frankly easy desire. But now, suddenly, it seemed immensely clear that Felipe was a struggling young Third World artist and I was a tourist, a patron, a middle-aged New Yorker with a disposable income. Guiltily and possibly irrationally, I wondered whether it had been the way I had whipped out my credit card. Maybe I should have taken it out less avidly, without such nakedly acquisitive excitement.

But that was absurd. Why shouldn't I be excited to buy it? Why should I have to pretend? Felipe had encouraged me to buy it, had practically engineered the whole thing. It made no sense why he should then withdraw from me, but maybe he didn't

know why it had happened, either. He probably hadn't anticipated this fallout any more than I had.

I drifted away without a word, escaped to the bathroom again,
and went into a stall and just sat there for a while, staring at the
closed door a foot from my face.

Maybe he was jealous; the night before, looking at his work,
I had been too attracted to him to see it and take it in, but I had
loved it. Had I seemed lukewarm, and was his pride injured? I
had absolutely no idea.

When I emerged, I saw Felipe across the gallery, laughing and
talking animatedly to Alfredo and the gallery guy. Paranoidly, I
wondered whether they were making fun of me, but I immediately recognized this kind of thinking as the irrational fear of a
stranger in a strange land. More than anything, I wanted to find
Raquel, my link to the familiar. The tequila seemed to be turning on me; I was suddenly so hungry, my stomach felt awash in
hot acids, as if it were gnawingly digesting itself.

I wandered through the gallery, staring into faces. No one
seemed to notice me; I felt invisible. In my shaky, hungry,
half-tipsy state, people's faces seemed to take on some of the
impersonal cruelty and rough beauty of the masks on the walls.
There was something very dark going on here in Mexico, some
ghostly but ever-present residue of the history of the place that
lay underneath the communally fatalistic, laughing, egoless
equanimity of the national character. The human-sacrifice tools
in the anthropological museum were beautiful things, carefully
crafted, professional almost, as precise in their intent as surgical
instruments; the Aztecs had absolutely believed that the sun, in
order to rise, required a live heart to be ripped from a live hu-

man and thrown before the gods. Heaped for sale on the Zócalo were ceramic skulls of every size; death was everywhere here, human death, not hidden away like it was up north, but on display, held close, a talismanic presence, stripped of some of its terrifying mystery through everyday use. The Catholic churches here likewise had a pagan, humble, homespun feeling; even the grandeur of the cathedral was tempered, rendered folksy and informal by the unmitigated humanity of its icons. The saints were luridly painted, not muted or romanticized, but frankly celebrated for their weirdness, the kind of obsessive self-mutilation and self-abnegation that, later on, caused people to be locked up in asylums and, these days, got them put on heavy medication. All the images of Jesus here were not saintly, not beatific, but desperately human, showing him in harrowing pain, grimacing and lamenting. Women cried and wailed openly sometimes during Mass; almost no one cried during Mass in the States unless it was for a funeral. There was no tasteful distance from darkness here: It was as common and ubiquitous as food, as light.

"Where's your little boyfriend?" came Raquel's voice from just behind me.

I was so happy to see her, I threw my arms around her.

She pushed me away and laughed up at me. "Lush," she said.

"I'm not drunk," I said to her. "Well, not too drunk. Hey, I bought some art."

"Yeah, this stuff is great," she said. "I might buy one of these masks, too."

"Is Chuy still around?" I asked.

"He went home this afternoon," she said. "I miss him already. It was so good to see him. I love him so much."

"Where were you just now?" I asked.

She waved the question away like irritating cigarette smoke. "Which one did you buy?"

I pointed to my wolverine. She squinted at it. "How much are they?" she asked.

"Five hundred bucks, plus shipping," I said.

"Not bad. I like that cougar over there."

I laughed. "That's a cougar?"

"Fuck yeah, it is. I'm gonna buy it."

Raquel looked happy and dreamy; her eyes were glittering, and she had lost her earlier expression of haunted tension. Oh no, I thought with a flash of protective dread, she's falling in love with David; she's desperate, on the edge, on the rebound, and he's some kind of safety net. I was beginning to dislike him, I realized then, for no reason I could identify.

"Talk to that guy there," I said, pointing. "With Felipe."

"Why aren't you talking to Felipe?"

"He doesn't like me anymore since I bought the mask. Suddenly, I turned into the elitist rich white turista."

"Bullshit," said Raquel. "You're being totally paranoid. Look at his skin color; he's descended from mostly Spaniards, not Indians. He's as white and probably as rich and maybe even as educated as you are. Come on, let's go see about the mask."

We went over to the small group of men, who smiled at both of us as we approached them. Raquel began negotiating with the gallery guy in rapid Spanish, pointing to the mask of a big cat face with a cruel laughing red mouth. Felipe and Alfredo looked at me expectantly, as if I had been about to say something interesting.

"Raquel is buying one of your pieces, too," I said to Alfredo slowly, in case he could understand without having Felipe translate. "They are very good."

"Thank you very much," said Alfredo in stiff English.

Felipe's hand went to the small of my back and rested there, and I felt that everything might be easy and okay again between us.

Raquel took out a wad of cash and counted out five thousand pesos; then the gallery guy said something to her and she added a few more bills, no doubt for shipping. She was conducting her own transaction in Spanish, in cash, and so her purchase didn't cause the same icky First World/Third World schism my own had. I had a strong feeling that I wasn't being paranoid about that. And I was glad Felipe seemed to have forgiven me for who I was, but now I was a little wary of our alliance, whereas before I had been completely and naïvely trusting of our parity. How dumb of me. I was glad to know now how things really stood, the possible pitfalls. My take was like Anthony's on the NPR announcers, measuring the world in even, serene, optimistic teaspoonfuls of good intentions and fair-mindedness. But this was only because I could afford to; or rather, I had no reason not to. I was a victim of nothing; I had the luxury of urbanely eschewing any jungle tactics, any savage teeth baring or snarling to protect what was mine.

I stood there feeling weak, silly, and mealymouthed. Eugenia came up and slid her arm around her husband. He said something in her ear, evidently telling her that Raquel and I had bought two of the masks, and her narrow face caught fire with joy. She beamed two radiant blue headlights at me, then turned to Raquel and gave her two kisses, one on each cheek, yakking in fast Spanish. She and Raquel huddled together in conversation for a moment; Alfredo and Felipe laughed at them.

"Eugenia seems thrilled," I said.

"Eugenia is very emotional about everything," said Felipe to me, teasing. "Like you."

"I'm not emotional!" I said.

"Yes, you are," he said, kissing my forehead. "You should have seen your face when you bought that mask."

"Why?"

"Like a little kid. Just like Eugenia now."

"How dare you laugh at me," I said, laughing myself. "I'll get you back for that."

"I am not afraid of you," he said.

So that had been it. He had just been teasing me, watching me, not recoiling. I really was an idiot. Jesus! I needed some dinner.

"Is anyone else hungry?" I asked.

"I am very hungry," said Felipe.

What seemed like hours but was really more like twenty minutes later, a group of us had marshaled ourselves into a few taxis and pointed them toward the same destination: Covadonga, an old, formerly all-male dominoes club that now allowed women, and which also, equally crucially, served food. According to Felipe, this was the destination of choice after all the art openings. Also according to Felipe, the entire art world of Mexico City had been present at the opening.

"What does Covadonga mean?" I asked.

"It's a region of Spain," said Felipe.

"Do they play a lot of dominoes there or something?"

"They must," he said.

We got out of the cab; it had been a very short ride, but we had all decided it was too cold to walk. We ducked under a red awning and went into a lobby that led into a great echoing hall filled with the clack of dominoes, cigarette smoke, and waiters rushing around in black jackets and pants, white shirts, and bow ties. I greatly loved the fact that seemingly all the waitpersons in Mexico, male and female, wore rather formal, old-fashioned uniforms. It seemed to translate into excellent, impersonally professional service.

Two of these waiters scurried around, pushing chairs and tables together in order to seat us all together. I had thought the place was jammed to the rafters when we walked in, but within five minutes, we were seated at four tables pushed together with exactly enough chairs to seat all fourteen of us. I found myself between Felipe and Eugenia; Raquel was at the foot of the table, deep in conversation with the large, sweet German girl. On Raquel's other side sat David. I was certain now that I had seen them at the gates to the mews, and that they had slipped off together into the street. I had a bad feeling about this, but why this should be, I wasn't sure.

Raquel was smiling at the German girl as if she found her very interesting and was enjoying herself; this was almost certainly genuine, since Raquel never suffered fools, never pretended to be interested in someone when she wasn't. She was not a people-pleaser, which naturally caused her to charm and en-

dear herself to almost everyone she met. She and David seemed
to be ignoring each other completely. If I hadn't known better, I
would have thought they had never met.

Mystified, I watched them out of the corner of my eye while I
asked Felipe about himself and learned that he was thirty-seven;
I was secretly relieved, because I had feared he might have been
much younger. Somehow, that would have been a bit unseemly,
although I had no problem whatsoever with Raquel sleeping with
a twenty-three-year-old. Raquel could get away with seducing a
guy half her age, but it would have made me self-conscious to
have a much younger man see my naked body. A guy closer to
my own age wasn't nearly as daunting a prospect.

Felipe had grown up in Tlalpan, a town to the south. His
parents lived in two different houses on the same street where
he had grown up. After their divorce, they had sold the house
where he and his sister had been born and raised, a big, sprawl-
ing, beautiful house his father had designed and built. His father's new house, which he had also built himself, was right next
door. Felipe could stand up on his roof and look into his old
bedroom, see the garden where he had played as a boy, where
a new family was now living, with new kids playing there. His
mother lived four doors away from his father's new house in a
simple cinder-block one-story house with a courtyard.

"Do she and your father get along?" I asked.

"My father goes over there for dinner all the time," said Felipe. "And every Sunday afternoon, we all show up and eat a big
meal, just like we're some regular Mexican family. Then afterward, we all leave and my mother gets to be by herself. It's exactly what she wants. My father keeps asking her to marry him

again, says he's sick of all these young girlfriends, that he loves only her, but she keeps saying no, she's so much happier with him four houses away. It's a perfect arrangement. He doesn't admit it, but he likes it, too. When he's sick, she comes over with *sopa de lima* and does his laundry for him, then goes home. He is more old-fashioned and macho and religious and philosophical, and she is kind of a hippie, more of a free spirit, into more untraditional spiritual stuff, and when they lived together, they fought all the time about everything."

I noticed that a waiter was standing above us, awaiting our order. "What's good here?" I asked Felipe.

"Nothing, really," he said under his breath. "You don't come here for the food. Get the shrimp; it's not bad. Want me to order for you?"

"*Los camarones, por favor,*" I said, surprising myself. "*Una herradura blanco con sangrita, y un agua mineral.*"

"*Y yo también, lo mismo de todo,*" said Felipe to the waiter, and then said to me, "*¡Qué bueno!*"

"*Gracias,*" I said. "Are your parents pressuring you to get married?"

"I am married," said Felipe. I think I must have given a slight gasp of surprise, but he didn't seem to notice. "My wife lives with her parents, with both our kids."

"So you have kids!" I said, even more surprised.

"Everyone in Mexico has at least two," he said, laughing. "But my wife and I can't live together; we fight all the time. I go over to her house on Sunday nights for a second dinner after I visit my parents, and once or twice during the week. I never spend the night there. We no longer desire each other at all."

"Why don't you get a divorce?"

"Too much trouble," he said. "Mexicans don't really get divorced much, my parents aside. It's not like I want to get married again to anyone else, and she doesn't, either. We worked it out; we're both happier like this. She goes her way, and obviously, as you might have noticed, except for the kids, I go mine." He offered me a cigarette; I took it gladly, and we lit up. "What about you?" he asked.

I looked at him, surprised. "What about me?"

"Are your parents pressuring you to marry?"

I laughed. "They're dead, first of all," I said.

"You're laughing at that?"

I shook my head, unable to explain. "I am married," I added. I had taken off my wedding ring on the plane from New York; it had seemed symbolically appropriate, somehow. "But I'm separated from my husband," I added. "Since last week."

He looked interested and didn't say anything, just waited for me to go on.

"I'm down here as a sort of vacation before I move out," I said. "I just realized right before Christmas that our marriage is over. I told him, and he took it okay. It really is over. I am going to divorce him."

"You must be sad," he said.

"A little," I replied. "We have a daughter named Wendy. She's thirteen. She's at home with her father right now. She decided to live with him. I'm moving out, to a place nearby, and I imagine I'll be at their house all the time. But like you, I'll be a lot happier living apart from my husband."

"How long are you here for?" he asked.

"I don't know," I said. "I came down here to help Raquel. She's my oldest, best friend, and she's in some trouble."

"What trouble?"

"She's . . . I'm not sure how to explain. She got involved with a young guy with a pregnant girlfriend. . . . You know, maybe she wouldn't want me to talk about it."

Felipe looked down the table at Raquel. "She's a great singer," he said.

"What do you think of David?" I asked abruptly.

Felipe smiled and ducked his head, picked a piece of tobacco from his lower lip. He was such a sexy boy, delectably good-looking. He had sculpted cheekbones and a beautiful mouth. My thigh was relaxed against his; I could feel how strong his haunch was. The urge to fuck him returned with a flash of wild heat from wherever it had gone into remission. I felt my face go a little slack with lust, watching him watch David.

"He is a close friend of mine," said Felipe.

"What's his art like? Not the stuff he does on the Zócalo, his real work."

"He used to be a sculptor," said Felipe. "Then he lost his arm. Now he takes photographs. Pictures of people, not portraits, almost abstract. I can't explain it well. You have to see it. He is very good."

"David?" Eugenia interjected, leaning in to talk to us. "Yes. I think he is a genius."

Our drinks arrived; the conversation halted momentarily while the waiter poured mineral water over ice into tall glasses, arranged glasses of tequila and sangrita in front of each of us.

As soon as the waiter had moved on, Eugenia said to Felipe, leaning across me, "Have you seen the new series he is working on? The mummies' faces." She tried and failed to continue in English, then added something in Spanish with an apologetic smile at me.

Felipe nodded at her and then translated for me: "He took digital pictures of twelve mummified people in a crypt in Ex Convento del Carmen in San Angel. You are not allowed to photograph them, but he bribed the guard. He's printing these negatives on the computer and then developing these pictures using simple chemicals and water and sunlight. So they are dead, dried faces resurrected first with technology and then with water and sunlight."

"Yes," said Eugenia to me. "Some of them look like they are screaming or smiling. It is very powerful to see."

"So how does he connect this work with the stuff he does on the Zócalo?" I asked, trying not to sound skeptical.

"That is separate," said Felipe. "To raise awareness of the prahleen in Chiapas and money for the struggle, it's what he is giving back to his village. His other work is what he does for himself."

"I see," I said. I looked down the table at David, who was listening to Alfredo, his back turned to Raquel, even though their shoulder blades were almost touching.

"Your show is excellent," I said to Eugenia. "Congratulations."

"Thank you," she said.

"I bought the blue mask," I said. "The one that looks like a wild dog. But they're all beautiful."

"We worked very hard," she said, unable to hide her pure joy at her and her husband's success; apparently, I gathered, their work had sold very well at the opening, unexpectedly so. Eugenia was the opposite of David; she flashed one strong, pure, intense emotion after another, as if she were a lighthouse of feeling, a beacon of blue-eyed light. I suspected instinctively that she was occasionally rash and impulsive in her passions, sometimes misguided in the way of the impetuous but compassionate and well-intentioned. I realized that this could be said of me, too. Come to think of it, she looked a little like me; she could have been my younger, fairer cousin. Anyway, she evidently saw nothing objectionable about David, to put it mildly, and she knew him much better than I did.

I was staring at David through cold, narrowed eyes, thinking about all of this. Suddenly, he flicked his glance over to me and caught my expression. Without reacting in any way, he flicked his eyes away again, back at Alfredo, but I knew he had seen how I felt. I drank another tequila and ate a plate of very good broiled garlic shrimp with rice and salad. The cantina was huge but felt warm and convivial because of its crowded bustle, waiters rushing to and fro with trays, dominoes clacking cozily, the constant buzz of voices and blue haze of smoke.

"Were you both raised Catholic?" I asked Felipe and Eugenia. They had been asking me about where I had grown up, who my family was, and my work as a therapist, and I was starting to get sick of the sound of my own voice.

"Yes," said Eugenia. "My mother is especially religious. But I am not."

"And my father is especially religious," said Felipe. "But I am not."

"So you're both like me," I said. "Religious parents, but you're not."

"Yes," said Eugenia, laughing. "My sisters are also not at all Catholic."

"Neither is my sister," said Felipe. "Most people our age are not. The Church is losing power with us. It is very complicated, the Catholic Church in Mexico. Ever since the beginning, it has been a difficult, violent, complicated history. The Church is as corrupt as our government."

Eugenia waved her hands. "Let's not talk about this with the dinner," she said.

"Anyway," said Felipe, "Josie, do you want to go to the bull-fight with me on Sunday? Unless you're like Eugenia and you can't take anything too violent."

Eugenia grimaced at him.

"I would like to see the bullfight," I said. "If *like* is really the word. I'm curious, but I don't blame Eugenia for wanting to avoid it."

"Thank you," said Eugenia.

"But don't you have to go to your two family dinners?" I asked Felipe.

"I can miss one week," he said. "My parents will survive the disappointment, and I'm seeing my kids tomorrow."

After we had all pored over the bill and paid our shares, we straggled out to stand in a loose-knit clump under the red aw-ning. It was 10:30, exactly the turning point at which a night ended at a reasonable hour or evolved into a drunken wee-hour revelry. Raquel stood at my elbow. "They're all thinking of going back to Luz and Miguel's to smoke some weed. And there's a chocolate cake Luz baked today for Eugenia and Alfredo."

I tried to disguise the excitement I felt about going back to Felipe's building and possibly ending up in his bed. "Do you want to go?"

"Sure," she said. "I love me some nice weed."

"Not to mention some nice cake," I added.

"Especially when it's beefcake."

"You should talk," I said.

"What do you mean?" she said. "I was talking about Felipe." A few people went off, waving good night, and the rest of us regrouped ourselves into a few taxis and disembarked in front of Luz and Miguel's house. Inside, we assembled around the dining room table, which was still draped in the cloth from the night before. Luz lit the candles; Miguel poured tequilas. Luz disappeared and came back with a large frosted chocolate cake, which she set on the table, along with a knife. She went back into the kitchen for forks and plates while Eugenia sliced the cake. Raquel and I sat at the far end of the table, Felipe on my other side and David on hers. The air between David and me was, I thought, fraught with growing animosity, but maybe it was just coming from my end. After my misunderstanding earlier with Felipe in the gallery, I wasn't sure anymore about anyone else's feelings, only my own.

Plates came around with wedges of cake on them. I took a bite; it was still warm, very dense and moist and bittersweet, with a lot of cinnamon. Next, a pipe, sticky from the cake, came around the table; I took a hit off it every time it passed, and soon, between the chocolate and the weed, I felt a warm glow in my chest, a beatific smile on my face. "I'm stoned," said Raquel with a big grin at me. "How about you?"

"Yeah," I said. "This is really good stuff. Sometimes when I smoke, my brain goes on a psychodrama Habitrail. I hate that."

"Oh my God, remember that time we were house-sitting and we ate brownies from the freezer and forgot we'd called out for Chinese food?"

"We thought the delivery guy was breaking in," I said, cracking up. "We called the cops, but we were too stoned to remember our address."

"But we thought we were thinking rationally," said Raquel.

"We didn't know the brownies had marijuana in them," I told Felipe.

Alfredo got out a guitar; Eugenia brought an accordion from another room. They pulled two chairs away from the table and started playing; Raquel drifted over to them and sang harmony with Alfredo. Listening to them, I missed Chuy. Raquel's voice overpowered Alfredo's light, amateur baritone, although I could tell she was throttling herself back.

Felipe's hand had snaked up my thigh. I was resting my arm across his shoulders and leaning against him, feeling like a twenty-year-old bohemian. This was extremely pleasant all around. Soon, maybe, we would go to his place and take off all our clothes and get into his bed naked and have dreamy, ecstatic, carnal sex. But I didn't feel any rush. This anticipation was one of the nicest experiences I had had in a very long time. The most amazing thing was that nothing had happened yet to cause my excitement about Felipe to ebb or lessen. He was so easy, so consistent and quick-witted and warm. My mother had once told me that you could know everything essential about a person in the first twenty-four hours of meeting them. She also claimed to have known she was going to marry my father after being with him for only one day, so I had always suspected there was something a bit self-justifying in this. Anthony and I had married after a year of dating; I supposed I'd known from the beginning that we'd get married, but I certainly didn't know everything essential about him after one day. However, there was something about Felipe that made me think, for the first time, that my mother might have known what she was talking about, and I could easily imagine remaining friends with him after this fun little vacation fling was over, after I went back home.

I flicked a glance at David. From the side, his face looked even flatter, more severe. He turned and met my gaze.

"Do you know this song?" I asked him, for something to say.

"I've heard it," he said. "It's an old tragic Mexican song about a guy whose wife ran off with a rich guy from another town."

"Did your family sing a lot of these old songs in Chicago?"

His eyes were hard and black and shiny. He smiled a little. "We didn't sing much," he said.

"My family didn't, either, come to think of it," I said.

"Hey," he said. "I have to go soon to pick up my sister from her job at the cantina. It's right near your hotel. Do you and Raquel want a ride back?"

"I don't know," I said, turning to Felipe.

"Come with me," said Felipe.

I followed him out of the candlelit dining room into the harshly lit kitchen with its overhead fluorescent tubing. Suddenly, I was self-conscious. Did I look haggard, I wondered, or was I having a youthful moment? It was hard to know, at my age. I hoped the gods were on my side right now.

Felipe leaned against the counter and pulled me to him. I slid my arms around his shoulders; he rested his forearms against my butt and held me close. "I want to make love with you very much," he said into my hair. "You know."

"Should I stay?" I asked.

"I have been thinking," he said.

"Thinking is no good," I replied, laughing.

"You are separated from your husband," he said. "You're not divorced yet."

"But it's okay," I said. "It's totally over."

"For me, it's no problem. He is up there; I am here—good for me. But for you, it's more complicated. *¿Claro?*"

"No," I said. "There's no complication on my side whatsoever."

"You are emotional," he said. He leaned back so he was looking directly into my eyes. "I do not want to take advantage of this."

"You have no idea how much that makes me want to fuck you," I said, laughing, my mouth on his.

"Yes, I do," he said with something like a groan. He tasted so good; he felt so good. It was a while before I let him talk again. But finally he emphatically kissed me and then pulled his mouth free of mine. "We'll go to the bullfight on Sunday."

I was quiet for a moment. "You're a good man," I said.

"Not so good, don't worry," he said, laughing at me.

A little while later, Raquel and I left the house with David and got into his beat-up old Volkswagen Rabbit. I sat in back. The inside of the car smelled musty; it was very cold. He turned on the heater; it blew cold dry air in our faces while the car warmed up.

"We have some time," said David. "Want to go for a little drive?"

"Where to?" asked Raquel.

"Down to Coyoacán? There's no traffic this time of night; the streets are empty."

"Coyoacán," said Raquel to me, "is where the rich folks live."

"Sure," I said. "Why not?"

David pulled into the street, and we were off. We drove through some sleeping smaller streets and merged onto an almost-empty, double-decker freeway that gradually lifted itself high above the city on stilts, snaking through the concrete sea of buildings, hugger-mugger. In dreamy silence, we drove for a long time, watching the billboards float by. In the distance were skyscrapers. We eventually came down off the freeway into more sleeping streets, but these were leafier and walled.

"Behind these walls are amazing villas," said David. "The government all lives here. The richest people in Mexico."

The street we were on twisted and turned like a country road; it was hard to tell, in the darkness, what it really looked like. We came out into a kind of square. David parked his car, and we all got out. We walked through the little square in the dark, deserted town. Dogs barked in the distance, but otherwise, there was an eerie silence. The night was so frosty we could see our breath. I could almost feel money oozing from every brick in the town. Suddenly, a car pulled up silently next to us. Two guys got

out, and David briefly talked to them in Spanish. They got back
into their car and drove off again. "They don't fuck around with
security here," said David. "Those are undercover cops."

We got back into the car. I sat in front this time. About five
minutes after we started driving, I could feel a dead space back
there where Raquel's wakeful presence had been. She had always
had the ability to fall sound asleep anywhere, anytime, at will.
We drove back along the crooked little tree-lined road with its
walled-off mansions, back onto the floating freeway in the sky.

"How do you like this city?" David asked after a while.

"I like it," I said warily. I sensed the question held some
implicit criticism. "But I imagine it's very different if you live
here."

"How so?" His tone was neutral.

"It's easy to be a tourist," I said.

"For you it is, maybe."

"What do you think you know about me?" I asked, my tone
as carefully neutral as his.

"I overheard your conversation on the Zócalo."

"Eavesdropper."

"You guys weren't keeping your voices down. Americans
never do in foreign countries; they always assume no one can
understand them."

"You're American," I said. "Come on. You grew up in Chicago."

We were staring straight ahead at the road, not looking at
each other at all.

"No, I'm a Mexican kid who grew up in Chicago," he said in
his flat midwestern accent.

"Identity is not that stable when you're little," I said. "My daughter is American. She was born in China, but she's as American now as you are."

"I never felt North American. The whole culture is rotten and lazy and corporate."

He spoke blandly, but there was a keen knife's edge in his words that felt personal for some reason, directed at me. "In other words," I said, "you despise North Americans. Well, I'm a North American, so I assume you mean I'm those things. But how can you think you know a single thing about me from one private conversation with my best friend?"

He was silent.

I said after a moment, when I realized he wasn't going to answer me, "I can't defend North Americans in general. And I certainly can't defend myself when I don't even know what you're accusing me of."

"I'm not asking you to," he said.

"Raquel is Mexican," I added defensively.

"Half," he said back. "And she was born up there."

"You think I'm a spoiled rich bitch from New York who cheated on her husband with a stranger and left her kid alone to come down here to do God knows what."

"Really," he said mildly. "You're putting words in my mouth. Raquel seems to need a friend right now. You came."

I subsided against the back of the seat. "I need a friend right now, too," I said.

I saw that we were rattling along the now-familiar cobblestones of El Centro. When David pulled up in front of the Isabel and stopped, Raquel said only, "Good night, David. Thanks for the ride," and got out. I thanked him, too, and we rang the door-bell for the sleepy hotel clerk, who let us in. Up in our room, we got ready for bed in silence. We climbed into our separate beds and Raquel turned out the light.

"That was fun tonight," I said into the sudden darkness, hoping we could parse out the whole night together, gossip about everyone, and that I could finally ask her what was up with her and David. My brain was still sparking and fizzing.

"Yeah," she agreed, and took a deep breath. "I'm going to sleep like an animal tonight."

And then we were silent. I went over the whole night in my memory, from arriving at the gallery until now. That moment at the gate, watching Raquel disappear with David, kept gnawing at me. I wanted to go over and get into Raquel's bed with her and hold on to her, keep her with me, but I imagined that she was probably feeling solitary, and that she would have laughed, called me a "lezbot," and told me to get back into my own bed. I couldn't help feeling that she had slipped out of my grasp, somehow, but I told myself this was the histrionic thinking of my hash-addled, tequila-soaked, lust-thwarted brain. Soon I warmed up enough, alone under my skimpy blanket, to relax and fall asleep.

PART THREE

CHAPTER NINE

T E R   N I N E

R aquel woke up sick the next day. I went out that morning and got her a cup of hot water for her detox tea, the morning papers, and a fresh pineapple juice, but no food; she had insisted that she couldn't eat. I delivered it all to the nightstand and announced its arrival to her humped and tiny form under the covers. All I could see of her was a spray of curly hair on her pillow. She acknowledged the delivery with a half-apologetic grunt of thanks that suggested to me that I would do well to go elsewhere for a while. I left her to it and went down to the hotel restaurant, where I robustly enjoyed a plate of *chilaquiles,* three strong coffees with foamy milk, and a big glass of the sweetest freshly squeezed orange juice I had ever tasted. While I ate, I watched the other hotel guests. Everyone but me seemed crabby that morning. Outside, it was very chilly and overcast, and the scraps of conversations I overheard at the nearby tables concerned the weird weather. *"Je croyais qu'il ne faisait* jamais *si froid ici,"* hissed a pinched-face Frenchwoman to the man who sat across from her—I assumed he was her husband by his air of stoic indifference to her pain. I was sitting over my third cup of coffee, bundled up in my warm wool hat and down jacket. I was feeling cheerful now because of this, but also because of Felipe, whose existence I felt in my solar plexus as a steady, radiating burn of joyful lust, and also because I seemed to have the opposite of a hangover. My reflection in the mirror earlier had shown that I looked as buoyant and optimistic as I felt, which had cheered me even further.

After breakfast, I checked my E-mail. Wendy had written back. Her E-mail said in its entirety, "Dear Mom, sorry I missed your calls. Daddy and I are fine! He cooked me some eggs this morning, but they sucked. He says to tell you hello. I hope you and Raquel are having fun. Love, Wendy."

I wrote back to her immediately, omitting, naturally, any mention of tequila, cigarettes, weed, Felipe, or mescal, then did my daily sleuthing for Raquel. Her nemesis was apparently leaving her alone for the moment; evidently, Mina Boriqua's spies had failed to track her here to the Isabel, so she had run out of ammunition. I browsed around her blog, reading about the various little girls she had dubbed "Wino," "Brit-Brit," and "LiLo." All of them looked malnourished, lost, trashy, and sad. I knew, of course, that they were famous, rich pop stars and actresses; I knew exactly who they were. But seen through the prism of Mina Boriqua's jaundiced purview, they were nothing but damaged waifs with ruined hair, amateurish makeup, and terrible clothes barely covering their sickly bodies. They all needed the cure poor little Heidi had been given in Johanna Spyri's novel, which I had read to Wendy as a little girl: a summer in the Alps with a gruff saintly grandfather, sleeping on sweet straw, drinking bowls of fresh goat's milk, and running over the clovered slopes all day in the sunlight, gulping lungfuls of fresh mountain air. Barring this degree of a wholesome extended cure, they seemed doomed to be choked by those Medusa-like tendrils of hissing snakes rising out of the poisonous L.A. or London air: drugs, mental instability, paparazzi, gossip hounds, and the fickle turning hearts of the public. Courtney, Pambo, and Posh, almost twice their age, were treated no better than the younger girls, but their faces looked more seasoned and weathered than their baby counterparts, as if they had purged themselves of vulnerability and tenderness and caused themselves to be eaten from within and flayed from without, consumed without being destroyed, to become tough, immortal survivor androids.

It shocked me that "Rock-Hell" had been pulled into their ranks. And this was the line of work my own daughter was so hotly determined to get herself involved in, my bright, pure girl with her nuclear-physicist IQ.

The computer beeped to let me know my ten minutes were almost up. Feeling relieved to stop looking, and slightly grimy, I logged off and went upstairs with another cup of hot water. Raquel was sitting up in bed with my blanket around her shoulders and her own over her legs, reading the paper. "Thanks so, so much, *chiquita*," she said. "Can you get another tea bag for me?"

I sat on my bed in my coat while she drank her second cup of tea. "This is much better," she croaked. "I've been rereading *A Passage to India*—sorry, I borrowed it. But it's so funny, the English fear of otherness. I mean, they were so insecure, the English. They had to turn every place they conquered into England."

"I know," I said. "I was thinking the same thing when I was reading it yesterday. Can you imagine Mexico as colonized by the English?"

Raquel laughed. "Brits in the Yucatán," she said, and laughed again. "They are so funny in hot jungle climates, with their roast beef and Yorkshire pudding."

"I shall take my afternoon tea under the mosquito netting," I said in a mincing voice.

"A spot of sherry, memsahib?" said Raquel.

"Colonel Whitcombe!" I cried. "What is that I spy through my monocle? I must consult my Baedeker."

"Unfathomably, I do believe it's a mongoose," said Raquel.

And for a moment, all was well; all was as it had been.

I went out again so she could sleep. I walked for miles, consulting that modern-day version of the Baedeker, the Lonely Planet guide, following the maps in the thick book. I walked for what seemed like an hour along a busy *avenida*, passing tarp-walled stalls of CDs, open tables of watches and underwear, then kitchen-implement stores, until I came to the Mercado Sonora, the witchcraft market. I entered hesitantly, with some superstitious misgivings, but it was a cheerful, bustling, well-lit place matter-of-factly stocked with bags of herbs, hanging bunches of voodoo dolls, pouches filled with various cures, incense, and good-luck candles, the sort of basic make-a-wish stuff found at any average New York City botanica.

I bought a pouch marked *Amor* for Raquel, figuring she needed all the good luck she could get in that department if she was really crazy enough to go from a twenty-three-year-old TV star to a one-armed, stone-faced ideologue. Then I wandered to the back of the market and had a plateful of spiced-meat tacos and a tamarind pop at one of the little food stalls. It was so cold, the steam rising from the stove bathed all our faces.

The guy to my left was chatting up the taco lady, who was about my age, a foot shorter than I was, with intensely dyed black hair under a hair net. She was wearing a down jacket very much like mine over a patterned dress. Her face was sharp and canny, and her eyes darted over to meet mine with laughter sparking in them as her gentleman caller got increasingly importunate in his courtship of her. He was about our age, too, with thin reddish hair on a bony scalp, a round, bland face, and thick, pursed, cherubic lips. I lingered over my pop just to enjoy the continuation of the drama. Finally, realizing she was not going to budge, he paid and left. She said something quick and sly to me in Spanish, and I laughed as if I had understood every word, and really, I had.

I wandered back through crowded streets in the general direction of the Isabel. I walked for a long time along a lovely tree-lined street that was hung with delicately cut paper streamers crisscrossing the street high above my head. It was like a fairyland. A band played on one corner. Stuff for sale was everywhere—so much commerce. How did these people do it? Massive quantities of clothes and watches and kitchen stuff and socks and CDs were everywhere in big piles on blankets on the ground, on tables. Where did they bring it from in the morning, and where did they lug it all back to at night? I imagined a stream of peddlers, like the olden days, with huge sacks on their backs, crammed into rickety little minivan buses going far, far away to all the endless concrete-building warrens on the outskirts of the city, noisy barrios with hanging laundry and cooking smells in every graffiti-festooned, concrete-lined alleyway. Such lives these people had, hard lives of complex mystery that my own life did not touch except glancingly as I met their eyes, passing by on my way back to my comfortable hotel.

When I got back to our room, Raquel was gone. I took a long, hot shower to warm up, then lay down in my bed and fell asleep for a while. I awoke, expecting to see her in her bed, but either she had come back and left again or she was still gone. I put on my coat and hat and went down to the lobby.

I looked in the hotel bar and restaurant—no Raquel.

It was nearly four; had she gone out in search of food? Why the hell hadn't she left a note?

I asked the two beautiful young women behind the desk whether they had seen her, whether she had left any message for me; they looked blankly at me and shook their heads. I wrote on a slip of paper, "I'll be in the hotel bar at seven. See you then and there? Jo." I folded it and wrote "Cecily Sweeney" on the front.

I left the note and room key with the desk clerks, went out of the hotel, passing the smiling but armed guard, and headed for the Zócalo. The intermittent sunlight was weakening, and the temperature seemed to have dropped. The pavement felt very hard against my heels; not for the first time, I wondered if they made it out of harder stuff than New York pavements. On Avenida Cinco de Mayo, I ducked into El Café Popular and stood at the counter right by the door. "*Café con leche, por favor,*" I said to the woman behind the counter. She poured hot black coffee from a carafe into a Styrofoam cup and then tipped in foaming hot milk from a metal pitcher. She slapped a lid on it; I tipped her, paid for it at the cash register, then went back out into the blast of icy air. I sipped my hot coffee as I crossed the Zócalo toward David's spot. The enormous Mexican flag over the square whipped in some wind that existed only higher up, apparently, because down on the ground it was perfectly calm. The flag snapped taut, crumpling, then snapped taut again, as if it were constantly disintegrating, then magically reintegrating itself.

David was sitting on his chair, bundled in an authentic-looking Indian wool blanket over a puffy down jacket. Over his head, he wore a black balaclava with cutout eyeholes that covered the lower half of his face completely. He had set up four finished framed landscapes on the ground near his chair; instead of working on a new one, he was reading a book. He wore a black leather glove.

"Hey, Marcos," I said. "How's business?"

He looked up and saw me. I couldn't tell what his expression was because of the balaclava. He didn't say anything. His eyes were watchful.

"I'm looking for Raquel," I said. "Have you seen her today?"

He was silent a moment, as if he was trying to decide whether or not to tell me. Suddenly racked with dark fears, I fought an urge to fly at him with fangs and teeth bared and rip his arm off.

"Yes," he said finally. "I saw her a while ago."

"When did you see her?"

Again I had to wait while he processed the question and

weighed its merits and worthiness of being answered. Again I fought that same urge to attack him, which was getting stronger.

"About an hour ago," he said.

"I don't suppose you know where she was heading."

He inclined his head, but the movement was so subtle, I didn't know whether or not it was a nod or a twitch.

"Does that mean yes?" I asked, trying not to sound livid.

"I have an idea," he said. He waited.

A light dawned, vaguely: Does he want me to bribe him?

"I'll give you ten bucks to tell me where she went," I said.

He shook his head emphatically.

"Twenty," I said. "Two hundred pesos."

"No," he said. "Listen, she asked me for my sister's phone number, but I wouldn't give it to her. The same thing happened the other night. She went off by herself; I wouldn't help her. I think she went over there a while ago to find Maria at the cantina."

My heart thudded cold and damp in my chest. The suspicion that had been coiled in my brain released itself now with a *ka-ching* like a pinball and went ricocheting down various hot spots and sand traps to the pit of my stomach, where it vanished into a hole.

I said in a low, hard voice, "So your sister sold her drugs?"

After a brief pause, he said with a pained sound that suggested this was true even though he would have given anything to have it be otherwise, "I bet she's still at the cantina right now."

"David," I said, "is that what's going on?"

"Maria's boyfriend," he said. He looked back down at his book, shaking his head.

"Did you know Raquel's an ex-junkie?" I asked him accusingly. He turned a page of his book.

"You're not really reading," I said. "You're pretending to read so I'll leave, but I want you to know that my friend is an ex-junkie who OD'd and almost died twice and finally got clean ten years ago after three trips to rehab. She's desperate right now and self-destructive and maybe suicidal. If you're helping her get drugs, you deserve to rot in the lowest hell in the universe. I mean it. You're vermin. If you sell her any more drugs, I will kill you with my bare hands."

"I'm sure you will," he said, not looking up. "But you're attacking the wrong person. I'm on your side. I tried to stop her from going there, but she wouldn't listen to me."

"Why didn't you tell me?" I said. "At the opening, right? When you guys disappeared. Why didn't you warn me what was going on?"

"She got herself a cab," said David. "She asked me to help her and I said no. She went off in a cab. I am not her keeper, and I am not your informant."

"Right," I said. "We're rich gringos, not Chiapan peasants, so why should you care what happens to us?"

"If you're worried about her," he said, not unsympathetically, "then go and find her."

I stood there impotently. He kept his eyes on his book, then turned another page. I gave a small gasp of frustration, then left him and walked back across the Zócalo toward Avenida Cinco de Mayo, trudging with my hands in my pockets over the hard, high sidewalks to the taxi-dancer cantina where we had introduced ourselves to David the other night. I went up the stairs and ducked into the red-draped room. Even though it was afternoon, loud music played, people sat drinking at the little tables, and several helmet-coifed, stout women jogged on the tiny dance floor with various drunk, stout men. I saw David's sister Maria dancing with El Borracho from the other night, or maybe it was one of his two million doppelgangers.

I went to the back of the room, peering through the dimness, and found Raquel at the table nearest the bathrooms, sitting alone with a shot of tequila and a bottle of mineral water in front of her. Her eyes were closed. I sat down next to her and shook her gently. She opened her eyes, but they fluttered shut again. I shook her again. She focused on me with some evident difficulty. Her pupils were tiny pinpoints.

"Josie," she said with a puckish little smile. "I thought I'd get a start on my day's drinking."

"What are you doing?" I asked.

"Living my life," she replied.

"Are you doing that stuff again?"

"Josie," she said, "I'm on vacation."

"Do you remember how hard it was to get off that shit?"

"Yeah," she said, "but it was always there, waiting for me to come back."

"Bullshit," I said. "This is such bullshit. You're acting like some idiotic bullshit rock star cliché. If you do any more, I mean even once more, I'm going to leave you here and get the next plane back to New York."

"I know," she said. "I deserve that. You're right. Tough love."

"Shut up," I said. The waitress came over. I ordered a tequila and shook a cigarette out of Raquel's pack and lit it.

"You're smoking," she said. "You're drinking."

"That's within the bounds of acceptable immature behavior. Weed is okay, too. But heroin is out of bounds. Heroin is a breach of contract."

"Actually, I relapsed with the first tequila," she said. "I'm just continuing what I started. Don't you know anything?"

"You were never an alcoholic," I said.

"Doesn't matter," she said. "That's what they told me in rehab. The brain doesn't distinguish between intoxicants. I've been completely straight for ten years. You should have started worrying about me days ago, Jo. You're a little late now."

"Addiction is obviously not my area of expertise," I said ruefully. "But that isn't the point."

My tequila arrived. Recklessly, because I was angry, I tossed it off at one go and signaled to the waitress for another one. She nodded without expression; she wanted no part of our personal business. She probably thought we were two dykes having a lovers' quarrel. I ignored the horrible cough-syrup sangrita. She took the empty shot glass and went away.

"Then what is the point?" Raquel asked with a smack-addled grin.

"Are you trying to kill yourself?"

"Maybe," she said seductively. She was still smiling, but I knew she wasn't kidding.

"Please don't," I said. "Raquel, please. I need you."

"You *need* me," she repeated. "Oh, sweetheart, you do not."

She laughed. "No one does. I do not say that with self-pity, believe me."

I didn't answer. I watched her and waited. I wasn't sure what I was waiting for; I had a feeling she needed some silence for a moment so she could realize what we were really talking about.

After a while, she said with a flash of sheepish ruefulness, "Sorry."

"I don't take any of this personally," I said. "You don't owe me an apology."

"Okay," she said. "But I wanted to say it anyway."

"I can well understand the temptation," I said. My second tequila arrived. I took a sip of it. "You're in psychic pain, and heroin's a psychic pain reliever."

"Really the best," she said. "Everyone would agree."

"You're taking Advil for your headache," I said. "I understand. But in this case, the Advil is addictive and eventually maybe lethal. Better to suffer through the headache till it goes away on its own, don't you think?"

"Blah blah blah," she said, but she didn't say it nastily; she said it with comical subversiveness. I laughed. On the dance floor, David's sister allowed herself to be turned and spun by El Borracho's twin.

"Really, Josie," said Raquel, "I don't want to die of an overdose. You have to be under thirty for it to have any legitimacy."

"So I'm not going to have to watch you like a hawk till we both go home?"

"Please don't. You're on vacation, too. You're off duty."

"Did you get it from David's sister?" I asked swiftly, sneaking the question in like a shiv between her ribs while I had her softened up.

She raised her eyebrows and didn't answer.

"I saw David earlier on the Zócalo," I said. "He said I would probably find you here."

"Yeah, I saw him earlier, too," she said. "I told him I was heading over to watch his sister ply her trade."

"He told me her boyfriend sells it. Did you take a cab to his house to cop the other night?"

She leaned over and kissed my cheek. Her lips were warm and dry; she smelled of expensive shampoo. "You sound like a detective in a noir movie," she said. "Come on, Jo, let me have my nostalgic little bit of smack. My trip down memory lane. I'm floating here in a nice little bubble of relief. Analgesic relief. I know what I'm doing here. Okay?"

"You sound like Wendy when she's trying to talk me into letting her stay out past her curfew. 'Mom, it's not like I'm going to be sleep-deprived. Tomorrow's Saturday; I can sleep late.' I'm not your mother, Raq. I told you: I won't stay here if you keep doing it, but I can't stop you." I fished around in my bag and pulled out a paper bag and handed it to her. "Present for you."

"I love presents," she said, pouncing on it. She took out the *Amor* pouch from the witchcraft market and smelled it. "Thank you! I love it! I need ninety of these things. But I'm not sure how to use it. What do I do? Put it under my pillow? Brew it for tea? Maybe both." She hailed the waitress and ordered us both tequilas.

"I feel so much better right now," she said. "Tequila wasn't cutting it, and neither was weed. Maybe I can go home soon, get back on my feet. They didn't find me down here. I got a nice break from the shit storm."

"Good," I said. "But this is the second time you've done it. You could be sliding back into serious addiction."

"Listen to you," said Raquel. "And you say you're not a substance-abuse specialist."

I gave her a sidelong look. She was flushed and rosy and looked happy as hell. Our tequilas arrived. We clacked our glasses together and drank. I had a nice buzz going now. At this rate, I was going to be a wet-brained, raving alcoholic within a week. Maybe I would never make it back to New York. Maybe I'd be a taxi dancer here at this cantina. Felipe and I could live in sin. I giggled.

"What's so funny?" Raquel asked.

I told her my vision of where my life was headed.

"Are you at all worried about being single again?"

"I'm thrilled about being single again," I said.

"Yeah, I can imagine," she said. "How is Anthony taking it?"

"Like he takes everything. He's always prepared for the shit to hit the fan. He's so infuriating. Admit it. You never liked him."

"I always liked him! But liking Anthony is easy. He's a likable guy."

I looked skeptically at her. "Come on," I said.

"Okay," she said. "I didn't like how you were with him. It seemed to me that you made yourself smaller with him. That wasn't his fault, but you're so much more of a person than he is. He's limited in ways that you aren't. I mean, you're so much more open and aware, emotionally. He's closed off, right? Sort of emotionally unimaginative, or one-dimensional, or something. It's like you had to scale yourself down to fit with him. I always wondered if you liked being diminished like that."

I thought about this, looking at the tip of my cigarette as if it knew the answer. The question, coming from Raquel rather than Indrani, seemed genuinely curious, wholly without judgment.

"I guess I must have," I said. "Then I stopped liking it. You're pretty perceptive, to have seen that."

"I had to read between some lines there," said Raquel. "You always said everything was fine."

"I needed to think everything was fine. But you're right: That's exactly what happened. Indrani told me I'm pathetic."

"Oh, Indrani," said Raquel. She laughed. "She's like a little kid. She wants the fairy tale to be true. I love the girl, but she's so dumb sometimes."

"She's not dumb."

"Intellectually, she's brilliant. Emotionally, she's retarded. I should talk."

"I should talk, too."

"We're all retarded."

"Are you pissed off about me and Felipe?"

"Why, you think I'm jealous of your happiness or something? Possessive of you? Come on. I'm happy for you. You deserve it."

I smiled at her. "He asked me to go to the bullfight with him tomorrow."

She burst out laughing. "What a perfect date."

"Is the bullfight romantic?"

"No way," she said. "It's bloody and weird and beautiful and horrible. You'll go home after and fuck his brains out to forget what you saw."

"I'm still married," I said, as if I were warning or testing her.

"So what?" She rolled her eyes.

"I love you," I said.

"I love you right back. Thank God you came."

"I needed it," I said. I took another sip of tequila, then went silent and watchful, my eyes on Raquel's face.

Raquel waited, too, looking right back at me as if we were playing a game of psychological chicken. But I was a pro at this; she was just an amateur. "Oh man," she said on an exhale after a moment. "I don't know what to do next. All my life, I've felt like I had it going on. Even in my worst junkie days, I was still young enough to make a fresh start; I knew I'd get through. I don't know, Jo. I'm not feeling that way anymore."

I nodded slowly, watching her.

She was quiet, thinking. Then she said with sudden sober calm, deadly serious, "I feel like it's over. I do. The game is over for me, and I lost. My new album is not good enough. I know it, and it's killing me. It's trying too hard. It's the work of a washed-up has-been desperate for attention. It's a squawking, frenetic, empty, overproduced cry for help."

"Squawking and frenetic," I repeated. "I don't believe you."

"Well, believe me," she said. "When I go back to L.A., I have to face that. That's why Chuy didn't want to play on it. Because he knew, and I knew he knew, that it was bad. I held it against him, but he was right, and I knew that. The other night, he was trying to remind me who I am, musically. He was bringing me back to myself. It almost worked. I love that dude with all my heart."

She was silent again for a while. I waited. It reminded me of when Wendy was a little kid and got the stomach flu. She would vomit and then subside; I would empty the bowl and rinse it out, and then I would go right back to her, knowing she wasn't done yet. It was the same thing now with Raquel.

"But he couldn't," she said. "I mean, he can't save my album; I can't, either. I wake up every morning just dreading the day it comes out. The critics, if they even give a shit, are going to rape me. I'm already hearing the reviews in my head."

"You could be being paranoid," I said. "You always have these times of self-doubt right before a new album is released."

"If my album had been great, I would never have fallen for someone like Jimmy Black. I used him to distract myself, in part at least." She hesitated, and then she smiled with some effort. "It's funny that I always call him Jimmy Black. Some people always get called by their first and last names. I jumped all over him and licked his face like a puppy dog demanding to be kicked. So he kicked me. It served me right."

"No way," I said.

"Yes," she said. "I did. I was a puppy dog, and I got kicked. That's what I deserved. And you can reassure me or not; it doesn't matter. I know that was the end of love for me. My album sucks; love is finished. Might as well check out. I'm just talking, Joze. Don't worry. This isn't a threat."

"Yes," I said. "It is a threat. Don't you worry. I hear you loud and clear."

"No," she said, laughing. "No no no. I'm just talking out my ass here. Self-pity."

"I'm going to break the rules," I said. "I'm going to tell you what to do. Are you ready?"

"Ready," she said dreamily, apparently riding a fresh wave of heroin, or maybe it was the hard warmth of the tequila, or both.

I shook her shoulder gently so she'd focus on my eyes. "Raquel. I can't be your shrink; I'm too close to you. You need to go and check yourself into a private, secure place where the idiots can't find you and get some psychological help, somewhere where you can be taken care of twenty-four hours a day."

"I need to go to a *loony* bin?"

"A hospital," I said. "Otherwise, you're going to let yourself slide back into using again, and you will die of an overdose. I know you will. You will because you want to. This is my opinion as your friend and also as a shrink. You're suicidal, and you're begging me for help, and so I'm telling you what to do to save yourself, and I'm going to keep saying it until you do it."

"No way," she said. "I've already been to therapy. She filleted me and wrapped me in Saran Wrap and sent me home. I went through the whole litany: 'I worshipped my father, who was an indifferent parent and who probably cared more about the illegal immigrants he helped than he did about me. My mother was a needy narcissist who was incapable of maternal feelings, but nonetheless, she loved me and did the best she could.' Ecch! Fuck all that. *Fuck* all that."

"Retard," I said. We both laughed.

"Let's get out of here," she said. "Let's go see a concert or a movie or something distracting. A Hollywood blockbuster maybe. Or some fucking chamber music."

Outside, she took my arm. It was dark and very cold. We hurried along the street back toward the Isabel. We ducked into the lobby. Raquel dug out a ten-peso coin and handed it to me.

"I'm not going to torture you with this online gossip bullshit anymore," I said. "That's another rule."

"You're no fun anymore, Jo," she said half-gratefully.

The desk clerk handed us our room key. We climbed the two long flights in silence. In our room, we both flopped onto our beds and stared up at the ceiling, side by side.

"So my plan is that I have to go home sooner or later," said Raquel. "My self-pitying moment of weakness is over. No shrinks. No hospital. I will survive. I'll make another album."

"I bet this new one is much better than you think it is."

"Actually not," she said. "God, I am so sick of myself. I can't believe I let myself fall apart in front of you like that. It was the smack talking."

"It was you talking," I said.

"Well, maybe. I feel fine now, but I am going to come down so hard tomorrow and feel even worse than I felt this morning."

"You'll get through it," I said. "And someday you'll fall in love again, cliché though it may be. Hope springs eternal in the human breast, and all that."

"The human beast," she said. "Look in the paper and see what's playing at the movie theaters."

"You look," I said. "I walked all day. You just sat there nodding and blissing out."

She laughed and got up and found the paper and walked

around the room, shuffling through it to find the movie section. Then she threw it onto the armchair and flopped back down onto her bed.

"All I can say," said Raquel, "is that it is not fun to be a woman and to fuck up. The man is just being a guy, whatever. Good for him; he got some sex. But that was not my pregnant girlfriend; it was *his*. I didn't owe that poor little pregnant girl a damn thing. *He* did. But somehow it works out mathematically that I'm the villain."

"Maybe women are expected to behave better than men," I said, "because we are better than men. The world without women is *Lord of the Flies*. The world without men is *Little Women*."

Raquel laughed. "Tell that to Indrani."

"Poor Indrani," I said. "Here we are, down here in Mexico without her."

"Serves her right," said Raquel. "What did she say about me, again? How could I get myself into such a mess? What about her, letting that sleazy gigolo move in with her and fuck his little girlfriends in her own bed while she supported him?"

"Yeah," I said. "She was as in love with Vince as you were with Jimmy Black."

"So she shouldn't have judged me, then."

"You're right," I said. "Then there's me and whatever I'm doing with Felipe, which I know she'd have an opinion about, for sure."

"Whatever," said Raquel. "Knock yourself out with Felipe, that's what I say. He's hot. What kind of movie do you want to see?"

"A romantic comedy," I said. "Just kidding. Something bleak and violent. That Cormac McCarthy thing maybe."

"Hey, we didn't go to Mass today."

"Instead, we went to the slutty dancers' cantina."

Raquel plumped her two thin pillows and rearranged them under her head. "If I really believed in this album, I wouldn't care. If I knew it was going to set everyone on fire, I wouldn't give a shit. I think I'm especially vulnerable right now just because I know it's bad. I'm choking on it. That stuff I did with Chuy the other night was what I wish this album was."

"So go into the studio with Chuy for two or three weeks and record songs like those, and release them. How hard would that be?"

She was quiet for a while, tapping her teeth with her fingernails.

"Why not?" I said, pressing my advantage. "I bet he'd do it. It's time you guys actually collaborated, instead of you just playing on his stuff."

"Maybe," she said. She got up and picked up the paper from the chair and sat back down on her bed. *"No Country for Old Men,"* she said, looking at the movie listings. "A pulp B-movie all gussied up as great art. Just the ticket. What time is it right now?"

"Six-thirty," I said.

"But doing an album with Chuy . . . He's opinionated. He's tough. He does things his own way. I'm more flexible and easily influenced. He might railroad me, or something, make me feel like he wouldn't let me have enough of a say. But on the other hand, man, we could do some great stuff. Wait, six-thirty? Here's a showing at nine. We could get a drink first."

"I feel like I could drink forever," I said.

" 'Cause you're alive again," said Raquel. "The only way to live fully is to kiss the grape."

" 'Kiss the grape'?" I repeated, laughing.

"Dionysus has to beat Apollo; otherwise, you might as well be dead," she said.

"I could kiss a few grapes right now," I said. "Tequila grapes."

"Should we go down to the hotel bar or go out somewhere?"

"I hate the sangrita downstairs; it's that fake stuff."

"So let's get a cab to Roma. Come on. We can see a later showing of the movie." She leapt up and put on her coat.

Just outside the hotel, as we were getting into a taxi, I heard someone shout, "You guys, it's her!" and five thousand flashbulbs went off in our faces.

CHAPTER TEN

CHAPTER TEN

Something happened to Raquel in the explosion of cameras. All her years of performing came to her rescue; she didn't panic or fall apart. She was very quiet and regal; she ignored them and took my arm and calmly got into the taxi.

As we pulled away from the hotel, they piled into taxis of their own to follow us. Somehow, at Raquel's urging, our driver, a stout middle-aged man who seemed completely sober and rational, managed to shake the other drivers. We went to Roma, back to Pata Negra, and spent the night at the table where we'd sat when Chuy and Raquel had performed. We drank several rounds of very good mescal, but we didn't get drunk. We ate small plates of grilled squid, antipasta, salad, and potato tortillas. Shortly before midnight, Alfredo and Eugenia came in and saw us. They greeted us as if we were old friends, kissing us on both cheeks and asking if we minded if they joined us. I wondered whether this was a big night out for them without the kids and they were secretly disappointed to have to talk to us instead of getting to have a romantic date, but they sat right down at our table as if there were nowhere else they'd rather be.

"We sold two more pieces," said Eugenia. Her watchful, earnest, intense angularity was softened by success. Her eyes were bright and huge. "The reviews have been very good."

Alfredo smiled at her and took her hand. He was a large baby-faced man, bland-looking, innocuous-seeming, but there was a slow, sweet slyness to his smile that suggested there might be more to him than met the naked and casual eye. I had wondered, the other night, about his wife's obvious crush on David. How did Alfredo deal with that? I had watched them to see whether or not her behavior toward David changed when Alfredo was watching and had determined that it did not change at all, and that, in fact, Alfredo appeared to be totally unbothered by his wife's drooling admiration of another man. He was extremely oblivious, or extremely confident, or both. I knew from my own experience that this could be a sign of trouble. Who knew what lurked in anyone's heart?

Eugenia and Alfredo went off into the night about an hour after they'd arrived, trailing a chorus of *"Buenas noches"* and kisses.

"Are you scared to go back to the hotel?" I asked Raquel. "We could get a reservation somewhere around here for the night, if you would rather."

"We're staying put; it's the only way to get through this: Just let them get what they came for and not fight it."

"They're like bloodhounds to a fox," I said.

"If we get them on our side, we can make them work for us. That's the plan I came up with in the taxi. I'm not gonna cry about this. I thought I would when they found me, but it kind of got my blood up."

"Me, too," I said.

"Let's make them our bitches," said Raquel with a grin.

"Okay," I said. "But if you change your mind, it's okay. It's all right not to want your picture everywhere tomorrow morning. You know they're at the Isabel now, waiting for us."

"Well, then, it's show time," she said. "Let's get out of here."

We took a taxi back to the Isabel. And there they were again, waiting for us in the lobby. As they leapt up and aimed their cameras at us, I felt a momentary tremor of fright, and I imagined Raquel did, too, but she actually vamped a little for them while the flashes popped; I managed to stand my ground and tried not to look like an idiot. When Raquel evidently felt they had stolen enough of our souls for one round, she bid them a breezy good night and took my arm and led me out of the lobby. We went upstairs and brushed our teeth with bottled water, put on our pajamas, fell into our separate beds, and turned out the light. I was bone-weary all of a sudden.

"I'm feeling my age right now," said Raquel. "Tomorrow, I'm gonna feel ten times older, I know it."

"I am freezing," I said.

"Can I come over in your bed?" she asked like a little kid.

"Okay," I said like another little kid.

So we slept snuggled like birds in a nest.

The next day was as cold as the one before had been. Raquel

said she felt like a wreck when she woke up, and she looked a little puffy and wan, but she was able to get up and shower and dress. We ate breakfast in the hotel restaurant, reading the newspapers I had fetched from Sanborn's. There was nothing much new in the world. It was almost reassuring to see that all the corruption, bloodshed, greed, and persecution of the innocent were continuing exactly in the same way they always had; nothing had blown up or come irrevocably apart in the last couple of days, and no one had solved the world's problems. Our fellow tourists at nearby tables were bitching about the weather again in various accents and languages, and there was a comforting regularity in that, too.

I insisted over breakfast that Raquel go with me to the bullfight. I refused to leave her alone, and I wanted to see Felipe and the bullfight, so that was the only possible solution to this logic puzzle. Since they were going to tag along aggressively anyway wherever we went, we figured we might as well have the photographer boys as our enlisted allies, rather than as unwanted antagonists and tormentors, so we decided to ask them to go with us, as well. The idea was that they would take pictures of Raquel enjoying herself very much without Jimmy Black and without any apparent guilt about the pregnant girlfriend; this would show all the assholes, Raquel said, that she wasn't hiding out in shame and sorrow, that she had already forgotten about it all and was having an exotic and adventurous vacation with her best friend, or, as Raquel put it, "my MILF-type best friend."

I laughed. "That's a compliment, right?"

"Indeed, memsahib," she said.

After breakfast, we went out into the lobby and waved at

the paparazzi, a word I could not believe I was now applying to people who existed in my own social sphere. They were sitting around, reading magazines and waiting for us.

"How's it going, guys?" said Raquel as they photographed us both.

"Didn't sleep too well," said a snaggletoothed but appealing guy with a dirty-blond shag haircut. He wore a khaki jacket with many pockets. "The beds are hard here."

"They're *auténtico*," said Raquel slyly, half-mocking, half-proud of her determined lack of diva preciousness.

"How are you doing, Raquel?" asked a portly, swarthy, balding piratelike guy with long black sideburns.

"Oh, I'm ducky," said Raquel. She sat down on the couch across from them and tucked her legs up under her. "This is my friend Josie," she said.

They were a group of four guys, all in their late twenties and early thirties. They seemed very friendly but potentially dangerous. Their guard relaxed, like the bloodhounds I'd compared them to, once they realized the fox wasn't going to run and there was no reason to hunt her anymore.

While Raquel sat there charming them into falling madly in love with her, I went over to the computer, went online, and found the pictures of us that they'd all taken the night before. We were smiling, and we looked composed and halfway decent, both of us.

I checked my E-mail, assuming Wendy would have pounced on this right away, since, no doubt, she was spending most of her time on the computer now that I was safely in another country. Sure enough, she had written me. "Dear Mom, I cannot believe you're on Mina Boriqua and all those other ones, too!!! You look kind of cute!!! Call me if you have a minute in the midst of your famous life!! Love, Wendy."

"Hey," I called over to Raquel and our new pals. "Here we all are. Come and look."

They all traipsed over, except Raquel, who stayed put with an air of complete indifference, possibly for their benefit and admiration.

"I took that," said the quiet one of the bunch, a skinny kid with sticking-up hair and sticking-out ears.

The paparazzi accepted our invitation to the bullfight gladly, since they had nothing better to do and their flights home weren't until late the next afternoon, and it was just the sort of thing that naturally appealed to them. Also, "candid" snaps of "Rock-Hell" at a bullfight were exactly what they'd been paid to come down there for.

I went over to the hotel phone and had the clerk place a call to Wendy's cell phone. She answered on the first ring.

"Hi!" she yelled. Then she said to someone excitedly, "It's my mom!"

This had never once happened before with Wendy.

"Wendy," I said. "How are you doing? I miss you!"

"Mom," she said earnestly in a quiet voice into the phone, "I swear I didn't rat you out. I swear I kept the secret. I swear. It must have been someone at your hotel. God, that picture of you and Raquel is so cool!"

I heard girlish high voices in the background, the twittering of the teens.

"Where are you?" I asked.

"At Auburn's house. We're all here. I can't believe you're famous now!"

Who was Auburn? "Well," I said dryly, "I'm hardly famous."

"Well, I know, but you're on Mina Boriqua! My friends are, like, dying. Tamika said you look kind of hot. Are they gonna take more pictures of you guys? We're checking, like, every five minutes. I mean, Tamika's checking on her iPhone."

Who, for that matter, was Tamika? I laughed. "Well, you'll all, no doubt, be very excited to know that we're sitting in the hotel lobby with those very photographers, and we're all going to the bullfight later, me and Raquel and all four of them, so, yes, there will be more photographs. Probably just of Raquel. Don't count on seeing me anymore; I'm nobody interesting."

"Oh my God, Mom," said my daughter in tones of hushed awe. "This is just so awesomely cool. I so so so wish I could go to the bullfight, too. Please call me later and tell me everything?"

"How are you, Wendy?"

"I'm great! Really, Daddy and I are both just totally great! Stay down there as long as you want! I love you, Mom!"

After Wendy and I hung up, I called Felipe to let him know our date had been hijacked. When I explained why, he laughed and was very nice about it, although he was clearly disappointed, which flattered me.

"Can we at least have dinner alone afterward?" he asked.

"We can," I said.

"I am happy I get to see you soon," he told me in a low voice. "I missed you."

"Well, that was your choice," I said. "You didn't have to be so heroic the other night. I know you thought you had to save me from myself, but if you had taken advantage of me, I never would have held it against you."

"Don't tell me that," he said. We laughed. "I'll see you in front of the stadium at three-thirty," said Felipe, and we said good-bye. My heart was warm and gay and light for the first time in so long, I couldn't remember the last time I had felt like this. All seemed right with the world.

"Should we have the desk clerk get us a couple of taxis now?" asked the guy with thick gingery hair and a gap between his front teeth.

"We're taking the subway," said Raquel. "It's the fastest way to get there, trust me."

I gave her a look; sometimes she took all that "daughter of a Marxist, one of the *gente*" shit too far. But I didn't say anything. This was her show; I would let her run it.

"What?" she said to me, reading my feelings in my expression. "It is the fastest way. I take taxis all the time when it's more convenient. Come on, you'll see."

The six of us, Raquel and me and our new entourage, whom I'd privately dubbed "Ginger," "Pirate," "Ears," and "Khaki," but whose real names were actually Malcolm, Max, Wayne, and Chuck, traipsed to the subway. Together, in a clump, we underwent the journey underground to the bullfight stadium, which was called the Plaza México and which, according to the Lonely Planet guide, seated 40,000 people and was the largest in the world. Raquel and I sat side by side on the quiet, swaying train, reading about the history and ritual of the bullfight in our shared book, while our camera-hung pals stood grouped around us like a protective scrim or shower curtain, occasionally snapping a photo of us. I was getting used to the attention. In fact I found, to my own amusement, that I felt, unconsciously, a little miffed if too much time went by without our being photographed; I started to worry somewhere in a deep part of my insecure brain that we weren't being interesting or sexy enough. I could see, even at my advanced age and stage of life, how this might become a way of life very quickly, how one's private stock in one's own viability and worthiness could rise and fall according to the attention or lack of it.

We came up out of a huge, clean, near-empty subway station and set off across a huge *avenida* with traffic whizzing along. We marched down a quiet, narrow residential street. The "paps," as I was now calling them chummily to myself, were quiet, trailing behind us, obviously used to trying to make themselves invisible and letting the famous go about their business. Maybe because of Wayne's jacket, they reminded me of wildlife specialists studying ibises at a watering hole, trying not to change their behavior. But I could feel both Raquel and myself acting for their benefit, mounting thin plaster replicas of our natural, untrammeled personalities to create a puppet show of our friendship, ourselves. We neither diminished nor augmented ourselves; we projected parallel, false selves that were neither better nor worse than the people we were when unobserved.

The stadium was indeed huge, and I wondered how I would find Felipe, but he was waiting as promised right at the entrance, near a cluster of booths and kiosks selling bottles of water, seat cushions, souvenirs, and programs. He wore jeans and a dark blue shirt under a long wool coat. His face looked younger and more beatific than usual under a black watch cap. His cheeks were glowing. He looked so young, so healthy and vital. I wanted him again instantly. He seemed to see only me as we walked toward him. He kissed me three times, on one cheek, then on the other cheek, then back again to the first cheek, and then he held on to my shoulders and looked into my eyes and kissed my cold lips with his preternaturally warm ones. "Hello, Josefina," he said in his lovely, warm, accented voice.

"Hello, Felipe," I replied, hoping against hope that the cold air wasn't making my face look haglike and ancient.

Felipe greeted Raquel and allowed himself to be introduced to the silent crowd of camera-wielding men, who obviously had zero interest in meeting him or having anything to do with him.

We had time, Felipe told me, to go across the street for a quick drink and some lunch; the place was not bad. Raquel was indifferent to the idea of lunch, and the paps were busy sniffing around the place, so the two of us ran through six lanes of whizzing traffic to the other side of the *avenida* and tumbled into a warm, plain little restaurant. We sat on high stools at a high table and watched an American football play-off game on an overhead TV while we ate platefuls of grilled, spiced pieces of tender meat with greasy french fries and drank bottles of Negra Modelo. Felipe rested his knee against mine. We ate with unself-conscious concentration and intent; I was starving. When we'd finished, he offered me a cigarette and we lit up and ordered another round of beers. Just then, Raquel and the boys came in shivering and sat at the table next to us, chattering like old friends. Felipe ignored them, concentrated his attention on my face, and talked to me in a low voice.

TROUBLE

I was flummoxed by how much I liked him, how easy it always was to fall back into our attraction and rapport. I felt as if we were in cosmic alignment. Everything I said seemed to interest him; everything he said made sense to me. When Anthony and I had first started up together, our relationship had been immediately fraught with misunderstandings, missteps, doubts, and insecurities, which had been painful but had led to a lot of sex, which managed to obscure our differences temporarily, because we were so attracted to each other, but sex solved nothing; our problems always resurfaced again later. I had thought, when I married him, that by living together and building a life in tandem, over time, the deep, instinctive understanding we lacked would finally manifest itself. Then, when it turned out that I was infertile, I had thought that by adopting a baby and raising her together, it would happen. But it hadn't, obviously. And here it was, effortlessly, with this stranger I had met on vacation. I just hoped I got to sleep with him at least once before I had to go back to my real life.

Behind me, I heard Raquel bantering with the boys. I detected in her voice a thin wire of bright strain, but I was sure no one else would have noticed; no one else there knew her at all. One part of me smoked and drank and talked and laughed and flirted with Felipe; the other half of me was trained on Raquel, worrying about her, feeling empathetically how tightly wound she was, how brittle her laughter sounded. She was rising to the challenge, and I had no doubt that she intended to survive this, but I wasn't sure how much stamina she truly had. I wanted her to win; I wanted to help her. But there was only so much I could do. I could hold her hand and keep her warm at night and babysit her and cheer her on, but in the end, whatever she did next was entirely up to her. I knew that, rationally, and I knew she knew it, too, but it was hard for me to accept the fact that I couldn't do more for her than I was already doing.

"You're worried about your friend?" Felipe asked quietly.

I noticed that around his pupils were two golden coronas like rays of light around eclipsing planets. "How did you know?" I asked him.

Felipe paid our check; he insisted. We all went back outside, ducked across the avenue, and made our way back to the entrance of the stadium, where Felipe also insisted on buying my ticket for me. The seven of us traipsed down a very long, curving corridor and came out into our section of the stadium. We had bought tickets on the sunny side, where seats were both cheaper and warmer. Felipe maneuvered us a little apart from everyone else; the two of us sat huddled together for warmth, rubbing our four hands together. Flashbulbs went off around Raquel; under their cover, I leaned in to Felipe. We kissed as if we were just starting with our mouths and were about to devour each other whole. I pulled back, laughing at how turned on we both were.

The crowd roared as music played and three matadors ran out into the huge dirt ring and bowed. Then they all ran out again.

"Did you used to come here as a kid?" I asked Felipe.

"My father was a boxer; he's retired now. But he liked to bring me to the bullfight sometimes before his own fights. He thought it would bring luck and stamina; a macho superstition maybe, but he never got seriously injured, and he had a good career."

"Did you like coming here?"

"It scared me, but I kind of liked it."

"Like fairy tales," I said. "Darkness made manifest."

I caught Raquel's eye. She winked at me, but her face looked pale and pinched.

"I'll be right back," I said to Felipe.

I motioned for Raquel to follow me, and without looking back, I headed up the stairs to the back of the stands. I turned when I reached the top; she was right behind me. We stood side by side against the cement wall.

A bull burst into the ring. It bucked and ran and jumped, no doubt from the shock of hearing the huge crowd shouting and cheering. Two toreadors teased the bull, finally inducing him to chase one of them to the edge of the ring, where the toreador slipped through a doorway to safety while the bull leapt impotently around in the dirt.

"You okay?" I said.

"I feel like shit. Do I look awful?"

"You look beautiful, as always. Don't worry, the pictures will be good. You'll show them all. This is worth it; you'll be glad you faced them down."

"So what did you want to tell me that was so important?" she asked. I sensed something—not impatience, but a steely tone in her voice that hadn't been there since the beginning of this trip but which I had heard in her voice before, in years past, when she was angry about something.

"I wanted to give you moral support," I said. "You seemed like you could use a break from those guys."

She stared straight ahead and didn't reply.

"Are you mad at me?" I asked her.

She clutched my arm and buried her face in my coat as if she were wiping tears on it. "Oh God no," she said. "God no! I'm mad at myself. Here I am, courting these guys I would normally run away from. What a loser." I put my arm around her. She leaned into me and rested her head on my shoulder. "This bullfight stuff is freaky, I'm warning you," she said. "They hand-raise him and feed him like a king, and then—boom, out of nowhere—they shove him out in front of all these people and torture him until they kill him. He trusts people; he's never had any reason not to."

Two men on blinkered, leather-draped horses rode into the ring.

"The picadors," Raquel and I said in unison, having been good little apple-polishing students on the subway.

"He'll look like a pincushion in fifteen minutes if they do their job right," she said. "I remember this from last time. They're weakening him for the matador. By the time they get done with him, the bull will have lost a lot of blood." She looked a little bloodless herself at the thought. "In the old days, before they put leather blankets on the horses, they used to die all the time, too. Remember *Death in the Afternoon*?"

"You gonna make it through this?" I asked.

"Of course I will," she said. "Seriously, you can go home with your boyfriend tonight, I solemnly swear I will not fall into ruin and decay while you're gone. I'll be fine. I'll go to evening Mass, then show these boys a nice time at the cantina, give them something to talk about when they get home. That redhead's kind of cute."

"He is not!"

"I'm kidding."

"I can't go to Felipe's," I said. "I don't want to leave you alone right now."

"Don't treat me like a special-needs kid," said Raquel. "Like I'm riding the short bus in my helmet. I mean it. Let's go."

We walked back down to our seats. I slid in next to Felipe; without looking at me, he took my cold hand in his warm one and pulled me close. I winced as a picador plunged his lance into the bull's shoulder. I was trying not to look at the bull's face, but it was hard to ignore his expression as he was stuck full of painful things for no apparent reason. Of course I remembered Hemingway's terse and haunting bullfight descriptions of the beauty of the dance between the matador and bull. To me, this whole thing seemed like yet another manifestation of the deep, visceral, passionate pleasure men took in killing animals for sport in an organized fashion. Sure, there were female bullfighters, but I doubted that, left to their own devices, a country of only women would have engineered such a spectacle even once over the course of a thousand years, let alone in an ongoing manner. I wasn't sorry to be there, since bullfights went on every week all over the world with or without me and always would, but it wasn't the most pleasant thing to watch. Raquel had been right: The expression on the bull's face wrecked everything.

The bull went down on his knees, his face streaming with blood, and I got the feeling he would have liked to rest there for a moment to recuperate in peace, maybe have a few nurses come in with cool cloths to bathe his wounds and give him a little morphine, but he determinedly got back up again while the picadors rode around on their horses, circling for another attack. The matador, a lithe young man in a little bolero jacket and tight yellow satin pants that frankly outlined his package, waved a red cape at the bleeding bull dramatically, with an air of anticipation, as if there could be any doubt in anyone's mind as to the outcome of this encounter.

"Does the bull ever win?" I asked Felipe.

"Sometimes he does," said Felipe. "But usually not."

"So he's killed almost every time," I said. "I can see why."

"They cut him up and sell his meat outside. You know that, right?"

"Sure," I said. "But what happens to the bull if he wins? Is he taken home to live out his natural life in comfort?"

"Yes," said Felipe. "He's used for stud, which means he gets to have a lot of sex."

"I'm rooting for the bull," I said.

"Women often do," said Felipe in an indulgent tone that should have annoyed me but didn't at all. "Half of you anyway. The other half are thinking about how sexy the matador is."

I looked at the matador. I liked a little more meat on a man and a little less prancing.

"Are a lot of matadors gay?"

He shook his head. "Matadors are the luckiest men in Mexico for getting women."

"That guy has to be gay," I said. "Look how slinky he is. Look at his cute little butt in that outfit."

"No thanks," said Felipe. He put his arm around me and put his lips on my forehead. I leaned into him.

The first bull died a bad death. It was painful to watch; the matador failed to kill the bull cleanly the first time with his sword. He had to stab the bull again, and, horribly, again. Still, the animal finally staggered to his feet and tried to run away; then finally, at the edge of the ring, he collapsed, dead. Horses came trotting out to cart the big carcass away as the crowd booed the matador, who skulked off, probably to get drunk and sleep it off and try to forget the whole debacle.

"He's probably glad it's over," I said.

"For him, it isn't," said Felipe. "He has to fight one more bull, later."

There was a break, and then it all started again: the toreadors, the release of the bucking fresh bull into the ring, the picadors on horseback with their lances. This bull was testy, and the second matador of the day seemed phlegmatic and subdued. This bull did not seem to want to engage with him, and the matador, for his part, looked as if he would rather have been home on the couch watching TV and drinking beer; they had no chemistry whatsoever.

"This is the wrong bull for this matador," I said.

Felipe laughed.

When the second fight was finally over, the bull was carted off to be cut up, sold, and eaten.

The third matador had a finesse and grace the first two had lacked; he seemed to know exactly what he was doing. He stepped into the ring without fuss and began moving around quickly, efficiently, keeping his eyes on the bull, who was frantic and aggressive. The matador quietly stood his ground, controlling the bull with little drama, dancing him close to the cape, leading him in a swirl of movement.

"Olé!" the crowd shouted as he executed a beautiful pass.

This third matador killed the bull on the first try, but the fight seemed not quite up to snuff, according to the reaction of the crowd; they cheered him when the bull was dead, but I sensed wariness in their applause, something withheld.

The first matador acquitted himself slightly better with his second bull of the day; he managed to fell him with two swift stabs between the shoulder blades. But the second matador's second fight was worse than his first one: His new bull was as phlegmatic and resigned as he was. They engaged in a tepid, protracted pas-de-deux with many lackluster moments of listless standoffs when both man and bull seemed to be thinking about their grocery lists in their respective corners of the ring. It ended finally when the bull seemed to charge in a kamikaze rush of bravado, throwing himself on the sword out of sheer boredom, wanting to be done with it.

"Is it over?" I asked Felipe.

"There's one more bull."

"I don't know if I can take another one."

"You want to go?"

"I don't want to go."

"I will go if you want," he said.

"No, I want to stay."

"Then we'll stay."

When his bull had been weakened and readied, the third matador returned without seeming to notice the crowd. He approached the bull and feinted, stepped aside calmly as the bull charged him, as if he were letting a bus go by. Bull and matador circled each other, their gazes locked. Then the matador flicked his wrist and the bull charged. The matador waited until the last possible split second as we all watched in silent suspense before he slipped out of the way as the bull went pounding past, then spun around in time to meet the bull's eyes as the bull charged again. Then they circled each other for a while, each watching every move the other one made.

"This guy is good," I said.

"He *is* good," said Felipe. "He's a big star."

I was aware, as I hadn't been in the previous bullfights, which had been more like cartoons, that this very slender, slight man was all alone in the bullring with a very unhappy, lethal animal, and he seemed to have the bull completely under his control. The matador moved; the bull responded. The matador provoked; the bull charged. The bull's impending death began to feel like a release of tension we were all awaiting and committed to rejoicing in when it finally came.

"This is beautiful," I said.

"Very beautiful," Felipe agreed.

"Olé," the crowd roared again as the matador executed another flawless do-si-do. The bull was weakening, but he was menacing still, even with his diminished blood supply. I imagined that the matador's fixed attention and control was an analgesic distraction for the bull, a solid reality, an intimacy to organize his small brain around as he was being danced to his own oblivion. The matador elegantly sliced his body against the bull's, getting blood on his trousers, then turned and allowed the bull to graze him again.

"Olé," the crowd shouted, and "Olé!" again.

"It is very dangerous to do that," said Felipe.

The stadium was silent except for these unison shouts. We were all holding our breath as if we possessed one big collective lung, as if we were as much in the matador's thrall as the bull. Finally, the matador lifted his sword and, as the bull went by, plunged it with a snap of both arms into the bull's back, high up on his neck. It went in cleanly. The bull plummeted to the ground and was still. The matador bowed his head for an instant.

The crowd exhaled and leapt to its feet, I along with everyone else, and cheered. The matador finally acknowledged us. He made the rounds of the stadium, bowing to section after section as hats and flowers were thrown into the ring, piling up around him. Camera bulbs flashed all over the stadium. Finally, the matador was carried out on several men's shoulders, but he came back in to the ring a moment later to bow again as the crowd kept cheering and cheering. Finally, he was carried off again, and we all quieted down.

We slowly dispersed in a great mass of people out of the stadium. As our little group stood milling around outside, a limousine went by with the great matador's name and picture emblazoned on it.

"Where's he going?" I asked Felipe.

"Off to find food and drink and women."

"He's going to have a good night," said Pirate.

"He's going to have a great night," said Raquel.

All seven of us set off for the subway together.

"I'll come back to the Centro with you," I said staunchly to Raquel as we clattered down the steps of the station.

"No, you won't," she said. "If you do, I'll never forgive you, I swear. Hey, Felipe, where are you taking her?"

I looked over at Felipe.

"I'm taking her back to Roma," he said.

"Good," said Raquel. "Finally, I get a night off."

In the subway car, Felipe and I leaned together near the door in fizzy anticipatory silence, occasionally meeting each other's eyes and giving each other sneaky, triumphant smiles. I said good-bye to Raquel when we got out at Insurgentes. Raquel put her hands on my forearms for leverage and leaned up and kissed my cheek. I looked down into her; all I saw was resolution and self-reliance. "Have fun," she said, pushing me away. "Bring back some stories for me to enjoy vicariously."

"You're so bad," I said.

We both laughed, and then Felipe and I got off the train, climbed the stairs, and walked along the street. We walked briskly toward a bistro he knew.

"So were your families mad that you missed out on both Sunday dinners today?" I asked.

"They get plenty of me; you don't have to worry about them. What about you? Are you missing your daughter?"

We went into the bistro, which was small and lit with candles whose flames guttered in the breeze as waitresses walked by with plates. Some sort of earnest world music was playing, which would normally have bugged me, but right then I didn't care; it sounded beautiful. We sat at a small table near the back.

The hostess handed us a wine list and went away to let us decide.

"Yes," I said. "When I go home, I'll move my stuff into my new apartment, but I'll see Wendy as much as ever."

"What about your husband?"

"Anthony," I said. "I expect to like him a lot better when I don't have to live with him and be married to him. Maybe we'll be good friends in the end."

Felipe laughed. "That's exactly how it is with me and Carmen. We're better friends now that we've split up. We were never a good couple."

"Amazing how you can marry someone so wrong for you."

"Is rioja okay?"

"Rioja is great."

Felipe looked up at the waitress and ordered the wine. She brought it back, showed him the label, went through the ritual of pouring out a little for him to taste, then finally gave us a couple of full glasses and went away to let us talk and drink in peace. Here we were, on a date. It felt very proper and courtship-like. Over escargot, which here were called *caracol,* Felipe talked about his kids, Luz and Hector, who were four and six. Over soup, he asked me about Wendy. As we ate our main courses, I told him about some of my clients, and he talked about his upcoming show.

"What do you think of David?" I asked him.

"You asked me that once before," said Felipe. "He's my friend. Why?"

"I can't figure him out. He seems so noble and good, but there's something about him, something I don't like."

"David?" Felipe laughed. "What don't you like about him?"

"He seems too serious or something. I feel like he's hiding a dark secret."

"He is serious. He is from a very fucked-up part of Chiapas. He lost his arm. He has a sister with problems."

"She's a drug addict, right?"

"Yeah. He feels like he owes her because she raised him. It makes him really sad to see her live like that. Her boyfriend beats her. He tries to help her, but he can't save her. He thinks she wants to go down. She feels guilty for something, but he doesn't know what. He wonders if their father molested her. He is pretty tortured about her. If you see anything in him, it's a lot of worry about things he can do nothing about no matter how hard he tries—the situation down in Chiapas, his sister, this country, everything."

"Oh," I said. "I feel bad for saying anything about him, but don't you ever dislike someone for no reason?"

"I can see that you would," he said. He was teasing me. It was the same expression he'd had when I'd bought the mask the other night at the gallery, a warm, indulgent appreciation of some frankly immature quality in me, my rashness, I supposed, my transparent passions. I had a fleeting thought that maybe he found these things appealing or charming now, but if we were married, would they enrage him eventually? Would he wind up punishing me for the very things he'd cherished? I studied his face for a sign of incipient cruelty, lurking scorn, but I saw only a steady, intelligent, humorous sweetness; if we were married, I thought, he would never make fun of me for bringing home a blue wolverine mask. He would never undercook spaghetti if I told him I didn't like it that way. The thought made me suddenly sad, and to push it away, I said hastily, "Eugenia is in love with him, isn't she?"

He laughed. "*Who?*"

"Eugenia."

"Alfredo's wife?"

"Yeah, I watch her when he talks or when she talks to him. She drools. She can't hide her passion for him: Alfredo doesn't even seem to notice! I thought Latin men were supposed to be macho and possessive of their women, but he doesn't even seem to see it, and it's so obvious. I don't even know them, and I can see it."

Felipe was laughing too hard to speak. He took a sip of his water, but he couldn't stop laughing. "You are so funny," he said when he caught a breath. "You are the most adorable thing I have ever seen."

"Why am I funny?"

"David is gay," he said.

"What do you mean, he's gay?"

Felipe lifted one of my hands and kissed it. "I mean he likes men."

"David?" I sat back and let everything I knew and thought about David rearrange itself into a wholly different picture. "He's gay? Are you sure?"

Felipe kissed my hand again by way of an answer.

"Does Eugenia know he's gay?" I asked.

He laughed again. "Of course," he said.

"Oh," I said, laughing at myself. "So is it dangerous to be gay in Mexico City?"

"It's not so dangerous," he said. "It is no more or less dangerous here than anywhere else. But David is very careful and a little bit shy about it. If he seems secretive to you, maybe that's why."

"His sister and her boyfriend sold drugs to Raquel," I blurted. "David knew, and he didn't tell me."

"He probably didn't tell you because he figured it was none of his business to interfere."

"Maybe he's in on it," I said. "I've been wondering about this. Maybe that's how he really raises money for his village, and those weavings are a front."

"That is impossible."

"Why is it impossible?"

"Because David hates drugs. He is more against them than anyone else I know."

I stared at Felipe, thinking. He looked back at me with frank, laughing amusement.

"I feel like an idiot," I said.

"You are no idiot. You watch and pay attention and draw conclusions, and sometimes they're wrong, but not always. Often you are very perceptive. You were very perceptive about me, for instance, the night I met you. I knew right away that I could talk to you easily, say anything to you, because you really listen with all your attention."

"Thank you for saying that," I said.

"I imagine that you are very good at your work."

"Sometimes," I said.

"No more suspicion of my friend David, okay?"

"Okay," I said, shaking my head, finally laughing myself.

We shared a chocolate mousse and drank two snifters of co-
gnac and two espressos and drifted into silence, holding hands
on the table, smiling stupidly at each other. I pounced on the
check when it arrived and would not give it to him. After a real
and apparent inner struggle, because he was, after all, a Mexican
man, he thanked me and gave in. We left the restaurant and
walked through the cold night toward his apartment building. I
was on a date, and we were going back to his house. I was about
to have sex with someone who wasn't Anthony. It was all very
unreal and amazing; I wasn't entirely sure I was allowed to do
this, but I didn't care. There was no one around to stop me. And
even if there had been, I wasn't sure they could have.

CHAPTER ELEVEN

ELEVEN

*B*ack at Felipe's house, I felt suddenly shy for the first time since I had met him. He led me in and said, "Wait here. I'll make us some tea." On his way to the kitchen, he hit the play button on his CD player and music poured out, acoustic Cuban music, a woman singer with a guttural, haunting voice.

I paced around the living room, which was also his studio. The vines and flowers in the machine-strewn jungles of his paintings were alive with precision and vitality and weirdness, delicate but tough-seeming. The machines themselves were cunning, preposterous, improbable, as intricate as the vegetation but somehow comically naked and vulnerable, out of place in their jungle. I examined his bookshelf, which was full of poetry, philosophy, and novels, most of them by Spanish-language writers like Neruda, Paz, Bolaño, Fuentes, Márquez, and a lot I had never heard of, and a few translations: Dostoevsky, *The Magic Mountain, Catch-22*, Joan Didion, Robert A. Heinlein, Philip K. Dick, James Joyce, Saul Bellow, and *Under the Volcano*. Lower down were the big art books: Cézanne, van Gogh, Picasso, Kandinsky, Klimt, Guston, and so forth, all the big-league dudes with their swaggering artistic outputs and visions. A photo of two kids in a frame sat on the middle shelf; both of them were adorable little big-eyed versions of Felipe. On the floor by his worktable were a Lego set, a toy fire engine, a box of stuffed animals, and a toy stove with toy pots and pans and a matching toy cupboard containing tiny imitation food—little boxes of cereal and cans of soup—muffin tins, and a miniature tea set. I lifted out one of the tiny cups, remembering when Wendy had had a set a lot like this one. We had made cambric tea and drunk it out of these cute thimbles with animal-shaped cookies frosted pink and white.

On the coffee table were a ceramic skull, a tarot deck, and a vase of lilies. I was daunted by all of it. I sat on the couch, which was luxuriantly comfortable, and cursed my mother, who had been a devoted, self-sacrificing wifey-wife, and who had taught me nothing whatsoever about seducing men, about how to act in situations like these, probably because she had met my father as a young girl and had never, to my knowledge, looked back or around or askance. Anthony had been a seemingly irresistible force I had passively allowed to carry me off; I hadn't had to think about anything. I had been young, naïve, and overwhelmed by the power of his personality. I had subsumed myself in him. That was what I had learned from my mother. This was different somehow; this was a real situation. I was wide-awake and older now. I couldn't take refuge in blind ignorance, because Felipe and I were equals here. I was unequipped for this, now that the moment of truth was at hand.

I leaned back into the couch cushions, kicked off my shoes, and put my feet in their warm socks on the coffee table.

But this is nothing to be afraid of or intimidated by, I told myself, as if I were one of my clients. There is nothing here to cause self-doubt, and besides, it's just a vacation fling. This is just an experiment, and if it fails, I'll be back in my real life soon, and I'll never have to see him again.

By the time Felipe came in with the teapot and two cups, I had managed to talk myself out of my momentary squirrelliness.

"I made this tea," he said, setting everything on the coffee table and joining me on the couch, "and I don't know why. I feel like my grandmother."

I laughed. "I like tea," I said stupidly.

We were silent for a moment. The teapot steamed gently from its spout. Neither of us made a move to pour any.

"I'm a little nervous now," he said.

"Me, too," I said quickly.

We laughed self-consciously.

We were both silent again. I looked down at my hands. I don't know what he was looking at.

He made a noise, a cross between a grunt and loud exhale.

"I really like you," he said. His tone suggested that this aggrieved him as much as it surprised him.

"Sorry," I said, happy to hear this, laughing now for real.

"I was just having fun, before."

"I know," I said. "And you know that this is all your fault. We could have just slept together the other night when we were drunk and didn't care."

"That was so stupid of us not to," he agreed.

"I know!"

"What was I thinking?"

"You were trying to be gallant, and now we like each other too much to use each other for cheap sport."

He looked at me. "You were going to use me for cheap sport?"

I laughed. "I was going to objectify the hell out of you."

We smiled at each other silently; I started to feel breathless.

"Now what do we do?" he asked.

"You could read my fortune."

"What? Oh, that deck. I don't read tarot cards." He looked sheepish.

"Let me guess. They're your wife's."

He looked even more sheepish and didn't answer.

"You have a girlfriend?"

He looked over at me with a grimace. "I just met you three days ago. I can't help it. I have no girlfriend. She and I have an arrangement. Don't worry about her."

"Hang on. Is your girlfriend going to show up here and kick my ass?"

"She is not my girlfriend, I promise."

"She's some kind of special friend who spends the night?"

"She's some sort of friend who sometimes spends the night, but not very often."

"Well then, what am I doing here?"

He rubbed a hand over his face and sighed. "I didn't promise her anything. She doesn't want anything. She comes around sometimes. What can I say? She used to be my student."

"What do you teach?"

"I teach art," he said, as if he were surprised I didn't already know this. "That's how I mostly make my living. So this girl, I hired her to clean my apartment and help take care of my kids, and sometimes she—"

"Oh my God, the plot thickens. She's the babysitter."

"It is not anything like what you're thinking."

"How do you know what I'm thinking?"

He was quiet. I had just been bantering with him; I didn't care about this girl. But he looked truly upset.

"Maybe I should have told you before," he said. "But honestly, I forgot about her."

"Felipe," I said, "I don't really care. I don't give a damn; it's okay. Whatever happens with me doesn't have to affect whatever you have with her. I'm fine with it if you are. It doesn't matter."

"No," he said. He looked even more upset. "That's the thing. It does matter. Not about her, but about you. Anyway, I don't want you to go home. I don't care about her at all. I like you more than I've liked a woman in a long, long time."

"Really?" I said, startled and amazed.

"Yes!" he said. "So don't talk about that babysitter anymore. She doesn't care about me, either. We're friends and nothing more, I promise. Come here." He slid his arm around my shoulders and pulled me in to him. I didn't resist. I relaxed against him and buried my face in his neck and twined my legs around his. "Now I feel better," he said.

"You smell so good," I said.

"So do you," he replied. He slid his hand under my shirt and fondled my breasts as I ran my open palm under his shirt, touching the silky bare skin of his flat belly and then moving my hand up to his hard little nipple. His skin was velvety and warm and supple and so alive. My mouth and his mouth found each other. After a moment, we were both so heated up, we were gasping into each other's mouths. The music ended. In the sudden silence, our breathing sounded raspy and loud.

We stood up and pulled off each other's clothes with impatient clumsiness, and finally, by dint of determination, we both ended up naked. He was more beautiful without his clothes on; his body was creamy brown, muscled, and graceful. His cock bounced a little, sticking straight out from his thighs. I took it into my hand and began to slide my fist up and down the shaft; he slid his hand between my legs, where I was slick, open, and swollen. He plunged his fingers into me. He bent me slowly over until my hands were on the back of the couch and put his hands on my ass and slowly ran the tip of his cock back and forth to slide it against my wetness, teasing me with it, almost but not quite entering me. I was too far gone to worry about what I looked like from this angle. It felt like we were moving in slow motion; it drove me crazy. I wanted to do this forever. I finally tore myself away and turned around to sit on the couch, then took his cock into my mouth and engulfed it. I ran my open mouth and tongue over his cock, his balls, his inner thigh, and then put my mouth on his cock again and sucked it slowly, slowly, trying to match the slow motion he had almost, but not quite, fucked me with just before. Then I stood up and held his cock in my hand to keep it warm and kissed him while he put his hand between my legs and pressed hard, slid it gently but firmly back and forth, soaking it in my wetness. After about thirty seconds, I came hard, yelling out, while he rocked my pelvis back and forth with his hand until all the spasms had stopped. "Come into my bed," he urged me.

Dizzy with the force of my orgasm, I curled myself into him, wrapped my arms around him, clung weakly to him like a baby monkey, and burrowed my face into his neck.

"Come into my bed," he said again. We led each other by the genitals, laughing, into his bedroom and slid together under his ice-cold sheets, shivering with the sudden shock of cold. We found each other under the covers and pressed our bellies together like little kids. His cock throbbed hard against my stomach like a live animal trapped there. I slid on top of him and positioned myself over him and plunged him into me. I had been ready to fuck him for the past three days. It felt so good to have him inside me, I laughed out loud with joy. Gasping, he held my hips still and looked into my eyes and said, "Sssh, wait, wait. I need to put on a condom."

"I hate condoms," I said through gritted teeth.

"I hate them, too," he replied.

He fucked me hard for a moment, unable to resist. I moaned like a cat. Every nerve ending in my body was awake and electrified. Every part of him fit with every part of me; everything he did felt as good to me as it must have to him.

"But we have to," he whispered. "Come on, we have to."

"Don't stop," I said with urgent bossiness. I was being an idiot, but I was starving.

He pulled out with a groan, rummaged in the drawer of his bedside table, pulled out a condom packet, tore it open with his teeth, put the condom on, and slid inside me again. I stretched out along the length of him, put my hands on his buttocks, and plunged him as deep into me as he could go and held still for a moment.

"This feels insane," I said. "It feels so good. You are so hot."

"You're hot," he said. "You are amazing."

"You're amazing," I echoed with goofy ardor.

"The minute I met you, I wanted this," he said.

He rolled us both over so he was on top of me and began fucking me slowly, his elbows by my head, his mouth on mine, our stomachs slipping against each other.

"I know," I said into his mouth. "We were making out within half an hour."

"I would have attacked you within five minutes, but I was polite. I let you make the first move."

"I did not make the first move."

"You threw yourself on me," he said.

I reached up and cupped his face in both my hands. "I apologize," I said.

"You should apologize."

"You must have been so upset."

"I was so upset," he said.

We were talking absolute nonsense. I could not remember a time in my entire life when I had been happier. I felt as if the surfaces of our skin had some sort of weird subliminal communication going on. I lost all sense of time. We went deep into each other; his face shifted under my eyes from that of a young kid to an old man's, then became unfamiliar and otherworldly, then turned opaque and angelic, then looked like that of a feral boy, and then his face came back to me as the Felipe I was used to, and through all of it I felt as if I deeply knew and trusted him, as if I could easily find him, whoever or whatever he was.

Much later, we lay together, awake, our hands idly wandering over each other's bodies. I was sliding my hand along his thigh; he was cupping one of my buttocks with the arm he had around me and nestling the knuckle of the index finger of his other hand in the hollow of my neck. I could smell us both, a musky, sweet, good smell. We both sighed every now and then, but there was nothing to say. After a while, he slid himself under me and pulled my leg up so my pelvis was straddling his hips and then he slowly plunged his cock into me again as he reached for another condom. I was a little sore, which made it feel even better somehow, all the nerves on edge. I snapped awake, charged with renewed lust, as strong as ever.

"It's so hard to wait to get the thing on," he said. "It's almost impossible to pull out of you now." He inhaled sharply as he pulled out, as if it were painful, and managed to get the condom on, and then he was back inside me, filling me with hard heat. This time it lasted until I was dizzy from gasping, until we were both drooling a little from prolonged, intense pleasure. I felt myself spinning out on some plain of total rapture, hovering. "Hey," he whispered in my ear, "Josie," and then I stared into his eyes. His brown eyes were so close to mine, I could see again the gold coronas bursting around his irises. His skin smelled familiar to me now. We were both comically slack-faced, but we weren't laughing. We were earnestly focused, barely moving, moving very subtly, then almost not moving at all, just the slightest motion of rocking together with him deep, deep inside me, our pelvic bones locked together. I felt increasing heat and pressure building, then even more, slowly and inevitably, as if every part of my existence were concentrated in my groin and then my cunt, and then all of my entire being and consciousness was funneled into the tiny nub of my clitoris, and then, with a hard thunderclap of a shout in unison, we both came together in a series of long, slow throbs that emptied us into each other.

Finally, we fell asleep, naked and damp and hot under the covers. When I woke up, the air was bright with sunshine against my closed eyelids. Without opening my eyes, I stirred against Felipe very slightly so I could place myself in relation to him. His legs were between mine. One of my arms was under him and the other rested on his belly. My face was smooshed into the crook of his shoulder. The sole of my right foot was pressed against his calf. An aerial view would have shown me clinging to him as if I were drowning and him lying there flat on his back, one arm around me, his hand cradling my jutting hip, the other hand tucked with his legs between mine. I rose up through sleep until I was fully awake, but I didn't move. I lay there and savored this, knowing that the instant he woke up, we would fuck again, which excited me, but I also felt like I wanted to guard as long as I could this sleeping ease and fluency with each other's unconscious bodies.

He slept on. The room got brighter. His bed was wide and firm, but softer than the beds at the Isabel. He had a hard scratchy wool woven blanket and a thin down coverlet. The clock on his nightstand was the old-fashioned windup kind. It ticked loudly;

I couldn't see its face from where I lay. The room smelled of skin and breath and sex and morning city air leaking through the invisible pores and cracks in the outer walls. Suddenly, Felipe was staring right into my eyes, smiling. I smiled back. Then he was inside me again, groaning because he had forgotten again to put on a condom.

"Aren't we running out of condoms?" I croaked through a dry mouth.

"I have more," he said sleepily.

"Let me get it," I said.

With him still inside me, I leaned over, not caring whether or not my breasts looked saggy as they swung in his face; we were well past that now. I found a fresh condom packet, brought it back to our huddle, tore it open, lifted my hips so he slid out of me, rolled it onto him, and then tucked him back inside me all snug and hot and hard.

"This is how I like to wake up in the morning," he muttered into my ear.

"I am so sore." I laughed.

"Me, too," he said, laughing.

I repositioned myself so he went in deeper and I closed around him even more completely, so we fit together like a ball in a socket. We both grunted with the pain and pleasure of it.

"I think I'm chapped," I said.

"What does that mean?"

"Like when the weather is cold and windy and your lips get raw and dry and the skin rubs off them," I said.

"But it's not cold in here," he said suggestively.

Felipe's shoulder was satiny under my mouth, and his hips

were moving in the most slinky, sinuous way. "I just realized we're two lapsed Catholics committing double adultery," I said.

"I thought about that."

"Does some part of you think we're going to hell for this?"

"Do you?"

"The Catholics lost me a long time ago. It made no sense to me even as a kid."

"Me, too," he said. "It seemed crazy. All the things you had to feel bad about."

"Making people feel bad and then good again is how the Church keeps its power over them. I say, cut out the middleman and do your own reckoning."

He laughed.

"We're going to hell," I said. "Aren't we?"

"If you're there, it might be nice," he said.

After we finished, we took a hot shower together and almost fucked again, but then we admitted and agreed that we were too weak with hunger to go another round, so we got out and dried off. I put on the previous day's jeans, sweater, underwear, and socks, wishing I had fresh clothes but glad that at least I was clean myself. In the kitchen, Felipe made coffee and I rummaged in his fridge, which was surprisingly well stocked for a bachelor's.

"You have a lot of food in here," I said.

"My kids," he said. "Always hungry."

I took out eggs, tomatoes, butter, and cheese, along with a bowl of homemade black beans and some fresh hot peppers. I found a frying pan and a bowl to crack the eggs into and concocted a big, messy, spicy omelette oozing with melted cheese, with hot beans and warm tortillas on the side. We carried our plates and cups of coffee out to the courtyard and sat in wrought-iron chairs at a little table. It was sunny and almost warm, and birds chirped madly. The bougainvillea looked surreally bright and luridly hot pink against the scuffed whitewashed cinder-block wall. The enormous science fiction–y potted rubber plants reminded me of Felipe's paintings; I would have bet he'd used them as his models.

"*Buenos días*," said David, coming out of the door across the courtyard, carrying a newspaper and his own cup of coffee.

He didn't seem to blink an eye or miss a beat, finding me there with Felipe. I guessed our courtship had been as obvious to everyone else as it had been to us. We had been making out in front of them all since the instant we'd met each other.

"*Siéntate*," said Felipe, kicking a chair closer to him.

David sat and stretched his legs out under the table and almost, but not quite, smiled at us. "Did you sleep well?" he asked.

Felipe and I laughed and didn't answer.

"Did you?" I asked him.

"Just fine," he said. "How is Raquel?"

"I don't know," I said with a pang of worry. How indeed was Raquel right this minute? I hoped she was enjoying a nice breakfast in the hotel restaurant. "I'd better get back to the hotel soon and find her."

"Is she sick?" Felipe asked. "She seemed all right yesterday."

"Her life is sick, I guess." I looked over at David. "Sorry about the other day," I said.

"It's okay," he said. "You just wanted someone to blame."

"You want some breakfast?" I asked him.

"What is it?"

"An omelette," I said. "I'll be right back."

I went into the kitchen, put some food on a plate for David, and took it out to him. The three of us ate in silence. I could not believe how hungry I'd been since arriving in Mexico and how much I was eating. I didn't feel as if I had gained any weight; maybe it was all the walking and cigarettes.

Felipe passed cigarettes around when we'd finished eating and we all lit up. It felt so decadent and luxurious to smoke. I hadn't smoked since I was in my early thirties, before Wendy, in those fun early days of marriage when I had gone to parties or bars with Anthony, stayed out late. He had always been a big drinker, but back then he had been social about it rather than solitary. Every now and then he and I would tie one on; we'd buy a pack of cigarettes and smoke the whole thing between us in one night and wake up the next day relaxed, hungover, and euphoric. We had been good drinking buddies, my husband and I; I remembered sitting hunkered down with him in a bar years ago, our heads close together, talking and drinking and smoking. Of course, he had done the lion's share of all three, but I had tried to keep up.

It was remarkable how little I had thought, the whole time I had been in Mexico, about Anthony and Wendy, my clients, my "real life." I was undergoing something that had to do only with me. My subterranean tectonic psyche was shifting and heaving. My outer landscape was changing just as fast, but it was all coming from somewhere way below. I felt nothing but relief and a slight sadness at the end of my marriage, the emotional equivalent of getting a rotten tooth pulled. I knew in my bones that Wendy was okay. At that moment, I could hardly think about anything besides sitting in this funny courtyard. I felt the sated, soaring, goofy joy that came from the untrammeled, augmented commingling with another person, the pleasure of magnificent, requited lust, somehow suddenly right in myself. But I wasn't young or free; I had to resist being pulled into the opiated osmosis of a new love affair. My friend was in trouble; my daughter needed me at home; I had to get back and support myself while I disentangled my marriage, which was not going to be simple or fun. I needed all my faculties. This was not the time for falling in love. I was going to have to let Felipe go, I realized. It was getting harder and harder to accept this, but I hadn't forgotten it, and I wouldn't.

I covertly watched David's face. I had been so wrong about him. I hoped he had a nice boyfriend. I hoped those peasants could save their forest.

"What's going on in Chiapas?" I asked him out of the blue.

He said promptly, as if this subject was never far from his thoughts and he was glad to be asked about it so he didn't have to keep everything inside for a moment, "You know about the Belt of Misery?"

"What belt of misery?" I asked, picturing a chastity device or a self-torture leather thing.

"Tens of thousands of people live in a belt around San Cristóbal de las Casas in the most terrible conditions. It is a slum of slums. They converted to evangelical Protestantism, and the Catholics sent them away, violently."

"Your family did this?"

"My uncle is one of the worst," said David. "These used to be his neighbors and friends. Just thrown out of their lives to go and live in the dirt in shacks they've built from garbage, with no plumbing or electricity. All around San Cristóbal de las Casas, they've built these tragic shantytowns. San Cristóbal de las Casas is a beautiful little city in the most amazing mountain valley. The air is so clean, the mountains rise up, and the presence of God is everywhere if you swing that way. You know?"

"And these are your people," I said.

"You said it," said David. "I love my uncle and I want to help my father's town, but I think what they've done is as bad as anything the corporate loggers are doing. I tell him, 'You've got the most bizarre church I've ever seen, but you're not persecuted for your own deviance from orthodox Catholicism.' But he says the evangelicals are infidels and sinners."

"Life is complicated," said Felipe.

"Life is fucking complicated," David agreed. "And of course the reason the *caciques* hate the evangelicals is also economic. In their rituals, they use candles and a corn liquor called p-o-x, pronounced *posh*, and they're expensive. The evangelicals stopped using them, so the local economy was disrupted. Also, there's not enough farmland to go around. When you scratch it, it's all about money. The way of the world."

"Not everything is about money," I said.

"No?" said David.

"No," I said.

"Easy for you to say," replied David. He said it in a friendly way. "Who wouldn't be optimistic if they had just been to bed with my amigo Felipe here?"

I laughed. After an instant, when he saw that we were just

teasing and neither of us had anything but good will toward each other, Felipe did, too.

"I have to get back to the Isabel and find Raquel," I said. "Maybe we'll go to Mass after that lovely conversation. I'll pray for the Belt of Misery."

"They don't want your damn Catholic prayers," said David amiably. "Do you want a ride? I'm driving over to the Centro in a little while, after I run an errand."

"That would be great," I said. I collected the plates and took them inside. Felipe followed with the cups and ashtray.

"I'll wash the dishes," he said. "Leave them and come and sit with me before you go."

I followed him into the living room. He sat on the couch. I sat down next to him and curled into him. He put his arm around me and rested his chin on top of my head.

"I wanted to be a painter," I said, "when I was younger. I studied art in college, but I lacked both the talent and the discipline for it. All I had was a romantic idea about being an artist."

Felipe laughed. "That was your first mistake. It's not romantic at all."

"Do you think you'll go back up to New York to live again anytime soon?" I had decided not to bring up anything to do with the future, but I couldn't help myself.

"I wish I could," he said. "But as long as my kids are little, I want to be here all the time. I don't want them to forget about me. They need me."

"Of course." I was examining his hand, his broad, clean fingernails, his strong, stubby fingers, and the flat of his palm, which was paler than the rest of his skin and etched with dark purple lines.

"I want to see you every night," he said.

"Me, too," I said.

"Can you come back here tonight? I can cook a dinner for you."

Maybe because of our conversation about her making an album with Chuy, maybe because the photographers had found her and there was nothing left to hide from, I had a feeling Raquel was just starting to get itchy to go home, and without her here, there would be nothing keeping me here. I would leave when she did.

"I don't know if that's possible," I said. "I'm not supposed to be down here to meet a man. I came down to think about ending my marriage and to help Raquel. Actually, I'm feeling a little bad about leaving her alone all night."

"How bad do you feel, Josefina?" he asked sneakily.

I laughed. It was a smutty, dark, glutted chuckle I had never heard myself make before. "Okay," I said. "Not that bad."

"I agree," said Felipe. "Not that bad. Can you come tomorrow at seven?"

"Yes," I said. "I'll come tomorrow. What will you cook for me?"

"I'll make you a *cochinita pibil*," he said. "It's a big piece of pork in spices that's roasted in the oven all day. It's a Yucatecan dish. My mother was born in Mérida, in the Yucatán, and she made it all the time when I was a kid."

"My mouth is already watering, and I just had breakfast."

"You love to eat. How are you so thin?"

"I don't know," I said. "I guess I'm lucky."

"It's not bad to be fat," he said. "Just different."

"Is your girlfriend fat?" As soon as I said it, I regretted it.

He smiled at me. "She is not my girlfriend, Josefina."

"I know," I said. I was feeling an ache behind my eyes, in the bones of my skull, a sadness that meant I was saying good-bye to Felipe without really saying it. "She's the lucky one," I said. "To live so close to you and see you all the time."

He was silent. So was I then. We sat this way for a long time, entwined around each other but not talking, until David appeared in Felipe's doorway. I got up slowly. I brushed at my cheeks with the heels of my hands and turned to face Felipe. "See you tomorrow night," I said, thinking as I said it that I might very well be on my way home by then, but then again, I might not. Who knew?

"I'm going to the market tomorrow for the *cochinita*," he said, standing to face me.

"Thank you," I said. "I'll bring some good red wine."

I kissed him. He stood still, not kissing me back, as if, I thought, by withholding himself from me now, I would be sure to return later. He wanted this as much as I did; I had no doubt of that.

David's car smelled as dank and airless as it had the night when we'd driven on the raised freeway to Coyoacán. He pulled into the street and we were off.

"The other night at the gallery," I blurted. "How did Raquel know she could get drugs from your sister if you didn't tell her?"

"I denied it," he said. "I told her my sister was clean. I tried to steer her away."

"Then how did she know?"

"She has a nose," he said. "She knew I was lying."

"A nose," I said skeptically.

"She can smell them," he said. "She told me she always knows who's got them, that she honed her antennae when she was a junkie and she never lost the second sense. Then she came by the Zócalo the other day, before you showed up, to ask for Maria's phone number, but I wouldn't give it to her. She took off without another word."

"She found Maria at the cantina," I said.

"Yes," said David. "Poor Maria. She's in a very bad way. You can't blame her."

"Of course not," I said. "Raquel would have gotten the stuff one way or another, no matter what."

"She's in a bad way, too," he said. "Maybe you can help her. You're a therapist; you probably have some kind of magic spell to cure drug addiction."

I laughed. "I wish," I said.

He pulled up in front of the Isabel. "Hey, if I don't see you again, it was good to meet you."

"Likewise," I said. "Good luck with your work, all of it."

"You, too," he said.

I kissed him on the cheek and got out and waved as he drove off. I walked into the lobby, smiling at the guard, as I always did. I decided to call Wendy and check my E-mail later and see what Raquel was up to first. At the front desk, I asked for the room key in case she had gone out, but the key wasn't there, so apparently she hadn't left, which made me almost giddy with relief. I had been more worried than I'd known, I realized, that she had relapsed, afraid that I would find her again at the cantina, beyond my reach.

I ran up both flights of stairs to our room. I could almost do it now without getting out of breath. I knocked on our door, calling, "Raquel! I'm home."

While I waited for her to come to the door, I looked around the bright, cheerful courtyard. The plants on the balustrades were a little dry. They ought to water them, I thought. They would perk right up; plants always did with a little water.

I knocked again, even though I had a sudden strong feeling that she'd gone out and forgotten to give the key to the desk clerk and was now God knew where. "Raq," I called, "it's me." A maid came along with her cart; I indicated with sign language that I needed to be let into the room. Obligingly, with a smile, and without the least bit of suspicion, because no doubt she'd seen me around the hotel in the past few days, she unlocked the door for me. I tipped her twenty pesos. She looked surprised and happy and burbled off with her cart; the maids at this hotel were amazingly friendly and cheery, I had noticed. Actually, almost everyone in Mexico City was, no matter how menial their job. It probably had to do with what Felipe had pointed out to me the other night, the fact that their lives were communal and filled with ritual and festivity.

The room was dark; the doors to the balcony were closed, and the lights were off. I went in quietly, in case she was still sleeping. It was almost noon already, and we'd been waking up pretty early as a rule, but I figured she had probably tied one on with her new pals the night before. When I saw Raquel's tiny form in her bed, curled under the covers, her wild spray of hair over her pillow, I felt a second huge wave of relief. Thank God she hadn't gone back to David's sister's cantina, that she wasn't on some terrible destructive mission. I would never have forgiven myself for leaving her alone.

I climbed into my own bed and turned on my reading lamp
and opened *A Passage to India*, which Raquel had left on my
pillow. I looked over at her, afraid I'd disturbed her and that
she'd be pissed at me for waking her up, but apparently I had
been quiet enough, because she hadn't stirred. A piece of paper fell out of the book. Glancing at it, I saw her handwriting.
It reminded me of sharing books when we were in college. I
would find her comments penciled in the margins, something
like "Fucking crock of horseshit!" or "Stinks of ego" in Henry
James, or "I am so in love with this novel, I could scream" in *The
House of Mirth,* or "How much acid did she take?" in *Pale Horse,
Pale Rider.* I opened the sheet of paper, expecting a "Memsahib"
and snarky, affectionate jokes about the British abroad.

"Dear Josie," the letter said in that familiar loopy scrawl. "I
am so sorry to do this to you. Please try to forgive me. It's nothing but a big relief to get out of here. I love you, retard. Tell Chuy
if he's up to it, he can try to save my new album, remix it, sing
backup on it, turn it into Muzak, anything he wants. Raquel.
P.S. You don't have to do anything, but I want to be buried down
here, next to my grandparents. Here's my dad's phone number
and the name of the church. My will is with my lawyer. Here's
his phone number. Just so you know, I left you my house. You
can sell it or give it to Wendy when she's ready for it."

I put the paper down, my lips dry and my eyes wide and all
my veins running with cold fluid. I turned to look at her. She
looked like herself, asleep.

"Raquel," I whispered.

Of course she didn't move.

"Raq," I said.

I gave three harsh sobs, and then I pulled myself together with a strong internal slap, leaned over, and touched her face. Of course it was cold. I saw then that her lips were bluish.

I don't know why I did it, but I pulled the covers back to look at her whole body. I was flooded with love, and then grief so fierce I was paralyzed for a moment. She lay on her side, scrawny and beautiful and naked, curled into herself like a fetus, her arms crossed on her chest, her legs drawn up. She was marked by a green lizard tattoo on her ankle, a brilliant sunflower in the small of her back, and a line from Dorothy Parker on her shoulder: "What fresh hell is this?" I knew the stories behind all her tattoos, and had been with her when she got two of them, the ones on her ankle and the small of her back, such painful places to get tattoos that both times she had almost broken my hand, squeezing it. Nestled by her body were five glassine packets, all of them empty. Cradled in her arms was a mescal bottle, also empty.

There was a rapid, hard knock on the door.

"Who is it?" I shrieked.

"It's Malcolm," he said. "I came to see if you guys wanted to have some lunch."

I went to the door and opened it. The ginger-headed photographer stood there looking pale and scruffy and a little hungover. I was so happy to see a familiar face, I could have kissed him. "I need your help," I said. "Raquel is in trouble."

"Is she sick?" he asked in a low voice.

I looked into his face to gauge his reaction, to see whether or not I could trust him not to panic, to help me figure out what to do next: a doctor, an ambulance, all the phone calls, the funeral.

It suddenly hit me, what lay ahead, and I was suddenly enraged. If she'd stayed alive, we could all be on our way out to lunch now, I thought, and none of this would have to unfold the way it's about to.

"She's dead," I said.

"In there?"

"In her bed."

"How did it happen?"

I didn't answer, because I wasn't sure. She had overdosed, of course, but there was no needle, and she had no marks on her arms. Could one snort oneself to death? I wondered. She weighed only eighty-nine pounds, after all. Her tolerance was low now that she'd been clean for so long. She must have snorted herself to death.

While I stood pondering this, Malcolm pushed past me and went into the room and stood over Raquel's naked body. I crossed the room in three long strides and pounced on him, ready to tear his face off if that was what it took to get the camera away before he could photograph her, but I was too weak and slow, and he was too good at his job. While he fended me off, his camera flashed once, then twice; then he was out of the room, running, gone. It was too late, but I drew the covers back up anyway and tucked her in. I flushed the glassine packets down the toilet and put the empty mescal bottle into the trash can, and then I went to the phone and called down to the front desk and told the friendly round-faced boy what had happened.

CHAPTER TWELVE

*L*ess than half an hour later, three authoritative young men arrived in a blur of Spanish-speaking officialdom. I told them I had just come in and found her, and they took one look at her and all three of them nodded sagely in unison, as if they assumed she had wasted away from starvation or consumption. Probably because I was crying and couldn't stop, I was handed a pill by one of these vaguely medical-seeming bureaucrats, which I took without any questions concerning its identity. I sat on my bed and watched mutely as Raquel's body was examined, pronounced dead, wrapped in a white sheath, and taken away on a stretcher. After they'd taken her, I sat alone in the quiet, empty room for a few minutes, numb from the pill. From its subtly sedative effect, I assumed it was a Valium.

Finally, in a haze, I got up and went downstairs and began to set things in motion. None of the paparazzi was anywhere in sight. Maybe they had followed Raquel to the morgue or the funeral home and had bribed the officials there and were madly photographing her corpse right this minute, but there was nothing I could do about that.

I used the phone at the lobby desk, since the entire hotel already knew what had happened. This had become a comforting, familiar spot, standing on the phone by the hotel desk. I called Raquel's father in L.A. and then her mother in New York. Rafael Dominguez collapsed on the phone; his fourth and most recent wife, Maryann, a very capable-sounding, friendly woman I had never met, took the receiver from him and said good-bye quickly to follow him, she told me, to their bedroom to make sure he hadn't had a heart attack.

Raquel's mother, Suzie Weinstein, didn't break down or collapse. As the mother of a daughter myself, I knew right away that her instant organizational overdrive was a brittle dam holding back the howls of grief she couldn't let loose because she feared she might never be able to stop. My heart broke for her.

"I'll be down as soon as I can get there," she said at the end of the call, after I had told her all about our trip, Raquel's state of mind, everything I knew that had led up to her death. "What's the number of the place where they took her? I'll call them. Call me back for any reason whatsoever. I have my cell with me at all times."

I told her to bring a warm coat and promised to let her know everything I found out.

Indrani broke down; she was incoherent with grief. I cried with her. We were family to each other, and we had just lost our sister. There was almost nothing to say except how much we looked forward to seeing each other when I got home, how comforting that would be for us both.

Chuy shouted and swore at the phone and told me he was with me and to tell him what to do, that he'd do anything. I told him Raquel had wanted him to fix her new album, but I wasn't sure he heard me. I decided I would have to say it again, in a calmer moment.

Anthony wasn't home when I called my own number, so I had to tell Wendy, so at least she wouldn't learn it on the Internet or hear it on the news. She was hysterical, hiccupping into the phone. I soothed her, crying also, while the desk clerk kindly looked elsewhere and the other people in the lobby all eavesdropped openly. I didn't care what they thought or knew; I held on to the phone, talking with Wendy until I was dizzy, not wanting to release her, knowing she would be home alone after we hung up, but she finally said she was okay and made sure I was, too. She promised to call Anthony's cell phone immediately, and then we said we loved each other and hung up, both of us still crying. I went into the ladies' room off the lobby and washed my face, blew my nose.

When I came back out, I called the *Los Angeles Times* and asked about an obituary; they had already heard that she was dead. I didn't waste any energy cursing my stupidity at letting Malcolm into the room. What was done was done, and there was nothing they could do anymore to hurt her. Of course the photos of her corpse were already all over the Internet; I had warned Wendy not to look.

I ran upstairs for my coat and ran down again and asked the desk clerk to call me a taxi. I took it to Raquel's father's family's tiny, ancient church, which turned out to be a five-minute ride from the Isabel. I had a long talk in the dim, plaster-smelling sanctuary office with a very kind but unyielding old priest who spoke fairly good English and asked a lot of questions and nodded his large, wrinkled, totally bald head and, in the end, told me sympathetically but in no uncertain terms that the Catholic Church couldn't bury her. It wasn't possible, first of all because she had killed herself, and, second, because of the very public nature of the scandal she'd been embroiled in. He said I was welcome to wait for the official decree from the bishop, but he was trying to save me time and headache: He knew the Church would refuse her.

I took the waiting taxi back to the Isabel, and I tipped the driver so generously he almost levitated with happiness. At the desk, I called Suzie Weinstein back; she picked up before the end of the first ring. She was in a cab on the Fifty-ninth Street Bridge, she told me in a clipped, strident, heartbroken voice, on her way to JFK, and she had a reservation on a flight that would arrive that night, just before midnight. The instant I told her the Catholics wouldn't bury Raquel, she said, "Hold on a sec," and put her hand over her mouthpiece; I heard her telling the driver to turn around and take her back to East Seventy-eighth Street. Then she said to me in a rapid-fire stream, "That's good news. I'm frankly relieved. I'm going to have them fly her back here; that's what I wanted to do from the start. There's a plot for her at the family cemetery in New Jersey. She'll be the fourth generation to go in the plot. Listen. Don't worry, hon, I'll handle everything. I'll take it from here. And you should fly home tonight, sweetheart. Don't stay there alone. I'll make some arrangements for you."

"I have an open return ticket," I said.

"I'll book you a seat home tonight. I've got connections."

Gratefully, knowing she just wanted something, anything, to do right then, I gave her my airline information. I felt no hesitation; in fact, I appreciated being told what to do. I appreciated even more the fact that Suzie wanted to handle the repatriation of the body, which I imagined would involve a lot of red tape and hassle, which she sounded perfectly capable of dealing with from thousands of miles away.

I went upstairs, lay on my bed, stared at the ceiling for a while, unable to sleep but completely wrung out. I got up and went downstairs again. The lobby was all abustle with TV news cameras, photographers, reporters, and curious bystanders. I went to the desk, and the clerk called Suzie back for me and handed me the receiver. She picked up immediately. She'd already called the morgue, she announced, and a Mexican funeral home, and the American embassy in Mexico City; everything had been set in motion, and Raquel's body was practically on its way to New York as we spoke. I could not believe it had been so easy for her to arrange this, when burying Raquel in Mexico had proved to be impossible.

Suzie had also booked me a seat on a flight to JFK, which would leave at 6:05 that evening.

"You'd better get going," she said. "It's after three now."

I went upstairs and looked around at the room. There was Raquel's brush. There was her coat. There were her clothes. I felt desperate to get home, to get back to Wendy, to sleep in my own bed that night next to my soon-to-be ex-husband. It was excruciating to have to be in the hotel room anymore. As quickly as I could, I packed up my things and Raquel's.

I squirmed my way past everyone, headed to the front desk, asked the clerk to call me a taxi, and escaped from the Isabel— by some miracle, without attracting any attention.

Suzie Weinstein had upgraded my open ticket to a first-class one, to my eternal gratitude. I made my way to the gate, a bit shaky on my pins. When my flight was announced, I got onto the plane in an addled stupor of disbelief and accepted a glass of champagne, and then guzzled another one, settling back into my wide, comfortable, expensive seat, trying not to think about Raquel, wherever she was now. That isn't Raquel anymore, I told myself. There was no reason to feel bad about leaving her behind; she'd be on her way to New York soon enough.

The plane took off into dark air so impenetrable with pollution the lights of the city disappeared almost immediately. I realized as we climbed out of the valley that I hadn't called Felipe. In fact, I hadn't called any of our new friends, not David, and not Eugenia and Alfredo. I had forgotten all about them, even Felipe; I had barely known any of them, of course. Whatever fledgling feelings Felipe and I had been starting to feel for each other were almost certainly not fibrous or dense enough yet to stand up to this sort of calamity. But I would have to call him first thing the next day.

I fell into a deep sleep for the entire five-hour flight and woke up only when the pilot came on to announce that we were approaching New York City. As the plane circled Kennedy and came down over the familiar flat roofs of Queens, I felt a heavy phantom weight in my lap float away as I returned fully to consciousness, as if Raquel had been resting there, sleeping, too, while I slept. I had never believed in ghosts or spirits; I was as empirically minded as they came, but I felt her presence palpably.

The plane bounced down and hit the runway with Nevada salt flats all-out speed, then immediately slowed and taxied sedately to the gate. I was the first person off the plane. I walked along the empty hallway with my silly corporate vice president's bag rolling behind me and the bag I'd bought to hold all Raquel's stuff slung over my shoulder. It was clear sailing through the spooky midnight airport to customs; no one seemed to be there, and all the kiosks were closed. The airport was half-dark. I dealt with the usual slight amount of rigmarole with a very sleepy guy at the customs desk, and then I was free to go home.

I went out to the taxi stand, inhaling the cold New York winter air, which smelled clean and fresh to me for the first time ever in my life. I was first in line. A cab pulled up, and I got in, gave the driver my old address, and sat back to enjoy the ride. We sped through the dark, shallow canyons of the nighttime freeways of Brooklyn.

"Happy New Year," the Jamaican driver said liltingly, turning to look at me in the backseat.

"What?" I asked.

"It's twelve o'clock!"

"Yeah?"

"It's 2008!"

"Holy shit," I said. "It's New Year's."

I reached over to where I wished Raquel were sitting and took her invisible hand and held it all the way back to West Eighteenth Street. I imagined that I could feel her leaning against me, half-asleep, worn-out. It was the only way I could comfort myself, to feel her with me.

It took almost two hours to get from the airport to my old building, because of all the revelers thronging the streets, the honking, happy traffic crawling across Manhattan. After I'd paid and tipped the driver, I let myself in and climbed the stairs. As I dragged my bag behind me, I dimly recalled buying it a thousand years ago in a spirit of derring-do. And now here I was, back again, and everything and nothing had changed. I took out my keys and let myself in and stood in the tiny foyer, breathing the air. It smelled, of course, of hours-old undercooked spaghetti and a Christmas pine tree slightly past its prime.

As soon as the door shut behind me, I felt the suck of silence in my eardrums, felt the beat of darkness against my eyeballs. Trying not to picture Raquel's body in its coffin, or wherever it was at that moment, I left the bags in the foyer, crept to the bedroom, quickly undressed, and slid into bed next to Anthony without washing my face or brushing my teeth or even peeing. I was sure I wouldn't be able to sleep, but the next thing I knew, it was morning, and Anthony was still snoring next to me. I came awake all at once, without any memory of having been asleep. The room was too warm, for a change. Had Anthony fiddled with the radiator while I was gone? His snoring was soft and skeptical, as if he were unconvinced by whatever he was dreaming about. I looked at his profile, his chin slack, his nose jutting. Twenty-four hours earlier, I had woken up next to Felipe.

For the first time since I'd found Raquel's body, I missed Felipe with a burning, empty, sad feeling in my chest. To quell it, I slid out of bed as cautiously as I'd crept in, as if I had no right to be there anymore, and went into the bathroom. I brushed my teeth until it felt like all the enamel had worn off and then took a long, hot shower and scrubbed my skin until it felt raw. I dressed in clothes I hadn't seen in a while, black trousers and a sweater that now seemed as if they belonged to someone else, then went past Anthony's sleeping form to the kitchen. Wendy wasn't up yet, either. How long had I slept? I looked at the clock. It was only nine on a holiday, but normally Anthony was up by six every day, weekday or weekend, and Wendy had never been much of a late sleeper.

I made coffee and tried to collect myself. I was completely scrambled and disoriented. I could hardly remember how to work the coffeemaker. Had the kitchen walls always been this sickly yellow? I had been gone only five days, according to the calendar. The kitchen looked as if it had been totally rearranged in my absence. The toaster had moved to the table; the coffee cups now seemed to live on a paper towel by the coffeemaker. I opened a cupboard and saw a box of Kraft instant macaroni and cheese, a can of chili, and three boxes of Pop-Tarts. I smiled inwardly at my own scandalized shock, struck by the absurdity of domestic living, the hubris of caring where the toaster went, the fact that my daughter's nutrition had gone haywire for a few days.

I decided to re-create as closely as possible the breakfast I'd made the previous morning at Felipe's. Again, the thought of him gave me a shock of sadness, a delayed reaction made more poignant by its tardiness. I sat at the table and ate my omelette with a side of heated-up canned black beans with pickled jalape-ños. It wasn't nearly as good as my breakfast the day before, but at least the coffee was better. I paged through the newspaper. It was New Year's Day.

"You're back," said Anthony, padding into the kitchen. I stood up to meet him, and our arms went around each other. "Are you all right?" he asked, his mouth against my hair, his breath warm on my scalp.

"No," I said.

I stood there in his arms for a long, long time, both of us breathing quietly, feeling each other again.

He released me finally with a grunt of strong emotion and put one hand against my cheek and kissed me. "Ariel and Wendy are still asleep," he said. "They said they would be up all night waiting for you to get home, but I noticed their room got very quiet just after one o'clock. We stayed up to watch the ball drop on TV. I fell asleep shortly after they did. You must have gotten back at dawn."

"It took forever from JFK," I said. "New Year's traffic."

"I missed you," he said. "We both did."

"Mom!" Wendy yelled from the doorway. She pounced on me, hugging my waist while her friend Ariel, a sylphlike blonde who resembled a Victorian porcelain doll, watched self-consciously from the doorway.

"Hi, Wendy," I said, hugging her back, amazed at the trans-formation five days had wrought in my daughter's feelings for me. "There's an omelette on the stove. Sort of Mexican food."

"You made breakfast already?" Wendy asked, handing Ariel a plate.

"Hi, Josie," said Ariel in her slightly smarmy voice. "I'm really sorry about your friend Raquel."

"Thank you," I said. "She was my best friend. The best friend I ever had, and the most amazing person I've ever known."

"I miss her so much," said Wendy. Her face looked a little puffy.

After breakfast, I went into the living room and lay on the couch and stared out the window while Anthony washed the dishes and the girls went into Wendy's room for a teen conference, or whatever girls that age did behind closed doors. I rested my head against the arm of the couch, reached for the cordless phone on the coffee table, and thought about calling Felipe. I must have fallen asleep, because I was dreaming. In my dream, Raquel was singing in a spotlight on a bare stage. When I woke up, I had forgotten the melody, the words, but the sound of her voice stayed with me.

I heard water running in the kitchen, dishes clanking in the sink; I hadn't been asleep for very long at all.

I got up and rummaged through my bag and found Felipe's number and dialed it. As soon as I heard him pick up, I said, "Felipe!"

"Josefina," he said. The sound of his voice instantly brought him back. "I read about Raquel this morning in the newspaper. Are you still in Mexico?"

"I'm in New York," I said. "I flew home last night."

"I was worried about you when I heard," he said.

"I'm so happy to hear your voice," I told him.

"How is your daughter?"

"She's heartbroken. She loved Raquel."

"It's good you're with her."

"I needed her, too," I said.

"I can imagine," he said. "I'm glad you are safe at home."

We were both silent for a while, breathing into each other's ears. My eyes were closed.

"So," I said finally, "I was really calling to tell you I wouldn't be there for dinner tonight."

"I know," he said. "I understand."

"I'll call you again, okay?"

"I hope you will," he said. "We'll figure something out."

"We'll figure something out," I agreed, and, with heartfelt difficulty, we said good-bye and hung up.

Wendy and Ariel emerged from Wendy's room just then. Ariel had her backpack and coat on. She waved good-bye to me, then disappeared into the foyer as Wendy came and sat next to me on the couch. We sat together, curled up at either end of the couch, while Anthony fielded calls from reporters, friends, and other curious people who barely knew me or Raquel but wanted to hear firsthand what had happened. When I got up to make us some tea, Wendy put on *Big Bad*, and we listened to the whole album in tears, our untouched tea getting cold.

Anthony appeared in the doorway with the phone when the CD ended and said, "A reporter from *People* magazine." He handed me the phone. For the next half hour, I talked about how funny and brilliant and wild she had been in college, told a few anecdotes about the Shitheads, her first band, went on about her stage presence and charisma, and described our recent trip to Mexico, omitting mention of most of the things we had done and focusing on her pride in her Mexican heritage and her love for Mexico City in particular. I predicted that her new album would be her masterpiece. I raved about it, even though I hadn't heard one song on it.

"Was she very depressed in these final days of her life?" the reporter asked.

"She did not feel sorry for herself, ever," I told her. "Things were very hard for her, but she was scrappy and self-determined. She wanted to go, so she went. It's sad, so sad that I can hardly stand it, but mostly I just feel lucky to have known her and to have had her as my best friend."

When I hung up, Wendy asked, "Is that true, that she didn't ever feel sorry for herself?"

"Not really," I said. "She was pretty down about everything this past week. But it's what she would have wanted me to say."

"So you lied," said Wendy with a sneaky smile, nudging me.

It struck me anew that I seemed to have been admitted into Wendy's inner circle; this made me so happy I could hardly bear it, even though it was probably due to reflected gossip-blog glory from Raquel; I was in no position to be choosy.

"A white lie," I said. "Didn't your mother teach you that those are okay?"

"I was impeccably brought up," said Wendy. "I was told never to lie, even to avoid social complications or hurt feelings."

"You're right," I said. "It's wrong to lie, except when you're talking about your dead best friend to a puff magazine."

That night, Anthony stayed home, and Wendy and I dressed

up in party clothes and took a cab to the Upper East Side with a chocolate cake I had bought at a nice bakery and a bottle of good rioja, in memory of my bistro dinner the night of my date with Felipe. I was looking forward to this evening, because in my experience, sitting shiva, like going to a wake, meant a big alcoholic party with a lot of good food, and I imagined it would be cheering to huddle together and drink with a whole bunch of other people who had loved Raquel.

In the taxi on the way uptown, Wendy said, "Mom, I have a question for you that I didn't want to ask in front of Dad. Who was that guy in the pictures of you and Raquel at the bullfight? They were on Mina Boriqua's site. He was that really, really cute Mexican guy and you two looked like you were sort of holding hands."

I stared at her. "Wendy," I said, aghast. "He's a friend, Felipe, someone Raquel and I met down there. He's part of a group of artists who invited us to dinner one night and to an opening. He was our host at the bullfight."

"I was just curious," said Wendy. "Really, Mom, it's okay, you're getting divorced. You should have some fun. I thought he was cute. Really."

I stared at her with gratitude and a flicker of amusement. "Wendy," I said, "thank you for saying that. I can hardly believe you mean it."

"Of course I mean it. I never lie, except when I'm talking to a puff magazine." She smiled wanly. I smiled back at her and took her hand. She nestled against me.

As I had hoped, Suzie Weinstein's large, warm apartment was

filled with people holding wine and cocktail glasses, and her dining room table was covered in catered food, silver chafing dishes,
platters of crudités and hors d'oeuvres. The sideboard had been
turned into a makeshift bar with an array of bottles and an ice
bucket with tongs and dishes of cut citrus fruit, presided over
by an officious-looking young man in a white shirt and tuxedo
jacket. Suzie spied us and darted over immediately. She was, as
Raquel had been, a teeny-weeny, sharp-eyed woman, but she
didn't have Raquel's exotic brown-eyed beauty; she was blond,
helmet-haired, and blue-eyed, and her nose was a tiny button,
possibly due to surgical intervention. She was extraordinarily
well preserved, also, no doubt, due to artificial measures.

"Josie," she said, throwing her arms around me. She held me
tightly for a moment. She felt exactly like Raquel, like a tiny
tough bird. She let me go and kissed Wendy on the cheek. "I am
so glad you girls are here." She looked hectic and parched, as if
she had been crying all day and was about to start again. "And
what's this you brought? You sweetheart." I followed her stoical,
bustling little form to the kitchen, where I was relieved of my
offerings by one of the caterers. Then Suzie led Wendy and me
into her plush chintz-covered bedroom. She turned and looked
me in the eye. A flash of heartache passed between us. "I cannot stop crying," she said, starting again. "I don't know when I
ever will. Maybe never. You never get over something like this,
never."

"I know," I said. "I don't know how I'm going to live without
her."

"I don't know how any of us will," she said.

"We'll come up and visit you a lot," said Wendy. "If you want us to."

"Oh my God, do I want you to! I would love that," said Suzie. "I hardly ever saw her, but I knew she was there, you know, and now I'm so absolutely lonely, I can't stand it."

"We'll come whenever you want," said Wendy, sobbing. "Every day if you want."

When all three of us had finally managed to stop weeping enough to blow our noses, Suzie took us to the bar and instructed the bartender to take very good care of us.

"This was my daughter's best friend," she told him fervently. "Josie, you girls were so close for so long. She loved you more than anyone, except maybe her father."

"She loved you, Suzie!" I said.

"Oh, she had a million problems with me," said Suzie. She ran the back of a manicured finger under one eye to catch another tear. "I was too pushy and I could never say the right thing to that girl. I have to say, we weren't very well matched as mother and daughter. I often thought we had zero chemistry, and that was our real problem." She looked at Wendy and me. "I'm glad to see how close you two are," she added. "You're very lucky."

Wendy said sincerely, "I know," and put her arm through mine. My heart melted.

I asked the bartender for a glass of seltzer and cranberry juice for Wendy and a glass of wine for me. Indrani arrived then, looking flushed and distraught. She saw us all standing by the bar and made her way to us. I threw my arms around her and kissed her hard on the cheek. She clung to me for a moment and rested her head against mine, then we released each other, silently, with tears in our eyes. Suzie embraced Indrani and took her off to the bedroom to discard her coat.

"Indrani took me to lunch and shopping at Barneys while you were gone," said Wendy. "She wanted to make sure I was okay. We had a long talk about you and Dad splitting up, and she was very nice and sympathetic. She talked about her own parents' divorce. She said divorce is hard and that she's there if I need her."

"That was really good of her," I said sincerely. "Divorce is extremely hard on kids, and you have every right to feel upset and angry with me."

"I'm not angry," she said. "I swear I'm not. You're not really going anywhere; you're just getting your own place. And you will be so much happier living apart from Dad. You already seem different to me. I even think of you differently now."

"How?"

"I don't know," said Wendy. "I think maybe living with Dad all those years sort of crushed your spirit. He's not the easiest. He's very wrapped up in himself. You were probably very lonely with him."

"Wendy, how did you get to be so smart?"

"Precociousness," Wendy said with a sly smile. "The curse of the New York kid." I laughed, but she gasped and clapped her hand over her mouth. "Sorry to joke at Raquel's shiva," she added quickly.

"It's okay to joke," I said. "We need it."

"You promise?"

"There's no better place for a joke than a shiva," I said. "I promise."

Indrani and Suzie reappeared.

"That was great of you to take Wendy shopping," I said to Indrani.

"I loved it," replied Indrani.

The bartender handed Indrani a martini glass so perfectly full, the liquid trembled over the rim but didn't spill. It looked icy and viscous. Two enormous green olives stuffed with pimientos rolled slowly against the oily bottom. Indrani held the glass carefully in both hands and took a quick gulp to lower the level. I watched, imagining how it tasted and felt in her mouth. I loved martinis, but for some reason I always forgot to order them. I had become such a lush in the past week, it was amazing.

Suzie's face went very still; she put a hand on her breastbone and said, "Oh my."

She stepped forward and was swept up into an embrace by a solid but slightly stooped man: Rafael Dominguez. Behind him stood a stout redheaded woman, his wife, Maryann, I assumed. She was holding a small suitcase, hanging back.

Raquel's parents held on to each other for a long time, not saying a word, rocking back and forth.

"Oh, our little baby," said Suzie finally, crooning.

Rafael's face was crumpled.

"What a little girl she was," said Suzie into his shoulder. "Her temper, remember? Three feet tall and yelling at me like an overseer!"

He laughed through his weeping.

"She would give her toys away," she told him. "Her new doll! She loved it, but she gave it to that horrible girl down the street. She said, 'But Ma, she wants it more than I do.' The doll she had begged to have for months."

Suzie seemed to be holding Rafael up; he leaned on her while she chattered at him. I could see what had attracted them to each other all those years ago and also what had driven them apart not long after Raquel was born. I glanced over at Maryann to see whether she was jealous or pissed off, but her expression held nothing but sympathetic sadness.

"She was always singing from the time she could sit up," Suzie was saying. "I thought she had a funny voice when she was little. She sounded like sandpaper. 'Little Husky,' I would call her; then she would bark at me."

As if she had suddenly remembered where they were, Suzie released Rafael abruptly and wiped her eyes on her sleeve.

"And here I haven't even offered your wife a drink," she said, extending her hand to Maryann. "You must be Maryann. Hello, I'm Suzie Weinstein, and these are Raquel's best friends. Indrani, Josie, and Josie's daughter, Wendy."

"I'm so sorry, Suzie," said Maryann. "Hello, Josie, I spoke to you on the phone, didn't I. Was that only yesterday?"

"The funeral is tomorrow?" Rafael asked Suzie.

"Yes," said Suzie. "We'll meet at the funeral home at eleven for the service and then go out to the cemetery for the burial, and then come back here tomorrow night for the second shiva. The place is called Cedar Park, it's in Paramus. That's where my whole family is—my grandparents, my parents, my aunts, and a few cousins. I hope it's all right that she's going there, Rafe. I didn't even think to ask you."

Rafael nodded at her. "It's okay," he said. "Thanks for making all the arrangements. I couldn't do anything yesterday. Maryann got us onto the airplane this morning."

"Raquel's on an airplane now herself," said Suzie. "She's arriving tonight."

All six of us were struck all at once with mass weeping. We just stood there silently for a moment.

Then Maryann lifted her glass of wine and said, "To Raquel." We hit our glasses together vehemently, one after another, and then we all drank.

Much later that night, Wendy and I got into a cab in front of Suzie's building and directed the driver back to Chelsea. Wendy leaned against me, her head on my shoulder.

"I'm so sad," she said.

"Me, too," I replied.

"Are you moving out right away?"

"Maybe not," I said. "Maybe I'll delay it for a while."

"I would love that. It's too scary right now for me to think about you moving out right away."

"Me, too."

"But you have to leave, Mom. You can't change your mind. I command you."

We both laughed. A moment later, she fell asleep in the crook of my arm. I looked out the window as the cab jounced and bounced through the late-night streets. A Raquel-size hole burned black and empty in my mind. Someday, maybe, I would have the wherewithal to open the sluice that held back high violent floodwaters of guilt and anger: I had left Raquel for a night to go to Felipe's to do what I wanted to do, but she had told me to go, she had insisted, and she had promised me that she would be all right. I wouldn't have gone if she hadn't promised. But still, I had abandoned her when she needed saving. She had broken her promise that she wouldn't kill herself while I was gone. We had let each other down in two of the worst-possible ways friends can.

But maybe that wasn't the way it had happened. Maybe what had really happened, all moralizing and regrets aside, was that out of all the people who knew and loved her, Raquel had chosen me to be with her at the end. And despite having several very good reasons not to go, I had gone when she asked me and had been with her when she needed me most in exactly the way she required me to be. I had done all I could, and she was free.

Or maybe both things were true: Maybe she and I had failed each other by allowing each other the freedom to be ourselves, and maybe that was the inevitable consequence of true friendship.

Whatever. No matter how I looked at it, she was gone.

The cab pulled up in front of our building. I paid the driver, woke Wendy, and helped her up the stairs.

CHAPTER THIRTEEN

O n a strangely warm day in late March, Corinne, the surgeon who had been having a torrid affair with her colleague, came into my office. "It's time for me to end therapy," she said. "I've decided that this is our last session."

This was very like Corinne, to announce her termination of therapy as an instant fait accompli, but as far as I was concerned, she was well within her rights to do so.

"Congratulations," I said. "We've done a lot of good work together over the past two years."

"I ended the affair this week," she said. She looked pale, resolute, and unhappy.

"What did you—"

But she was having no interruptions. "I can't even be friends with him," she said. "I have to go cold turkey. We'll pass each other in the hallways, we'll sit in the occasional meeting together, and we'll probably have to consult on patients every now and then, but other than professionally, I'm through with him." She started to cry, deep, heaving sobs that racked her.

I said, "Good for you."

"I am going to miss him so much," she said.

"I know," I said.

"But I have to do this." She stopped crying as quickly as she had started. "I'm back in my marriage. I've been neglecting my life at home for months. My kids need me. My husband is an immature jerk, but he's the guy I married. I'm staying put and making the best of things."

"Are you sure you're ready to finish therapy, Corinne? Seems to me you might need a few more sessions just to work through this."

"No," she said. "I have worked it through. There's no more to say. I think I needed to go through this whole thing. That affair was like a malignant tumor growing in a healthy body. It diverted the blood supply. So I've cut it out. End of procedure."

"I see," I said. "What about post-op follow-up?"

"Nope," she said. "Thank you for everything, Josie. I'm all right now."

At the end of the session, she wrote me a check, shook my hand, and walked out of my life. I did not expect to see her again. I was sorry about this; I had learned a lot from her, had worked well with her, and now our paths had diverged, probably forever.

The next morning, I flew back down to Mexico City for a long weekend. I left my now-furnished, cozy, bright new apartment perfectly clean. Before I shut the door behind me, I glanced at the wolverine and wildcat masks on the wall above my new couch, and then I locked the door, pocketed my keys, and carried my wheeled bag down to the street.

In the cab to the airport, the biggest hit single from Raquel's new album came on the radio, a hard-driving, gut-wrenching ballad called "The Fall."

"Turn it up, please," I said to the driver, leaning forward. Without a word, he twisted the volume knob, and her voice filled the cab. Her album had come out a month before; it had debuted at number two on the *Billboard* chart, and the following week, it had gone up to number one, where it still was. She was now, of course, far more famous after her death than she had ever been in her life; that was the way it went. That was the deal.

I rolled down my window and sang along while the warm wind streamed in: "There wasn't any more time/There wasn't any more space/There wasn't any more breath/You came and got it all/You came and took it all/You came and stole it." I was almost shouting the words through the lump in my throat, not caring whether it bugged the driver. Chuy's work was all over this album; he sang backup harmonies and contributed guitar parts. He had brought in a Mexican mariachi virtuoso, an old friend of both his and Raquel's, to play on a few songs, including "The Fall"; now the searing, clean, impassioned sound of his trumpet cut through the noise of traffic on the Van Wyck Expressway and made me lean back against the seat and close my eyes with painful happiness.

On the plane, I finally read the ending of *A Passage to India*. I had not been able to bring myself to open it since Raquel's note had fallen out of it, but this seemed like a fitting time and place to finish rereading it. I found myself completely riveted by the story of the two Englishwomen in India, the friendship between the Englishman and the Indian, and the question of what had really happened in the dark and mysterious Marabar Caves, which was never answered. I finished the book just before the plane began its descent; it was even better than I had remembered from the first three times I had read it.

On the last page, at the bottom, Raquel had written, "Here I go, into the Marabar Caves."

I felt a stab in my solar plexus. "Raquel," I muttered to her, wherever she was.

The plane came down into the now-familiar yellow haze of soupy air. I walked through the airport, remembering Raquel's instructions: "Unleash your inner Catholic. Change money at an ATM. Use the taxi stand on the left."

But this time, I didn't need a taxi. David and Felipe had said they would come to get me, and there they were, waiting for me as I emerged from customs. Felipe took my suitcase in one hand and my whole body in the other, and we followed David out to the parking area, piled into his little car, and went trundling off to Roma.

About the Author

Kate Christensen is also the author of the novels *In the Drink*, *Jeremy Thrane*, *The Epicure's Lament*, and *The Great Man*, winner of the 2008 PEN/Faulkner Award. She lives in Brooklyn.